NEVER
ALONE

NEVER ALONE

— A Megan McGinn Novel —

C.J. CARPENTER

MIDNIGHT INK
WOODBURY, MINNESOTA

FIRST EDITION
First Printing, 2014

Book format by Donna Burch-Brown
Cover design by Lisa Novak
Cover art: iStockphoto.com/7739690/Denis Tangney Jr., iStockphoto.com/
    205391/Lise Gagne
Editing by Nicole Nugent

Midnight Ink, an imprint of Llewellyn Worldwide Ltd.

This is a work of fiction. Names, characters, places, and incidents are either the product of the author's imagination or are used fictitiously, and any resemblance to actual persons, living or dead, business establishments, events, or locales is entirely coincidental. Cover model(s) used for illustrative purposes only and may not endorse or represent the book's subject.

Library of Congress Cataloging-in-Publication Data
Carpenter, C. J., 1969–
  Never alone / C.J. Carpenter. — First Edition.
    pages cm. — (A Megan McGinn novel ; 1)
  ISBN 978-0-7387-4023-2
  1. Women detectives—New York (State)—New York—Fiction. 2. New York (N.Y.)—Fiction. I. Title.
  PS3603.A76855N48 2014
  813'.6—dc23
                                        2014000343
Midnight Ink

Llewellyn Worldwide Ltd.
2143 Wooddale Drive
Woodbury, MN 55125-2989
www.midnightinkbooks.com

Printed in the United States of America

DEDICATION

To Mary Ellen Carpenter, my mother and best friend.
She knew when to be the first and how to become the second.

ACKNOWLEDGMENTS

To my agent, Doug Grad, a huge thank you for your tireless work, the countless phone calls, emails, and especially your guidance. Actually, perhaps more so for your patience! To my editor Terri Bischoff and the great team at Midnight Ink for giving me the opportunity of taking a dream of over fifteen years and making it a reality.

To the authors who were so generous with their time and wisdom as I began this insane journey: Reed Farrel Coleman, SJ Rozan, Dan Judson, Jason Starr, Sarah Weinman, S. P. Lee, Todd Robinson, Bernard Whalen, J. D. Rhoades, and Terrence McCauley—and yes, I know I'm missing some people, please forgive my brain freeze. A very warm thank you to Otto Penzler for your candidness and generosity over the years. Larry Gandle, I would be lost without your sarcasm and dark wit; you're the best. Laura Lippman, Ken Bruen, Ali Karim, R. J. Ellory, Brendan DuBois—thank you for the wonderful advice you've shared with me.

Before the acknowledgments become longer than my prologue, thank you to my family and friends. I must point out a few lifelong friends I've been honored to have in my life: David Sonatore, Ani Nappa, Enza Golden, Amy Winner, and Susan Olsen. I thank you for your support when I'd throw myself on my couch and scream, "What am I doing?!" Thank you, Tony Duino Black, for giving me the actual tools: my desk, computer, pen, pencils, and paper.

It took a village to make this happen, and I'm very grateful.

PROLOGUE

HIS LAST KILL WAS *his favorite. He thumbed through the article with anticipation—until he was rudely interrupted by another patient's untimely demise. The soon-to-be-departed was named Roger.*

Roger mounted a chair to turn the channel on the television. Roger's favorite show had been interrupted with a special news report, so he opened his own vein.

"You son of a fucking bitch! Bitches! All Goddamn bitches!"

The disappointment had been too much for Roger. Two orderlies and a nurse ran over to him, covering his neck as blood sprayed out, but it was too late. Seconds later the show resumed with the exception of one viewer; so much for the Nielsen ratings at Hudson Psychiatric Center.

Fintan glanced over, ambivalent to Roger's self-inflicted expiration date as he searched for the continuation of the article. They'd crowned him The Executor. He was proud of that moniker. Eight people of different ages, sexes, ethnicities—all dead through his doing. Since his capture, the only enjoyment he experienced was in perusing the articles, viewing the evening news for his accomplishments, and hoping to see an interview or a ten-second clip of the formidable woman responsible for his capture. He didn't hate her. If anything, he viewed her as a worthy opponent. After all, she'd caught him when no one else was looking in his direction.

The patients in the common area were being told to go back to their rooms. Fintan didn't understand the big deal; it's not as though the man bleeding out on the floor had anything to offer the world. Roger was nuts, crazy off his ass. He thought the walls spoke to him. He would talk to the invisible little man on his shoulder and smack him off when he felt agitated. There was one week when Roger thought he was a Rockette and started kicking the staff while singing show tunes.

One definition of insanity is to be in a state of mind that prevents normal perception, behavior, or social interaction. Fintan wasn't insane. FBI profilers would write books about him, he'd be added to the list of Bundy, Gacy, and the like. Yes, his atrocities, his motives, would be hypothesized over for years to come, and that would amuse him because the diagnoses would be incorrect. And he'd be the last person to offer any reasoning for his actions. There was only one four-letter word that would be appropriate to describe Fintan D. Worth: evil.

Fintan turned to the last page of the story, and there was her picture next to his. Captor next to captured. Deciding too much time had passed, he tiptoed around the pool of blood, stopped at the nurses station, and asked for paper and pen.

ONE

"Did you give my mother a sedative this morning?" Megan whispered to the nurse. The nurse nodded and crossed her fingers as a sign of hope in answer to her question. Megan's mother, Rose McGinn, sat next to her in front of the casket, staring blankly. Michael Murphy, Pat McGinn's best friend and partner in Homicide, was speaking of his life knowing Pat. It spanned over thirty years. He reminisced about standing up for each other on their wedding days nearly thirty-eight years ago. Megan avoided looking at her mother, knowing there would certainly not be a glint in Rose's eye. *Scraps*, she thought. *Alzheimer's leaves a brain with nothing more than remnants.*

So fucking unfair.

She'd looked around at the number of people in attendance. She was hardly surprised to see so many paying their respects in their full dress uniforms. They had traveled from church to cemetery. Her father would have done the same for every person there, if he'd been given the chance.

Megan returned her attention to the eulogy. She couldn't think of anyone better than Uncle Mike to give the tribute. She listened as he spoke of their time together as partners in Homicide and how their friendship had quickly turned into a brotherhood. It was nice to listen to him reminisce about all the summer vacations the families shared. Uncle Mike was a sky-scraping, first-generation Irish-American. His ruddy complexion, due more to his lifestyle than anything else, displayed uneven dimples and a Jack Nicholson mischievous grin. His head was a mop of previously black hair now speckled gray. Megan was sure his smile and playful demeanor managed to land him more than his share of fleeting romances. Before he'd settled down with his wife, Maureen, of course. Megan knew there were far more devilish stories to be heard than the ones he was relating, and someday she hoped he'd share them with her. It brought a small smile to her face before she felt a quivering hand over her own. She turned to find her mother staring at her in a way she hadn't in some time.

"Angel face."

"Momma?"

"He's gone, baby girl. I've lost my husband."

Megan squeezed her mother's hand. "I know, Momma."

Rose turned toward the casket, slipping back into oblivion while tears fell over her cheeks. Megan turned to look at her older brother, Brendan, standing behind Rose's wheelchair. They shared a painful glance knowing they truly had lost both parents.

As Uncle Mike continued, Megan's thoughts trailed back to the moment she'd found her father. She'd called him last Wednesday morning to confirm their weekly dinner: one large pizza with extra cheese and sausage accompanied by a few cold beers at her parents' house. Nothing seemed out of the ordinary when they spoke that morning. Pat said he was going to take Stubbs out for his morning walk and then run a handful of errands early. Stubbs was a black-and-white mutt Megan had adopted from an animal rescue shelter for her father when he retired, not knowing how fast her mother would spiral into dementia. Pat refused to send the dog back even though just taking care of Rose was a full-time job. They managed to arrange for a day nurse to visit and do the majority of the care: the bathing, feeding, organizing her medicines.

The time gave her father a level of reprieve, and he enjoyed spending it with Stubbs. Pat gave him the name because his tail was docked too close to his rump. When he got excited, the thumb-sized black stump would wiggle but not wag. Pat thought everyone had their own cross to bear in life, even the furry among us.

Megan always knocked before letting herself in, followed by yelling, "Hey, McGinn, I'm home," but that afternoon she was met by a locked front door and silence. The only sound was Stubbs's barking. But it wasn't the excited bark she knew, the one dogs let out when visitors knock. It was a frantic, high-pitched squeal. She walked around the outside of the house to look in through the side window. She could see Stubbs in the living room, panting and nervously walking in circles. Rose stood motionless at the opposite window.

Megan had banged on the door. "Mom! Mom! It's Megan. Open the door and let me in!"

No response.

Megan dug out her set of house keys. When she turned the knob and opened the front door, the foul odor she was far too accustomed to assailed her senses. Her hands began to tremble as though it were a cold winter night, not an autumn day.

She ran over to Rose, who'd soiled herself multiple times.

"Jesus, Mom." *Where is that fucking nurse?* "Mom, it's Megan. Where is Dad?"

Rose pointed to the living room. "He's asleep."

No. Please. Please let me be wrong. "Mom, you stay here. Don't move. Do you hear me? Don't move." Her voice trembled as she called out, "Dad?"

Megan had no idea why she called out for her father. Clutching at straws was the only reason she could offer herself in the days that followed. Stubbs ran over to Megan and raced back into the living room. He did this twice before actually tugging at Megan's pant leg for her to follow him. She did.

Pat McGinn was slouched to one side in his recliner. His reading glasses were lopsided on the end of his nose, and he still wore his morning slippers. Crime-scene photos lay in his lap; one even remained in his hand. Megan knelt down before her dead father and took the photo from his cold grasp. She released an exasperated sigh. "Right up until the end, huh Dad?"

———

"You fucking asshole!" Rose yelled at the casket.

Yanked from her unpleasant trot down memory lane, Megan swung toward her mother, bending down and saying, "Momma! Please!"

"Don't talk to me, you little bitch." Rose slapped Megan across the face.

Brendan bent over to hold Rose's arms before she took another swing. "I thought you said she'd be sedated so this wouldn't happen," he snapped at Megan.

"She was supposed to be." Megan glared over at Rose's nurse for assistance, ignoring the searing pain spreading over her cheek.

"When is she going to be put in a hospital? You were supposed to have taken care of it by now." Brendan was a delegator, not a doer. It never dawned on him that *he* could have looked into a hospital for their mother, or at the very least asked his spoiled wife, Jill, to do so. As far as Megan could see, Jill's only commitment to the family was spending Brendan's money.

Jill apparently viewed Megan as a source of competition, having a tight brother-sister bond with Brendan that, although tested at times, always survived. Megan just had zero patience for gold-digging trophy wives.

Still, Megan and Jill had long shared a white-flag distance—up until the moment, only *four hours* after Pat's death, when Jill asked if she and Brendan would get the family lake house and pontoon in upstate New York.

Hence the demise of the white flag.

"Are you fucking kidding me, Brendan? You're bringing this up now? Give me a break—I had to make all the funeral arrangements the last few days. Let's just get Mom out of here." Megan was exasperated. "Okay Momma, it's time to go. Say goodbye to Dad."

"Why do I have to say goodbye?" Rose's confusion mounted, her anger now completely forgotten.

Megan began moving Rose's wheelchair around. "Because he's dead, Momma. Dad's gone," she whispered in her mother's ear.

"I'll take her. You guys stay here." The voice came from behind Megan's seat. It was her partner, Detective Sam Nappa. "Stay. I'll take her to the van."

"I'll do it. I'm her son," Brendan said, glaring at Nappa.

"Brendan!" Megan snapped.

"I was just trying to help," Nappa said with an apologetic look.

"I'm sorry. He's not handling things well," Megan whispered.

Rose started to sob like an overtired child who needed a very long nap, except that Rose's mind had been dozing for over a year. The nurse took over the duties of the wheelchair once they reached the van parked on the road near the interment site. Megan then returned to her seat, but not without noticing more than a handful of astonished faces. Sheepishly Megan answered their stares with, "Alzheimer's." She then refocused on her father's casket, covered in the green, white, and blue police flag.

Fucking hell.

The priest ended the ceremony with a prayer and information regarding the wake being held at Uncle Mike and Aunt Maureen's house in Cobble Hill, Brooklyn. People were leaving the service when the bagpiper, requested in Pat McGinn's short will, began to play "Danny Boy."

Megan found she couldn't move. It started to sink in that she'd never see her father, her mentor, ever again. People touched her on the shoulder as they passed, offering condolences. It took all of her strength to acknowledge each mourner. Minutes later Uncle Mike and Aunt Maureen approached.

"Meganator," Uncle Mike said in a soft voice. "We'll give you a few minutes and then meet you at the limo. Okay with you, kiddo?"

"I guess Rose won't be coming to the wake." It was more a comment than a question from Aunt Maureen.

Megan cringed. "Oh, I don't think that's a good idea."

"I'm sorry, sweetie. Take as much time as you need. Brendan is going in the van to take your mom back home with the nurse. He'll come over to the wake after she's settled."

Megan nodded, then waited for the rest of the people to leave. She hesitantly walked up to her father's casket and put her trembling hand on one end. "Hey, Ginty. This *just* can't be happening. I thought there'd be more years ahead of us before this day came." She looked up at the sky, not wanting to confront the tears welling up in her eyes. "I'm going to miss our morning phone calls. I already do." The lump in her throat felt like a horse pill lodged in her larynx. "Remember? You'd call me every morning before work to tell me to watch my back. And always ending with a 'Love you, kiddo' before hanging up?" The tears were now flowing full force. Megan was embarrassed by her own rare show of emotion. She released an awkward laugh. "I love you, Dad. I love you so much." She patted the casket. "I'll take care of Momma, okay? Maybe every once in a while I'll bring you a Guinness, and we'll catch up."

She started to walk toward the limousine, but not without taking one last look back.

"Bye, Daddy."

————

The limo ride to Brooklyn was silent, allowing Megan to gather her thoughts. She was glad for the bit of quiet time. She knew she wasn't going to get it later because Irish wakes are anything but silent. And that was exactly what Megan would need—noise and people and laughter and, oh yes, alcohol. One of the first people Megan saw upon entering Mike and Maureen's home was Nappa. His face was a welcome relief.

His Italian-Hungarian heritage practically begged for the clichéd "tall, dark, and handsome" description. Park Avenue socialites would give their husband's last dime to have his high cheekbones and sharp jaw line. His dark brown eyes, set deep within his chiseled features, were softened by dimpled cheeks and an I've-got-a-secret boyish grin. His ordinary presence brought her solace on this difficult day.

"Nappa, thank you for trying to help earlier. I guess Momma just snapped. Do you think many people noticed?"

He looked to the side to see if anyone was listening. "Well, you know those foam fingers people wave at football games?"

"Oh Christ."

"That would have been less conspicuous."

This put an awkward smile on Megan's face, and she let out a small laugh. "Great."

"Don't worry about it." He looked intently into her eyes. "How are you holding up?"

"I'm fine." But her red, puffy eyes couldn't hold out the lie she'd just told. "Really. Now, make yourself useful and get me a drink. I have to get into hostess mode for all these people."

Brendan snaked through the crowd. "Baby sister."

Megan smiled. It was true, she was younger, but not by much. She and her older brother were Irish twins, born ten months apart. Brendan was closing in on thirty-five, and Megan was thirty-four. Two months out of the year, they shared the same age. It felt comforting, she was never sure why; most likely because very little else ever did.

Megan knew an apology was coming, which meant the funeral bitch-fest was nearing an end.

"I'm sorry. I lashed out at you for no reason. It was wrong. I miss him."

Megan nodded in agreement.

"You're the one who has had all the parental responsibilities. You've been helping out with Mom. You're the one who found… I'm sorry." He was sincere, and Megan knew that. Having only two or three real fights their entire lives, they were as close as a brother and sister could be. Megan could never figure out why the few fights they'd had were over their mother.

"Still my kid sister?"

"I don't know. Still going to lend me money when I need it?"

He smiled. "You're living virtually rent-free in my Upper East Side apartment, that's not enough? I thought you were making the big bucks now that you're a high-profile detective." He smiled. "Look, once I got Mom back and settled—which wasn't easy, believe me—I realized I was wrong."

Megan gave her brother a small hug. "Thanks."

Nappa returned with a drink for Megan.

"Nappa, I'm really sorry for how I acted back at the cemetery. I was a jerk," Brendan said.

"Don't worry about it. It's been a long day for both of you. And my condolences about your father."

"Thanks. Well, I better get mingling." Brendan excused himself.

"Nappa," Megan said, "we need to talk, and it's as good a time as any, I guess. Actually, you just listen." She let out a hard sigh. "I'm serious about this. I'm thinking about leaving the force."

Before Nappa could object, Megan said, "I need to, Nappa. For my own fucking sanity."

"McGinn, your father was the reason you joined the force. Seriously, think about this. I know the last few cases have been grueling, *especially* the last case. You may want to leave, but the job will never leave you, and you *know* that. Take some time off."

She shook her head. "I'm burned out."

"Please, as your partner, promise me you will take some time and really think this over."

She promised him, knowing full well her decision had been made. Megan clanked her glass with his. "To my dad. The late, great Detective Pat McGinn. God bless."

For the next six hours people talked, laughed, and filled the Murphy household with the occasional alcohol-induced tear. More than once she glanced over at Uncle Mike and felt more pain for his loss than for her own. He'd just lost his best friend—the one friend who had his back, no matter what. Knowing someone has your back rarely happens in this world as far as Megan could see. That part of Uncle Mike's life just ended. He had Aunt Maureen, but it's different between men, especially men on the job.

By midnight Megan was sure she'd pass out if she didn't get home to her Upper East Side apartment soon. "Time for me to go."

"Oh, Meggie, please stay here tonight." Aunt Maureen was a short woman with wide hips and a warm smile. She still bore the wedge haircut made popular by skater Dorothy Hamill in the 1976 Winter Olympics.

Megan began putting on her coat. "I need my own bed tonight, Aunt Maureen."

Uncle Mike interrupted. "Leave her alone, Maureen. She knows what's best for her right now." He heaved himself up off the couch and declared, "But, kiddo, you are not taking the subway. I'm calling you a Town Car." He held up his palm. "No arguing."

Megan complied, and thirty minutes later Uncle Mike walked her out to the shiny black Lincoln. Before she got in, he gave her a hug. His voice shook as he said, "We lost our Ginty, kiddo."

"Yeah, we did." Megan's tears returned.

"You remember: we're family, blood or not." Uncle Mike quickly regained his composure. "Here, take this for the tip." He tucked a twenty-dollar bill in her pocket.

"Uncle Mike, I'm not going to—"

"Yes, you are. Now, go and be safe. I'll call you tomorrow."

———

The Town Car crossed the Brooklyn Bridge into Manhattan and zipped up the FDR Drive along the East River. Megan stared out the window at all the lights, thinking of her empty apartment, her empty bed. All that quiet, and the long hours before dawn. When the car was two blocks away from her building, she told the driver to take a left and then stop. Kinsale's Bar would be in full swing, and she wanted to be too.

TWO

Through an exhausted breath, he asked, "What did you say your name was again?"

The room smelled of pot and booze. Pitch-black with the exception of the Manhattan lights filtering in through the curtains. Moaning, the occasional grunt, and the sound of the headboard banging against the wall filled the bedroom.

"I didn't." *This is not the time for small talk, dude,* Megan thought. She was straddling him with her eyes closed, gyrating his cock between her legs, deep inside her. She ran one hand up and down his sweaty chest, while the other rubbed her clit. She noticed he had large, soft hands as they played with her nipples. She liked that, especially when the sex was rough, especially with a stranger.

They'd met in Kinsale's. Just past one in the morning, he sat down on the stool next to her. A half hour later they were back in her Upper East Side apartment. She wasn't looking for a romantic evening, obviously, just a fuck-fest. It's funny how few men ever denied her that.

He moaned and came long before she hoped for.

Jackass.

He whispered, "God, that was incredible." She barely had time to dismount before the next noise coming from her bed was a gruff snore.

"Christ."

She went to her dresser to get her jackrabbit and gave herself what the man sleeping in her bed couldn't: a nice hard, make-your-eyes-roll-to-the-back-of-your-head orgasm.

Thank God for Duracell.

She decided a quick shower was in order—not out of shame, just cleanliness. Megan kept shame at bay when it came to sex. An unmarried woman in her thirties had as much right as a man to get her needs met. Besides, there were plenty of other places in her life where shame could plant itself.

Afterward she toweled off, threw her hair back, put on a pair of boxer shorts and white T-shirt. Then she opened up the medicine cabinet and popped an Ambien. Not only did she find herself grateful for battery companies, but pharmaceutical companies made her top-ten list as well.

———

It was one of those nightmares when you know you're dreaming, but you don't know it enough to wake yourself up. She'd had the dream a thousand times, so she knew how it would end. Not that that made waking up any easier.

She was walking down the street, drunk, a three-beer kind of drunk for being a senior in high school. She'd left a party and was on her way back to her girlfriend's dorm. Two blocks. The longest two blocks she'd ever walk in her life.

He grabbed her from behind and pulled her through trees blocking an empty house. The FOR SALE sign had weeds growing around it. His hand tasted of cigarettes and sweat and something she wouldn't recognize until later. Blood. She kicked, tried to scream, but the only sounds available were muffled pleas. Two pit bulls were tied to the radiator. They lunged at her, lusting for fresh meat. Their gritted fangs dripped saliva. The sound of their ravenous barks was as clear in the dream as it was sixteen years ago.

He gripped her by the back of the head, slamming it down onto each step of the staircase as he dragged her to the second level. She grabbed onto the banister as if it were a life raft. That's when she caught sight of the lit candles, garbage, ripped newspapers, and, oddly enough, dolls strewn about the musty-smelling house. Most of the dolls were complete in form, others just headless torsos. And the thought came to her, just as the glare of the blade passed in front of her face: *Headless torsos. Headless torsos.*

The feeling of the knife entering her was always responsible for catapulting her eyes open to the present day. It was the feel of warm blood trickling down her breast that Megan would be hard-pressed to forget.

Nightmare toll: one thousand one.

———

The room was on its side. At least that's what she thought until she realized she was lying on the bathroom mat. The combina-

16

tion of alcohol and Ambien must have knocked her out before she could make it back to her bed. She sat up—too quickly, she realized. Suddenly nauseated, she was glad that at least she was already in the bathroom and didn't have to go far to get sick.

After what seemed like an eternity, Megan didn't think it was possible to have anything remaining in her stomach. She thought wrong. She clutched the sides of the porcelain bowl with her palms tightly clasped, elbows resting on the rim, looking as she did years ago at Our Lady of Lourdes Elementary School during confession with Father Dwyer. Both experiences left her abdomen in agony and her face waxen.

She sat back on the white tiled floor of her bathroom. The cold soothed her legs as the rest of her body continued to rebel while she paid homage to the porcelain God. She then leaned against the wall, dabbing her face with toilet paper and wondering if there would be one more heave.

"Christ, Meg—are you done yet?" she asked herself through the pounding in her head.

Rubbing crust out from the corners of her eyes, she stared down at the floor. "Jesus, when was the last time I cleaned this?" Megan's idea of cleaning was the twenty-second-typhoon approach. If someone called to say he was on the way over, she'd blast through the place, throwing most everything into the closet or under the bed. A domestic diva she was not.

She picked up a tampon wrapper, a piece of lint, and a used cotton ball and rolled them into one, tossing it into the trash. During this intense bathroom cleaning, her phone rang.

"Shit, what now? What time is it?" A tuft of her strawberry blond hair had escaped the ponytail holder. She pushed it behind her ear before raising herself to the edge of the tub. Turning on the tap, she drenched a washcloth with cold water before placing it on the nape of her neck. The cold compress felt like the only thing keeping her head from falling off her shoulders. Her other body parts were in equal, if not worse, condition. She felt one large, continuous cramp riffling through every muscle.

Megan knew it wouldn't be long before she'd have to answer the damn phone.

The sound of her own voice on the old answering machine broke the silence. "Hi, you've reached Megan, please leave a message."

"McGinn, pick up the—" It was Nappa.

Megan took a deep breath, pulled herself up off the edge of the tub, and ambled her way into the bedroom. She cleared her throat as she grabbed the receiver, trying to sound as if she were in full form. "Hey. What's up?"

"McGinn, there's a new case. I know what you're going to say, and you'll probably still say it, but you need to see this."

She waited a moment before answering, "No. Nappa, I told you I'm done. I'm *done*."

"You need to see this. *I* need for you to see this crime scene."

She responded with silence.

"If not for your partner, then for the memory of your father."

Her silence was now coupled with anger. "That was a cheap fucking shot." Megan hung up, then yelled in the direction of her bed, "Hey, wake up! You have to go." She threw on her clothes and ran a brush through her kinked hair.

The twenty-something stockbroker groaned as he turned over, exposing his firm ass. "Come back to bed, we're not done yet."

"Can't. I have to get to work."

"Just for a few minutes."

"The meaning of a one-night stand is that it's once, and at night. That's why it's not called a one-morning stand. C'mon, you have to get out of here. I'm in a hurry."

Stockbroker guy turned on his back, pushing the pillows up behind his head. The sheet fell below his hips, revealing dark pubic hair and the increasingly stiff reason for wanting her to return to bed.

"Technically, it was three times during the one-night stand." He waved three fingers in the air.

Megan picked his pants up off the floor and threw them in his direction. "You dropped the ball on the third time, dude. Seriously, I'm in a hurry. Get up. Get dressed." She went back into the bathroom to brush her teeth and put some distance between her and Stockbroker stud.

"When can I see you again? I like you, I want to get to know you better," he yelled from the bed.

Megan rolled her eyes at the absurdity of his comment, answering with a mouthful of toothpaste, "Leave me your number, I'll call you."

So many lies, so early in the morning.

"I'm serious, I think you're great," he said.

She wiped the remaining toothpaste from the corner of her mouth before walking back into the room. "You're right, I am great. I'm a sexual Olympian. Now get up."

"Can't you tell? I *am* up."

"I meant the rest of you."

Stockbroker guy watched as she zigzagged around the apartment, gathering her things while he put his clothes on.

"Do you mind if I ask where you got that scar from?"

When you're naked and straddling a man during sex, a scar positioned slightly above the left breast and under the collarbone can rarely be missed, even in the dark.

She ignored the question, even though his tone was sincere. "Listen, I had a great time, too. I'll call you." She fastened her watch while scanning the room for one last item.

"Looking for these?"

Handcuffs dangling from the headboard can cause either a flurry of excitement or a terrible lull in conversation. This was the latter. She took a moment before acknowledging him with a sarcastic glare.

She pointed toward the door. "Get out."

THREE

It was so easy. She opened the door with that wide-eyed morning smile, so happy to see me. I told her I didn't come empty-handed. Within minutes, my hands held her lifeless neck. Today is a good day.

———

Megan arrived at the crime scene wearing more black than a ninja. Her customary Manhattan attire—black pants, black turtleneck, black leather blazer—set against her pale skin emphasized the gold highlights running through her hair. She held up her shield for the officer standing in front of the yellow police tape as she ducked underneath.

After they figured she was out of earshot, the officer clicked on his walkie-talkie. "You guys better be awake up there. Detective Super Bitch is on her way up."

There were two officers posted outside the apartment door of the crime scene. The one not grazing on a bagel responded, "Got it, but what's *your* problem with her?"

"I don't got a problem with her."

"No, I can tell you don't. What, she's a detective and you're still hanging the yellow tape outside of scenes, that bother you, bro?"

"That ain't the reason and you Goddamn know it. I just think she's a bitch who could use a good hard pounding, if you know what I mean."

The officer, bug-eyed and red-faced, stared at Megan as she quickly approached him. The other officer stopped in mid-chew of his breakfast.

Yellow-tape cop continued via the walkie-talkie, "And lemme tell ya, I'd give her one good hard pole of a time. Bitch would feel it for weeks."

Megan had been halfway up the last staircase when she'd caught wind of the officers' conversation. It put a smile on her face. She loved to take the piss out of people. She placed one finger up to her lips, motioning both door officers to be silent, taking the walkie-talkie away from the embarrassed man. "This is Detective Megan McGinn. Trust me when I say this: if the size of your cock is in proportion to your IQ, or to your potential to move up in the ranks of this department, I am in complete assurance that not only could you not hold a hard-on for five seconds, but it couldn't fill half a hot dog bun." She kept the button pushed in. "One of you go down and get his shield number for me." She returned the walkie-talkie. "Nappa inside?"

Both men just stared like boys caught spray-painting a school.

————

Entering a crime scene was an adrenaline rush for Megan, as odd as that seemed. Her first month on assignment, she'd witnessed overdosed hookers in alleyways, the needles still sticking out of their arms; countless double murders or murder-suicides; a man who stabbed his fiancée to death because she overcooked his dinner; and numerous welfare mothers killed by their drug-dealing boyfriends. The number of bodies she'd seen in gang killings alone could fill a book.

She stood at the threshold of the living room now, donning a pair of latex gloves and paper booties over her shoes as she scanned the room like an eagle surveying a field before dinner. The forensics team was deep into their work. She didn't bombard them with her questions yet.

Nappa was speaking with the first officer on the scene, getting the usual information: confirm the body hadn't been moved, ascertain whether anyone had entered the apartment after his arrival, note anything suspicious when he arrived (besides a dead body on the floor). He then delegated the usual laundry list of duties: start taking names and phone numbers of everyone in the building, check if anyone had any priors, find out if there were any disturbances reported in the building recently, etc.

Megan liked Sam. He knew his business, and he knew how to work a crime scene. He had started out in Narcotics and had made some big drug busts, but in the end you're always one step behind the drug dealers. One would get knocked off or arrested and there'd be another waiting in the wings ready to take his place.

Nappa was getting close to burnout mode when he decided to switch to Homicide. He thought helping to solve murders would give him some kind of closure. That was about a year ago. So far, there had been little in the way of closure.

Megan waited while the crime-scene photographer took some shots before she went over to the dead body.

"I wasn't sure you'd come."

"Fu—" Megan paused to stare down at the position of the victim. "Fuck you," she whispered.

"Sorry for the earlier comment about 'do it for the memory of your father' bullshit."

Megan scratched her forehead, hearing his apology as mere white noise. "Hmm."

Nappa continued, "Young, maybe late twenties, early thirties. Looks like strangulation. No sign of a break-in." Nappa released a heavy sigh. "So far, no sign of prints. Forensics just got here, so they've really just started. She's fully clothed, in workout clothes, so I doubt there was any sexual assault. Nothing's been torn on her. The super found her this morning when he came to fix the kitchen faucet."

"Where is he now?" Megan asked.

"He's with a uniform downstairs. He's pretty rattled. We're working on getting the contact information from the lease to see if we can get in touch with next of kin. The super said her family lives somewhere in Connecticut. We should have the information soon."

"What's her name?" asked Megan.

"Shannon McAllister."

"Can I take a look?" Megan asked the crime-scene photographer.

The photographer stopped chewing a large wad of gum to respond. "Go ahead, I'm done. I'm moving into the next room."

Megan walked around to the other side of the couch to inspect Shannon McAllister's dead body.

Oh Christ.

"This was exactly how she was found?" Megan asked.

Shannon lay on her side, her head placed delicately on a pillow. Her hair was brushed neatly over her shoulders and her hands lay peacefully cupped one within the other in front of her forehead. Her legs were bent at a ninety-degree angle. She looked as though she could have been sleeping peacefully, if her eyes weren't bulging open and gray.

"Exactly," Nappa replied. "I spoke with the first uniform on the scene. He said he didn't touch her."

"What about the super?" she asked.

He shook his head.

Megan knelt down beside Shannon. She looked hard into her vacant stare, then moved Shannon's jaw side to side, inspecting the contusions on her neck. She was as gentle inspecting Shannon's lifeless corpse as she'd be placing a baby in a crib. She looked around the immediate surroundings: books sprawled across the floor, an empty Tiffany's jewelry box.

"You're sure she wasn't touched?" Megan asked again, hoping the answer would somehow be different, though knowing it wouldn't be.

"Positive."

Megan read the inscription on the heart dangling from the bracelet on Shannon's wrist. *Carpe Diem.* Megan tugged at her own necklace, a compulsive habit she'd developed when she was deep in thought.

"I guess seizing the day is no longer an option for you, Miss McAllister," she whispered.

Megan picked up Shannon's right hand to see if there were traces of anything under her fingers. She found bruises near her wrist and an Irish Claddagh ring, the crown turned outward. There was a faint scent she couldn't place.

Nappa crouched down beside Megan and whispered, "McGinn, tell me what I'm thinking is wrong."

She raised an eyebrow in sympathy, whispering, "Sorry, Nappa." Megan started to walk around the apartment to view Shannon McAllister's body from different angles. "Obviously, she was deliberately placed in this position."

"It looks like she's sleeping, almost in the fetal position."

Megan paused. "Maybe." It was a good theory, but there was something more to it; at least that's what her gut was telling her. But it was also telling her something else.

This won't be the last victim.

Two policemen were in the corner of the room chatting about the score of whatever sporting event took place the previous night. When their conversation got above a whisper, Megan snapped. "Hey, is our investigation interrupting your conversation? Take it outside, for Chrissake."

Judging how everyone else in the room responded, mannequins had better circulation after one of Megan's outbursts. Nappa was immune to them by now. "Jesus, McGinn, get up on the wrong side of the bed today?"

Got up on the wrong side of the wrong man, is more like it.

She just shrugged. "Something like that. Keep going. What else is there?"

"Wallet's still here with money and credit cards inside. Jewelry is still on her. Maybe boyfriend trouble?"

"I doubt it. She's wearing an Irish Claddagh ring."

"Doesn't that mean she's in love or something?" Nappa asked.

"She's wearing the Claddagh ring on her right hand with the heart facing outward and away from her body. She's single, offering her heart."

"Are you sure?" Nappa asked.

Megan looked over at Zachary Jones, the assistant medical examiner on the scene. "Hey, Jonesy, the Italian is questioning his Mick partner about Irish Claddagh rings. What's up with that?" she joked.

"Beats the hell out of me. I'm not Irish, what would I know about Claddagh rings?"

Zachary Jones, commonly referred to as Jonesy, was thin and had precision-cut brown hair. He always wore Oxford shirts with matching ties—which Megan joked were clip-ons—underneath his blue medical examiner's windbreaker. He was smart and young, and had a direct sense of humor. Megan considered it a dry humor, while most people meeting Jonesy for the first time thought he was bleak, sometimes bordering on crass.

"Do you want to know why there's a dead girl in the middle of the room, or are we going to chitchat about jewelry some more?"

Megan could see why people thought Jonesy insensitive. She smiled, remaining quiet as Jonesy explained how Shannon Mc-Allister was murdered.

"Carpe jugulum."

"Sorry?" Nappa interrupted.

"Go for the throat." Megan had trouble grasping as well as remembering the Ten Commandments in Catholic school, but Latin had always fascinated her.

"Very good, Detective. You two have a fresh kill on your hands."

Megan shot a look over at Nappa, then back to Jonesy. "What do you mean *fresh*. It's barely eleven o'clock."

"Maybe three hours, if that. I'll have a better idea when we do an autopsy, check the temp of the liver."

Fucking ballsy unsub, Megan thought.

Jonesy continued, "I think he wore surgical gloves, two pairs, specifically. Based on the bruising around the neck, I think the killer first attacked from behind. Then, because of the abdominal bruising, I'd say he put his knee on her side to hold her down while he strangled her. So far no fingerprints, and I mean not *one* print, even from the victim. It looks like he wiped the whole place down."

"Don't forget to bag her hands," Megan said.

"I'll bag 'em, but I don't think we'll find anything," Jonesy said.

"Why not?" Nappa asked.

"Look," Jonesy knelt down and held up one of Shannon's wrists, moving her clutched hand side to side. "He cleaned her hands and trimmed the nails down to the quick. It looks like he used nail polish remover or rubbing alcohol to do it. I'll do a chem test to tell for sure."

"The killer cleaned her hands?" Megan asked.

"Yes, and he was extremely thorough about it."

"So he kills her and gives her a manicure." She looked up at Nappa. "I doubt he threw any cotton balls, or whatever he used, in the trash can."

He shook his head. "Nope."

"He killed her, gave her a manicure, and cleaned her apartment. That's a hell of a Merry Maids service, isn't it?" Jonesy said.

"This has not been a good fucking morning," Megan whispered to herself. A moment later, her cell phone vibrated. She turned away from the group for the slightest bit of privacy. "Detective McGinn." The call was one she'd receive every now and then. "Well, is she okay? Did she hurt herself? Okay. Good. I'm going to have to call you back." She hung up without saying goodbye and reconvened with the others. She stood with her arms crossed as if preparing for a fierce chill.

"There aren't any signs of a break-in, so she knew him, or he had a key and waited until she got home," Nappa said. "What do you think? Any connection to the murder on the Lower East Side?"

"Could be. It's too early to tell." Megan muttered again, "Could be." She walked a few steps around Shannon to look at her from a different vantage point. "The other vic didn't have anything under her nails, right?"

"Totally clean," Nappa answered.

Megan thought a moment. "She was found a few days after being killed. Maybe there's a time issue with what he used to clean under the nails, something that couldn't be detected after a few days." Megan stepped back. "But the other victim wasn't placed so ... *thoughtfully*. Maybe the killer didn't have time with the other vic."

"Yeah, something could have rushed him, but the Lower East Side girl was a hooker. There are so many more possibilities with a vic like that," Nappa said.

"A hooker who's murdered and still has nine hundred dollars on her was definitely not killed for lack of performance. And she wasn't murdered by her pimp or a john wanting his money back."

The details of the other murder were sketchy. A young girl, probably a runaway at one time, fell into prostitution. She was found strangled in her studio apartment with no signs of a break-in. Megan knew something wasn't right, but nothing added up. The girl was placed in the cold-case files.

Megan smelled her surroundings again, thinking it odd there was an odor more fitting for an Entenmann's factory than a room housing a slowly decomposing body. She looked around to see if there were scented candles nearby. There were none. "Nappa, what's that smell?"

"That's what else I want to show you," he said.

Megan followed Nappa into the kitchen.

"Open the oven."

"Why?"

"Open it."

Inside Megan found a loaf of bread slowly warming. "It's bread, Nappa." She checked the stove. The oven had been set to 150 degrees. "But . . . baking bread wouldn't cover the scent of a decomposing body. We both know there is nothing more putrid than that." No human being could ever forget the first time such a pervasive smell entered their life. Megan's first experience was investigating an odor neighbors called in on the Lower East Side. She entered the apartment to find a man, once Caucasian, now black, bloated and dead on the floor. He'd been there for five days. A fetid pile of human remains surrounded by feces and dried urine made even the toughest cop dry heave if not run for the hall to retch completely.

Megan looked again into the stove. "It's Irish soda bread. Mom would buy it on the weekends to have with breakfast." Saying those words made her wince with sadness knowing her mother no longer had the memory of cooking those old-fashioned Irish family breakfasts. She glanced around the kitchen. "Awfully clean for someone who just made homemade bread."

"And murdered a girl before breakfast," Nappa said glancing back at now-deceased Shannon McAllister.

The vic let you in, you sneaky bastard, Megan thought. "Let's go talk to the super."

"I'm not sure how much help he's going to be."

Megan released a heavy sigh. "Dot the i's, cross the t's, right Nappa?"

Few crime scenes sent a chill down her spine. This was the second in as many months.

FOUR

MEGAN AND NAPPA MADE their way to the basement level to speak with the building's super, Mr. Mendoza. There were a handful of cops standing outside his office. An EMT attended to Mr. Mendoza, giving him oxygen, checking his pulse and blood pressure.

They squeezed through the narrow entrance into his office.

"Mr. Mendoza, I'm Detective McGinn," she began. "This is my partner, Detective Nappa. I think you met earlier. I know this has been a difficult morning for you, but can you tell me everything you remember from the moment you entered Ms. McAllister's apartment?"

Mr. Mendoza took a long drag of oxygen before pulling the mask below his chin. "Oh, that poor, poor girl. She's the nicest girl in the building. Most tenants ignore me when they see me in the hallway, not Miss Shannon. She's an angel, I tell you, an absolute angel." He turned his head in Nappa's direction, as if trying to convince him of Shannon's saintliness. "She stop and ask how my wife and children are all the time. My wife, she had these things removed from her feet a few months ago." His index finger shaking as he pointed down toward his feet. "Bunions? Something like this. Well, Miss Shannon made my wife her favorite *galletas*... um ... cookies." He stopped to take a sip of water, most of it missing his mouth. "A lovely girl. Just lovely."

"I'm sure she was, sir," Megan said.

"Well, she leave a note in the basement last week. We have a message board. Tenants write down what they need me to do." Looking at Nappa, he repeated nervously in Spanish, "She maybe put her name down once in the last year. Miss Shannon never made a fuss."

Nappa, in his broken Spanish, told Mr. Mendoza to continue.

"I was hosing down the sidewalk in front of the building this morning. Miss Shannon came back from her jog."

"What time was that? Was she alone?" Megan asked.

"Yes, alone. I think maybe six thirty? She ask me would I mind checking the faucet in her kitchen today. I tell her no problem. She said she be gone by eight thirty. Any time after that is okay. I ring the bell twice to make sure no one is there. I don't like to bother my tenants. I unlocked the door, bring in my toolbox, and then I see that poor girl just lying on the floor like ... like ..."

Mr. Mendoza started to break down again and pulled out a handkerchief from his back pocket. He abruptly pulled it away from his face, shaking his finger. "I tell you whoever did this to that girl is a monster. I tell you, *un monstruo!*"

Megan took a small step back so the EMT could administer more oxygen to Mr. Mendoza. His color soon returned to normal.

"Mr. Mendoza, have you noticed anything suspicious lately? Anyone hanging around the building or going in and out of Ms.

McAllister's apartment? Any male visitors for Ms. McAllister?" Megan asked.

"Boyfriends, you mean? No, no, not that I know of. She's a quiet girl, a good girl. I can't remember anyone." A few seconds passed when he looked up at Megan, tapping his index finger against his left temple, stunned he could recall such an uneventful moment. He stammered, sure this would be of no use to them, "I remember she had a party at the end of the summer. She worked at a camp, a summer camp for sick city kids. She and a few other people got together to celebrate the end of the summer. Nothing big, just ordered a few pizzas, no big thing. No neighbors complained or anything like that."

"How did you know about it?" Nappa asked.

"I run into her when she was paying the pizza guy. I help her into the apartment with the pizzas. There were six, maybe seven people. Nice kids."

Megan glanced over at Nappa. A small something is better than a big nothing when it comes to leads.

"We noticed there's a video camera at the entrance to the building," Nappa mentioned.

"Yes, but I have trouble with it. It works, but not too good. The company was supposed to come last week to fix it. We never had no trouble at this building, never! I been here twenty-two years and not once, not one bad thing ever happen here!" Mr. Mendoza pulled his handkerchief out again, attempting to mask his emotion, as much as a man who just found a murdered woman could.

"Okay, Mr. Mendoza. Thank you, thank you." Megan placed a business card on the desk next to him. "If you wouldn't mind providing us with information we'll be needing, sir. Names, phone numbers of everyone in the building, and if there is anything at all that you remember, please call us immediately."

———

Megan and Nappa walked up the back stairwell to the lobby level. They were at the front door of the building when a uniformed cop attempted to warn them of the onslaught of press, but it was too late. Megan opened the door to find television reporter Ashley Peters in her face. Ashley Peters was a twenty-something pain in the ass who mastered the art of pancake makeup without all those nasty, dark foundation lines. She was glam without the glitz or the intellect, but she was driven to get the story out first, and she usually did.

Ashley Peters pushed a bulbous microphone in Megan's face, the network logo prominently in view. "Detective McGinn? Are there any leads as to who committed this outrageous murder? Is this in any way related to the tragic, *unsolved* murder of the young woman on the Lower East Side recently?"

Megan was not in the mood for one-on-one combat with a hyper, career-obsessed, ethically challenged moron from the evening news. Ignoring Ashley Peters completely, she confidently spoke into the microphone, directing her answer to the other reporters surrounding her. "There are no suspects to report on at this time. We are treating this case as an individual incident unrelated to any previous crimes, and we will not be giving out the victim's name until the family has been properly notified."

Ashley barely gave Megan time to finish her statement before asking, "Detective, isn't it possible that these murders are connected? The fact you have been unable to solve what appears to be two related murder cases, doesn't that suggest perhaps more *man*power and stronger insight is needed to prevent any future killings?"

Without a bat of an eyelash Megan responded, "We have New York City's finest team working this case, and I am confident justice will be found for these victims. Thank you. That will be all for now." Megan knew how to handle the press. She hated them, but she knew how to handle their moxie.

But Ashley Peters worked hard for her afternoon sound bite and wasn't about to get it from Megan, nor was she about to get bumped to the "psychic cat saves family from house fire" news segment. "Detective, given your recent celebrity having solved the Worth case—"

Megan suppressed the urge to rip the head off the microphone with her teeth and spit it back on live television. "*Celebrity* is an exceptionally heightened term." A figure skater could have performed a double axel on the iciness of Megan's response.

"I think there are those who would disagree."

"That's all I have for now, if you wouldn't mind taking a step back. You're so close I can tell you're not a natural blonde." Megan offered a feigned smile and an even less sincere thank you as they walked past the cameras.

After signing off with her audience, Ashley Peters drew the microphone away from her perfectly Clinique-drawn lips and leaned toward her cameraman. "Cut it, Mitch. It looks like we're done here." She glanced back at Megan. "What a bitch."

FIVE

THE ELEVATOR OPENED TO the basement level of the medi-cal examiner's floor. Simultaneously, Megan and Nappa took a deep breath as they exited to follow the CORONER'S OFFICE sign marked in bold red letters. They didn't need an arrow to direct them to Max Sutherland's office. It was a hallway they had walked down many times before; if they did need a reminder, the noxious smell immediately notified them of their location.

Everything was white: white walls, white floors, white blinds hung in the identification rooms separating life as it identified death. Even the tissue boxes were white, something used often by visitors to the lower level. The minor exceptions were the thin black lines separating the floor tiles and the steel table and chairs occupying each exam room. Megan was bewildered by the notion of calling them *exam rooms*. No one was being examined. It wasn't a turn-your-head-to-the-left-and-cough room or a time-to-put-your-feet-in-the-stirrups appointment. The doctors down in the basement didn't take down vitals. They wrote down the cause of death while sipping Starbucks lattes and weighing body parts in scales just like ShopRite used to weigh fruit. No one got a free Zoloft sample or a B12 shot when exiting the lower-level exam rooms. Nada.

The walk to Max Sutherland's office was long, not because of its location, but because of its purpose: to tell complete strangers they'd lost someone they loved. The reality being they hadn't *lost* them. Their loved ones weren't aimlessly wandering around Grand Central Station. They had been violently taken from them and would never be seen by their relatives again. Period. It never got any easier for Megan. She knew no matter how delicately she handled meeting the families, they would always remember her as the person who told them of their loss. She was a part of a moment that would never be erased from their minds. It made her hate the perpetrator even more.

Christ, we're supposed to be the good guys, she'd catch herself thinking.

Conversations rarely took place between the two detectives while en route to the office of Dr. Max, Megan's little nickname for her favorite medical examiner. The two long hallways led to swinging doors; yes, white swinging doors. Two doors down on the right they turned into Dr. Max Sutherland's office.

Dr. Max was not one for city-regulated and -approved decor. Entering his office was similar to walking into the Ethan Allen showroom, where you could find entire rooms filled with sets of perfectly matched furniture. An oversized oak desk was centered on a maroon tapestry rug, faced by two custom-made leather chairs. The walls were covered with tokens from his many travels: African tribal masks, hand-carved sculptures from Ghana, framed black-and-white photographs he'd shot himself from all over the world. Dr. Max couldn't stand the fluorescent lighting in the lower level, so he placed a green banker's lamp at the top of his desk pad. His fedora rested on a bust of Socrates in the corner. Max opted for *Illegitimi Non Carborundum* instead of his name inscribed on his desk plate. Translated: Don't let the bastards grind you down. It was one of Megan's favorite sayings, and something she tried to remind herself of daily in her job.

"Knock, knock," Megan announced as they entered.

Dr. Max Sutherland's glasses sat on his barren forehead as he wrote copious notes on what Megan assumed were medical forms. He skipped the formalities. "These stupid expense reports. I can quote the Latin term for every single body part of the human anatomy, but to fill out New York City expense reports is complete Greek to me. Stupid regulations. Why did we change mayors again?" Max asked as he completed his anti-city-bureaucratic-duties speech, a speech his secretary heard every few days prior to the monthly expense-report deadline.

"Are we having fun yet, Dr. Max?" Megan asked.

"I detest that phrase, Miss McGinn," Max said, expressionless.

"Not as much as I hate that one. I mean, *Miss?* What is it, 1950?"

Max released a sigh of relief at having been interrupted, so he tossed the expense reports into the bottom drawer of his desk.

"So, Dr. Sutherland, what can you share with us about the McAllister case?" Megan asked with a mock-authoritative sound to her voice.

Nappa stood next to her as a tiny grin found its way to his face. If anything, the verbal sparring took the edge off the impending events.

"The lab identified two blue fibers," Dr. Max said.

Megan's eyebrows catapulted upward.

"Hold on"—he held up a hand—"before you get those Irish eyes smiling, they're extremely generic. One hundred percent cotton. The blue dye is consistent with a color The Gap, as well as countless other stores, use. There's no way of determining where they originated, at least for the time being, unless you bring me the exact sweater they came off of."

Megan was visibly disappointed. She allowed those emotional displays in Max's office.

"There's something else." Dr. Max placed his glasses on his desk, rubbing his tired eyes.

"What?" Megan asked. She could tell by the grim look on his face that things had just gotten worse.

Dr. Max sat back in his chair, staring down at the files piled high on his desk before him. His eyes took on a level of revulsion Megan had never seen in any of the ME's before.

For a moment Dr. Max Sutherland's office had become a black hole of silence. Then he spoke. The news hung in the air like the proverbial elephant in the room.

After several moments, Megan broke the silence. "*Sewn shut?*" Megan shook her head. "What are you talking about?"

"The victim's labia majora and labia minora were sutured together so ..." Dr. Max paused; this had to be a first for him. "So no penetration would be possible."

"Jesus Christ," Megan whispered.

Nappa rubbed his forehead.

"Now, here is what I can tell you. The thread used is very common. You can get it from any sewing kit from any pharmacy. I need to do more research on the type of suturing and the knot that was used. I've never seen anything like it before."

Megan ran her fingers through her hair in disbelief they were having this conversation.

Dr. Max continued, "I'll have photos for you as soon as possible."

"Was this done postmortem?" Megan asked.

Please God, say yes.

Dr. Max nodded. "The stitching is quite precise. It was definitely postmortem."

"Is that where you found the fibers?" Nappa asked.

"Yes, within the thread, but not one pubic hair. Nothing. No vaginal hair on your victim at all for that matter."

"He shaved her prior to sewing her shut?" Megan asked.

"No, your victim had what looks to be an allover bikini wax one to two days prior, based on the limited hair growth and small traces of body wax I found."

Megan was about to ask another question when Dr. Max held up his palm. "Wait, I'm not done." He pulled out a small plastic bag from his desk drawer, the kind extra buttons come in with a newly purchased shirt or pair of pants. "I found this when I cleared the stitches. It was lodged within the victim's vaginal area."

"Oh my God," Megan whispered staring at the item. Neither detective really wanted to take it, but Megan forced her hand to move.

She turned the plastic bag around in the air. It was a gold wedding band, nothing ornate about it, but one thing was for sure: few dead women have a gold wedding band sewn shut in their crotch.

That was the only remarkable attribute about the ring, though. She tried to see if there was an inscription.

"I checked. Nothing was inscribed. And if it had an inscription or stamping, it's long since rubbed off by wear," Dr. Max said while Megan handed the bag over to Nappa.

"So, we know one thing: it's old. I'm not all that familiar with wedding bands, but it's not that large. I'm guessing it was a woman's. Not a huge clue," Megan added.

"And, hold on to yourself, not *one* print was found."

"Max, that's impossible. He'd have to have worn a hazmat suit to do all that and not leave any trace." Awe mixed with revulsion filled the air. The sound of Dr. Max's phone broke the silence. Max took the call.

"Christ, Nappa," Megan whispered. "This means the killer took the time to undress her, stuff her with a wedding band, do this fucked-up tailoring, reclothe her, and ..." Megan shook her head.

"Position the body in the manner he did," Nappa finished the thought for her.

"Jesus." Megan grabbed the Magic 8 Ball off Max's desk, cradling it in her hands while they waited for him to finish his call. The oversized billiard ball filled with blue liquid and a white plastic die was used to answer questions about the future, which was about as accurate as a quack psychic on crack. Megan silently asked the ten-dollar toy a question, turning the ball over and over in her hands while listening to Max's end of the conversation.

"Yes? Yes, the detectives are here. Please escort them down. Thank you." Max laid the receiver down. "The victim's parents, Mr. and Mrs. McAllister, are here. You're in exam room five."

"Thanks, Max. We'll get back to you." Megan returned the Magic 8 Ball to Max's desk, but not without first checking out the answer to her question. The triangle read, *Try Again Later*. She shook her head and looked at Max. "Get rid of this thing, will you?"

Megan and Nappa waited for the McAllisters outside the exam room. "I hate this, I really hate this part of the job."

"Me, too," Nappa agreed.

"Did you have to do this much when you were with Narcotics?"

"Some. The vics were usually heroin addicts, cokeheads, or drug dealers, so the family or friends identifying them were never that shocked. Don't get me wrong, they grieved, but they were never really shocked. It was more like they expected it, at one time or another."

She raised an eyebrow. "I guess they would."

Megan was about to continue when the white doors swung open. She could tell immediately they were Shannon's parents. Shannon's mother looked identical to her daughter. Mrs. McAllister walked toward them, grasping her small black purse in one hand and her husband's arm with the other. Somehow she managed to greet Megan with a crooked smile, one filled with hope that maybe this was all just a terrible mistake; that her baby girl was fine, somewhere.

"Mr. and Mrs. McAllister. I'm Detective McGinn. This is my partner, Detective Nappa."

Immediately Mr. McAllister asked, "Is it her? Is it Shannon? The police officer who contacted us couldn't give us very much information. We got here as soon as we could," he offered.

"If you wouldn't mind, Mr. and Mrs. McAllister," Nappa said as he motioned them into the identification room. A small chrome table with three chairs filled the room. The blinds were drawn closed. "Please have a seat."

Mrs. McAllister couldn't let go of the grip she had on her purse as tears filled her eyes. "No. Detectives, please, if it's my baby, I want to know. I want to know now."

"We'd first like to ask, when was the last time you spoke with your daughter?" asked Nappa.

"Well, she left a message for us last night. We went out to dinner and a movie. She said she was going to review some papers and go to bed. We missed her call by fifteen, maybe twenty minutes. I didn't want to call her back, in case she had already gone to bed," Mrs. McAllister answered.

"Well…" Megan looked at Nappa. She just wanted to get the identification over with, as did the McAllisters. Megan went over to the window and softly spoke into the intercom as she held the button down. A few moments later the white blinds opened.

Shannon's parents walked up to the window. Shannon lay on a pewter table, her hair brushed away from her face. A white sheet covered her just below her naked shoulders, displaying pale skin that now had a yellowish green color. Dark circles surrounded her closed eyelids.

Mrs. McAllister pressed her hands firmly against the glass, tears streaming down her cheeks. "My sweet baby," she whispered as her breath formed a cloud on the glass.

"Shannon…" Mr. McAllister clamped his eyes shut, making a full turnabout. Any direction was better than the one toward his daughter's dead body.

Megan noticed the men always turned away first. The mothers wanted to go in and hug their children one last time; they displayed such stout. It wasn't that the fathers were weak; they merely handled the pain differently. The men couldn't accept that they hadn't been there to protect and save their children.

"That's our baby girl in there," Mrs. McAllister said. Her voice was monotone, empty. "Who would do this to our daughter?"

Nappa pulled a chair out for Shannon's mother. "Please, Mrs. McAllister. Please sit down." Shannon's father stood at the other end of the table. His hands gripped the back of the other chair, propping his body up as he stared at the floor, shaking his head in disbelief.

"Was there anyone? Anyone you can think of who may have had something against your daughter? An old boyfriend, maybe?" Megan asked.

"No. No. She was someone…" Mrs. McAllister trailed off in thought, realizing she just spoke of her daughter in the past tense.

"Has she lived in that apartment long?" Nappa asked.

"The apartment is Shannon's grandmother's. She snowbirds in Florida but pretty much lives there full-time, except during the holidays." Mrs. McAllister took a deep breath. "My mother never wanted to give up the apartment. She's lived there forever. It's extremely low rent, a huge apartment. Well, you saw it, I guess." That was all she could handle; her face collapsed down into her hands. Mr. McAllister quickly put his arms around his wife, not that anything could lessen the pain.

"What or *who* do you think did this? Shannon didn't have any enemies. Who could have done this to her?" Mr. McAllister looked at both detectives with a level of desperation Megan was sure he'd never experienced before this day. "Was it a robbery? Is that it?"

"No sir. Nothing was taken that we can tell of at this time. Her wallet and credit cards were intact. There was a set of Mikimoto pearls in her drawer," Megan answered. She paused before adding, "Actually, when you're allowed back into the apartment, that could be something you might be able to tell us: if any other jewelry may have been stolen, such as gold rings, necklaces, anything of additional value." Megan swallowed hard regarding the "gold ring" comment and how they were about to tell these people their daughter had been used as a fucking piñata.

Mrs. McAllister lifted her head. "They were her sweet-sixteen present, the pearls. Shannon never wore gold, only silver, or pearls."

"We need as much information from you as possible. Information on her friends, coworkers, anyone she socialized with. We have her address book here. If you can just go through it for us and tell us who some of the people are, it would save us a lot of time," Nappa said.

"Of course, of course we'll do whatever we can to help," Mr. McAllister said.

"Did she have a boyfriend or any close male friends?" Megan asked.

"She didn't have any boyfriends, at least not that I knew of. MaryEllen, did she talk to you about anyone?" he asked his wife.

"She mentioned a boy she worked with on and off. They were just friends. Nothing romantic was going on. Shannon would've told me. We're very close. She would have told me if there was someone in her life. She was too busy. My God, between school and some of the charity programs she's involved in, she barely had time for herself, let alone a boyfriend. If she did have someone in her life, I would have known. I'm sure of that. She was my baby," Mrs. McAllister said, looking up at the now-closed white blinds.

"If there is anything you think of, please let us know as soon as possible."

"We missed her call by fifteen minutes. *Fifteen minutes,*" Mrs. McAllister said, looking up at Megan.

Megan could only offer a sympathetic look at the woman facing her with mascara-strewn tears and red, swollen eyes. Mrs. McAllister would never be the same. Some sick bastard had taken away the most precious thing in her life, and there was nothing Megan could do to change that. She doled out crippling news, unable to answer the questions families had a right to ask and deserved answers to.

"There's one thing we're particularly interested in. We were unable to find a cell phone anywhere. She must have owned one, I'm assuming?" Megan asked.

"Shannon owned a BlackBerry once, but she never got the hang of it. She did have *many* cell phones."

"I'm sorry, I don't understand," Megan said.

"Shannon had a knack for misplacing things. Last month she left her purse on a bus. She had to cancel every credit card and order a new cell phone. Last weekend she forgot her laptop at the house. I still need to get it back to—" The pain caught her mid-sentence.

"What we'd like for you to do is keep the account of the cell phone open, and give us her number, if you don't mind, so we can start checking records."

"Of course. Of course," Mr. McAllister offered.

Now was the point in the conversation neither detective was anxious to get to. They shared glances that had not gone unnoticed.

"What is it? You haven't told us everything. I can tell," Mr. McAllister said warily.

Mrs. McAllister hadn't caught the hesitation between the detectives. Horrific thoughts ran through their minds but none as awful as the news they were about to receive. "Oh, God. Was she"— she put her hand to her face, barely able to get the word out— "raped?"

Nappa fielded this question. "No. Our medical examiner said there had been no sexual assault."

"Well, then what in hell is it?" Mr. McAllister demanded.

Megan took the small plastic baggie out of her pocket, handing it to his wife. "Have either of you ever seen this ring before? Do you know if this belonged to your daughter?"

Mrs. McAllister took the bag, examining the contents. "I told you Shannon never wore gold. I don't understand. What—" Her hands started to shake as she passed it to her husband. "What's going on here?"

"This—this is very difficult for us to tell you, but it seems that whoever killed your daughter placed—"

"What do you mean, *placed*?" Mr. McAllister's voice began to rise.

Nappa took a step toward him. "Sir, please."

Megan continued, "The killer inserted this within your daughter's vaginal canal."

Mrs. McAllister grabbed her stomach, doubling over in her chair. Megan went to her side. "I'm so, so sorry."

Mr. McAllister clutched the back of one of the folding chairs before slamming it against the wall. He could withstand no more. Nappa tried to catch him as he fell to his knees. He grabbed Nappa's shoulder and released a scream so primal you could feel his soul breaking as he wailed the only word possible:

No. No. No.

SIX

Following the identification of Shannon's body, Megan and Nappa completed the remaining paperwork needed at the coroner's office. Emerging into the crisp New York air, Megan nosed her surroundings. She was reminded that not every breath of the day bore the lingering scent of formaldehyde.

"Nappa, this is going to be a motherfucker. I can feel it in my bones."

"I'm sure you're right, which is why I need you on this case, McGinn."

"Fuck all, Nappa—" Megan halted mid sentence to face him, "You and I both know this is a football field away from a lover's-quarrel-gone-bad murder." She shook her head and started pacing back and forth. "I can't do this one. Not now. Not after the whole Worth case."

"*You* were the one who got Worth. *You.*"

"Yeah, and because I spent all that time on Worth, I fucking missed the last few months with my father!"

And now the truth was out. Megan hated admitting it, but her guilt for not spending more time with her dad was starting to come to light and into her heart. "I'll never get that time back. I was too busy chasing a fucking psycho!"

Nappa smoothed his tone. "That's what this is about?"

Megan tightened her fists, pressing her fingernails into her palms in hopes of pushing down the rising lump in her throat, "I don't know. Maybe."

"McGinn," Nappa whispered, "he's gone."

"I can't say those words." She moved away. "Not right now. Not yet."

They walked in silence for the next few minutes. Nappa slowed his pace, allowing Megan to walk ahead of him. He knew to switch gears and give Megan the space to regain her footing after her emotional disclosure. "You think this is the unsub's first?"

"Not a chance."

People bustled past them. The noise and the traffic did little to distance them from how they spent the last few hours. Metrosexual men resembling Ralph Lauren ads strutted while texting aimlessly into iPhones. One particular guy caught Megan's eye. He wore a perfectly fitted ribbed turtleneck covered by a dark suede jacket. Nice contrast. A new TAG Heuer peeked out from under his suede cuff as he nonchalantly ran a hand through his overly product-filled hair. Megan glanced in his direction, but men like him did nothing for her, especially today.

"How do you think they'll do?" Megan asked as she took her cell phone out to check for a signal. She knew she had to dial it. Just to check. Just to see if anyone would pick up.

"The McAllisters?" asked Nappa.

"Yeah."

"Oh God. I don't know. I can't imagine it. I don't know how any of the families handle it." He winced, partly from the chilly breeze, partly from thinking about the horrific circumstances of losing a family member in that manner. "It's just so vicious, so sudden. I'm not sure how anyone could get through something like that." He looked back at Megan as she started dialing the phone.

"You're trying the number the McAllisters gave us?"

She nodded, waiting. "It doesn't mean I'm staying on this. I was waiting for you to think of it, but as usual everything falls on me."

Nappa stared straight ahead. "Hmm."

It went directly to voicemail, and then she experienced another first. Listening to the dead. Some people sound stiff when recording their outgoing message, uncomfortable. Others are at the opposite end of the spectrum: obnoxious, like an insecure actor overdoing a scene. But Shannon's voice was sweet, buoyant, and now silenced forever.

Nappa could see the discomfort in Megan's face. He took the phone from her, closed it. "Let's go, McGinn." They walked in somber silence for a few minutes. Hoping to lighten the moment, he said, "By the way, very nice interview today. You're a natural in front of the cameras. A very calming force."

"Yeah?" Megan smiled. "Thanks. There was a real organic feel to the conversation."

"A respectful give and take"—he rolled his eyes—"especially when she thought more *insight* was needed on the case."

"Oh yes. The zen was definitely flowing then," Megan said.

"Okay. So what's next? Max is running everything ASAP and—"
At that moment Nappa's cell rang. "Nappa." It was their boss, Lieutenant Walker. "We just left Max's office. It went as expected. We're on our way back now."

Megan waved goodbye to Nappa's cell phone as he closed it.

"She wants us back for an update," he said.

"I feel another zen moment coming on."

"Isn't one enough for today?"

Megan took a serious turn. "Do you think we should have told them about the vaginal canal being sewn shut?"

"I thought about that, too, but I think we made the right call. It's important to keep that information confidential, especially—"

Megan interrupted, "—if we get another victim. If *you* get another victim."

Just as she finished her sentence, Megan's cell phone rang. She answered it.

"Megs, it's Brendan. Good news—the Olsen Facility has an opening for Mom. I managed to get a private room. The hitch is you have to get her over there *today*, or we lose it."

"What, can't you do it? I'm on a case."

"We're about to get on a plane back to Ohio."

"You're going back already?"

"The kids need to get back into school, have their routines back on track."

"Jesus Christ, Brendan."

"Do you have any idea how fucking expensive a private room is at one of these places? And plus I'm taking Dad's stupid dog for Chrissakes." Brendan took a deep breath before he continued,

"Shit. I'll come back in a few weeks and we can start clearing out the house. You won't be the only one, baby sister. We'll all chip in."

"Okay, okay. I'll get her and go right now." Megan checked her watch. "Have a safe trip home." Instead of a goodbye, she slapped her phone shut. "Nappa, this facility that we've been waiting to get Mom into has an opening, but I have to get her over there today. Why don't you go back and get the lieutenant up to speed? I have to go to Brooklyn."

"Is Brendan going with you?"

"No. He's on his way back to Ohio."

"Come on. We'll both go. You shouldn't do this alone."

Megan didn't fight him on his offer; if anything, she was relieved. "Thank you."

———

"Jesus, this is a nice place," Megan said staring into the lobby. "I may move in here myself if I ever wanted to move back to Brooklyn." Nappa pushed the wheelchair carrying her mother through the sliding doors. He looked around, equally impressed.

"What do you think this costs?"

"I don't know, but I'm definitely glad Brendan is paying," Megan answered. They went up to the front desk. "I'm Detective Megan McGinn. I was told you have an opening for my mother, Rose McGinn?"

The woman seated behind the desk clicked into her computer, "Yes, right here, Rose McGinn. Private room. First three months paid in full. Let me get the doctor, a nurse, and the social worker assigned to her so we can do a full admission proceeding. It looks like from my records she will be in Room B16. That wing was just updated, so I'm sure she'll be quite comfortable. We will need all of her medical records to be transferred here as soon as possible."

Megan nodded, looking back at her mother. It was becoming all too real what she was about to do. The guilt rose in her like a balloon released to the sky. An orderly showed them to Rose's room, and they waited for the staff to arrive.

"Hey, Mom. What do you think? You have a big room all to yourself." Megan knelt down by her mother, tucking the blanket into the wheelchair. "You're going to love it here."

Rose replied by smacking her daughter's hand. Megan was relieved it wasn't another left hook.

The nurse was the first to arrive. "Megan McGinn?"

"Yes."

"I'm the nurse handling your mother's admittance."

"So, you're the head nurse?"

"No, I'm Breton. Your mother's full-time nurse is Marcie. I'm covering for her while she's at a luncheon seminar. She'll return shortly."

"She's very agitated. My father passed away this week so, she's been very, well—" Megan swallowed hard. "Combative."

"I understand. I'm going to help her into bed, since you have basically an hour's worth of forms to fill out." She handed Megan a folder with Rose's full name and birth date printed on the tab. "If you don't mind starting this while I take down your mother's vitals?"

"Of course."

The nurse shifted the wheelchair closer to the bed. She locked the brakes and hoisted Rose onto the bed. This was familiar territory for the day nurse, but Megan was less than comfortable with tactile maneuvers involving her mother. She was always waiting for the outburst or the aggressive comment that would be forgotten as soon as her broken mind lashed out with it.

"I'm just going to take her blood pressure, temperature, basic vitals. The doctor will be in soon." The nurse moved Rose's hair away from her cheek when Rose grabbed her by the wrist. "Rose, it's alright. This isn't going to hurt."

Rose's grip was unforgiving. Nappa stepped in before Megan had a chance to react. "Mrs. McGinn, it's okay." It took some doing before he was able to free the nurse's wrist from Rose's grasp. His cuff became caught on her jewelry.

"It's okay, it's okay. You're in a new place, sweetheart." The nurse tried to calm Rose down the best she knew how. "I'm sorry, until the doctor arrives I can't administer anything unless it's listed on her chart."

Megan hovered over Rose. "Momma? Momma, it's Meggie, everything's okay." She turned toward the nurse. "I'm so sorry."

She offered an empathetic nod. "Please understand this is very typical; it's okay. I'm fine." She turned toward Nappa. "Thank you."

After Rose's outburst, Megan continued to sign form after form. By the time the doctor arrived, there was little left to be done other than confirm Rose's medication. With that completed, it was time to say goodbye. The nurse was kind enough to add, "This really is a wonderful facility. She'll be well taken care of."

Megan couldn't speak without fear of tears forming. She smiled and nodded. Nappa put his hand on her shoulder and told her he'd wait outside.

Rose was sitting up in bed staring out the window. Megan sat beside her and did the same. "Time for me to go, Momma," she said and patted her mother's leg. "I'll be back soon to check on you." She leaned in, hugging her mother tightly, wishing she'd hug back. "Love you much, Momma." She kissed her on the cheek before walking out of the room.

SEVEN

LIEUTENANT PEARL WALKER FLIPPED a pen back and forth with one hand while the other held her forehead, probably trying to comfort a headache before it transformed into a migraine. Megan spied her boss through the open doorway and knew neither of them was looking forward to this meeting. News of an Upper East Side woman being murdered provoked major concern from Megan's bosses and, in turn, her bosses. A homeless man being beaten to death or a drug deal gone wrong was merely a sad reflection of the society we lived in today; a young upper-middle-class woman pursuing a degree in social work viciously murdered in her own home, however, held all the ingredients of a public-relations nightmare. Walker needed this case to be solved quickly, and she knew one of the few detectives who could deliver was Megan McGinn. Given the recent death of her father, the lieutenant was undoubtedly worried Megan might not be emotionally equipped to handle the high-pressure case. But, being a frequent visitor to the track, Walker knew where and when to place her bets. This meant she was putting her money down on Megan to win, place, *and* show.

The lieutenant had a Newton's pendulum set on her desk. Five metallic silver balls hung from a frame in alignment. Pull back on one of the balls, drop it down to collide with the others, and it produced a calming *click-clack-click-clack*. Or so it was supposed to; this seemed like false hope from an office-supply catalog when Megan knocked on the open office door.

"Come in."

Let the clicking commence.

Lieutenant Walker's office wasn't a large, ornate room, but it possessed a strict level of style and power, a reflection of the woman who occupied it. A credenza faced her desk displaying her many achievements, both professionally and personally. A photograph of her with the current mayor and governor at a charity event sat next to a plaque honoring her work with Big Sisters of America. A certificate of mentorship from the New York Urban League was proudly displayed on the top shelf. Her desk held her family photo: her and her dentist husband with their two daughters.

"Lieutenant, you wanted to see us?" Megan asked.

"Take a seat."

Megan sat in the only chair while Nappa leaned against the wall.

"First off, I'm sorry about your dad."

Megan solemnly replied, "I saw you at the funeral. Thank you for coming."

"Second, I'm sorry to hear about your mom. Nappa told me you just put her in a nursing home. I hate those places."

"Well, at least this is a nice one," Megan said.

"Third, are you up for this case right now?"

Images of herself as a young girl waiting for her father to come home from work, giving her a warm hug and telling stories of his day, filled Megan's mind. The sound of his voice calling every morning and how that was now silenced filled her heart.

My father is dead. My father is dead. It's real.

It was as if he were standing next to her in the room at that moment and whispered in her ear, *Go get 'em, Meganator.*

Megan raised her head and looked straight into her boss's eyes, "Yes. I need to be here. I need to work on this, Lieutenant."

Walker paused a moment to study Megan's determination. "Okay, so what do we have?" She sat back, taking in a deep breath to brace before beginning what she seemed sure would be a taxing conversation.

"Strangled. No signs of rape. No prints. Forensics is still working the scene, but it looks like the whole place was cleaned from top to bottom," Megan answered.

"Witnesses? Anyone in the building see or hear anything?" Walker looked over at Nappa.

"None so far. We still have some officers canvassing the building. We spoke with the super. He went into her apartment to fix the kitchen sink, and that's when he found her," Nappa replied.

"So what are we talking? Botched robbery? A jilted boyfriend?"

Megan jumped in then. "Definitely not a robbery. Her purse held her wallet with cash and credit cards in place. Jewelry was still there; a pearl necklace was sitting on top of the dresser. We asked her parents and they said she didn't have a boyfriend."

"That they knew of anyway." Walker, being the mother of two daughters, had experienced on more than one occasion how daughters can self-edit what they share with their parents.

"The mother was pretty adamant about that," Nappa said.

"Mmm." The lieutenant wasn't convinced. "Non-doorman building; any security video?"

"Yes, but the super said he's been having problems with the system. We're going to take a look at it anyway," Megan said.

"Well, I'm sure whatever problems he's had with it will be fixed after today. Unfortunately, it's a little too late for Miss McAllister." Walker's dry wit failed to mask her parental reaction to what she encountered at her job. "Max Sutherland is the ME on the case, right?"

Both detectives nodded.

"I'll give him a quick call. I'm sure he knows this is priority, but it doesn't hurt to give a reminder. Next steps?" Walker asked.

"Before we go to next steps, there are a few others details we need to discuss." Megan took a deep breath.

"Like what?"

"The victim had a gold wedding band inserted into her vaginal canal and her vagina was sewn shut." Megan hated the way she heard the news exit her mouth. She sounded sterile, unaffected, when the exact opposite was true.

Disturbing news such as this had a way of stifling all the members in a room, no matter how many times one heard it. Walker was no exception. The woman sat back in her chair. "You're serious."

It had been an emotional day. Megan's fuse was short with herself, even shorter with others. "No, Lieutenant, we make this stuff up because our jobs are *so* boring we want to see how much whacked-out crap people will believe."

"McGinn!" Nappa stepped over. It wasn't often that he got in the mix, but if he saw his partner was about to throw herself or her career off the cliff, he jumped in. "Cool it." He grabbed her shoulder, not in a strong-arm fashion, but in a go-sit-the-fuck-down-now-I-have-to-pull-damage-control way.

"Listen, Lieutenant, there's more." Nappa paused to gain footing in his explanation. "When the victim was found, she was positioned very specifically." He was waiting for Walker to move her slow-burn stare from Megan to his face. It wasn't close to happening. "She was placed very neatly. As if she were asleep."

Walker continued to stare Megan down a few more seconds before deciding to take the high road. "What makes you say that?"

"Look at her, you'd never think a murder had taken place," Nappa answered.

Megan added, with a lot less attitude, "Her hair was brushed to the side; there was a *serenity* to her position. Well, that's the best way I can describe it."

"How much do the parents know?"

"We had to show them the ring. We kept the suturing to ourselves," answered Megan.

"Good call. The press will have a field day if this leaks out."

"Her parents are providing us with a list of friends, past employers, and so on. We didn't find a cell phone, but we have her datebook, so we'll start there as well as speak to the people where she interned. She was a counselor, so there could be a whacked-out patient, something along those lines. And we'll also check out who she interacted with at the university. She was getting her master's at Columbia," Nappa said.

"Good. I've assigned Palumbo and Rasmussen to help you with the legwork. Give them anything you think may slow the two of you down. There's another matter, McGinn. From now on, I want Nappa to handle the press."

"What?" Megan looked at her boss as if she'd just said smoking was good for you. "Exactly what was wrong with how I handled the press this morning?"

"What was *wrong*? You came close to having a catfight on live television. For Chrissakes, Vegas had a five-to-one spread you'd bitch slap her if she had asked another question."

"I'm a professional. I would never do anything to embarrass this office."

"Yes, McGinn. You are a professional. You'd also lose every poker game ever played because you can't hide any of your one thousand emotions. You think you can, but you can't. I'm serious; no more impromptu interviews. Nappa handles the press. You stick to the case."

"Excuse me?" Megan sat forward. "Stick to the case? Who in the hell do you think sat with the victim's family today? I didn't see you there when Nappa and I had to tell two parents their only child was dead. What were you doing, having lunch with the mayor?"

Not a drop of zen could be found in the air.

Megan knew it, too.

Lieutenant Walker rarely shouted. When she wanted to make a point, she simply spoke very slowly. "You are out of line, Detective, for the second time in my office today."

Megan stared at Walker, knowing she was walking a thin line; she also knew she didn't want to be taken off the case. After a few seconds, Megan swallowed hard. "Fine. I apologize." She turned to leave. "I'll get Palumbo and Rasmussen up to speed." Megan walked out, giving the door a slight but perceptible slam, ratcheting up the pissing contest by half a notch.

"That was sincere," Walker said as she resumed reading a pile of messages. "She needs to switch to decaf or O'Doul's. Or both."

"I'm right on it." Nappa walked to the door, adding, "Give her a break. Look, she's fine; she can handle this. But it's been a rough day." He raised his eyebrows, hoping to make Walker less upset with Megan's outburst.

"Shit." She rubbed her brow. "I'm counting on both of you to handle this. You'll let me know if she begins to lose her footing." It was less of a request and more of a demand.

Nappa didn't acknowledge the comment. "We'll give you an update when we get some leads."

"*Lunch with the mayor?* Is she kidding me?" Walker grabbed the Newton pendulum off her desk, throwing it in the bottom drawer. "Thanks for nothing." She slammed the drawer shut as Nappa left.

———

Megan sat with Detectives Palumbo and Rasmussen, sharing what little information they had on the case. Both men were professionals and team players. They had no problem being directed by a woman. Rasmussen was a big man with blond hair and blue eyes—a modern Viking dressed in a suit and tie. Palumbo was third-generation on the job. What he lacked in height, he made up for in muscle. He accentuated his barrel chest with dress shirts that were just a bit too tight. He had to show off his long hours at the gym somehow.

Megan glanced up when Nappa approached. *"Stick to the case?"*

"Megan, you know what she meant. She's going to be under a lot of pressure from downtown to make sure this gets solved. She was posturing. That's all. And by the way, thanks for putting me in the middle of whatever *that* was in there."

Palumbo and Rasmussen exchanged looks, acknowledging they were out of the loop in the conversation and didn't much want to be in on it, either.

"Sorry." Megan didn't want to rehash her meltdown. "Sorry. It won't happen again." They both knew that was a lie. "I'm giving them everything we have so far." By the grim look in Palumbo's and Rasmussen's eyes, Megan had told them the more heinous aspects. "They're going to go back to the victim's building and speak to the neighbors, store owners, et cetera. Let's also get a copy of the building's security camera. It doesn't sound like it was in great condition, but we'll try."

"That reminds me, check back in with the super, Mr. Mendoza. He's the one who found her. See if he's remembered something," Nappa suggested.

"Got it." Palumbo had a gravelly voice, with a hint of a Queens accent.

"You want us to order phone records? Or is that being done?" Rasmussen asked.

"Rasmussen, you work on getting her apartment line and her cell phone records. We'll see if we can track who she's been in contact with lately. Also, see if we can get the phone records from the place where she interned. I have the name of it in my notes. That may be a pain in the ass for confidentiality reasons. She was a counselor at some center, so specify we're only getting *her* records, not those of the whole place. If she was being harassed by some nut, then he would probably be calling her there. Palumbo, I want you to check any and all databases on homicides that have the same MO, specifically the vaginal suturing. This can't be the killer's first time. Check it all. City, state, country."

"We're on it," said Rasmussen as they returned to their desks.

Megan knew Palumbo and Rasmussen asked the right questions and knew how to get around roadblocks. Walker made the right move assigning them to the case. Megan sat at her desk reflecting on the McAllister murder scene. Nappa sat opposite, starting what was sure to be a very thick case file.

"What's on your mind?" he asked.

"There's something at the crime scene that didn't feel right. I mean besides her head resting on the pillow so perfectly, and her arms folded. That was definitely intentional. There's something else, something I'm missing."

One of Megan's habits when in the zone was to push her long hair back and twist it into a bun, a subconscious habit she'd had since junior high school. Within minutes, it would fall out of place, cascading over her shoulders once again. The thought of buying a hair clip never seemed to cross her mind.

Nappa began making a list of Shannon's contacts from her datebook. "It's been a long run today."

"Yep." Megan noticed the message light blinking on her phone and was not at all surprised to hear whom it was from.

"Hey, Meganator, it's Uncle Mike. Judging by the newscast this afternoon, you're probably knee-deep in it. I just wanted to check in on you and see how you're doing. Call me."

She had a faint smile on her face listening to the concern in his voice.

"Uncle Mike?" Nappa asked.

"How did you know?"

"I'm a detective."

"Good one." She dialed the Murphys' number. Uncle Mike picked up on the second ring.

"Hey, how's my Mini-Ginty?"

Megan rubbed her eyes. "Holding my own."

"Brendan called earlier. He told us about Rose. Maureen is going to check on her tomorrow. Olsen Facility, right? Pretty fancy—that place advertises on the radio."

"Tell her thank you for me."

"Like I said yesterday, kiddo, blood or no blood, we're family. You working this case I'm hearing all about?"

"Yeah. It's gotten interesting, to say the least," she released a heavy sigh.

"Watch your back."

Megan laughed. "That's what Dad would say to me every morning before I'd leave for work."

"I know, kiddo, I know."

There was a brief moment of silence, both thinking back at the loss they'd endured.

"Okay, Meganator. Get back to work. We'll talk soon."

"Love you big guy."

"Back at ya."

EIGHT

Megan leaned against the window staring out at the mid-afternoon storm. Rain pelted down on the city streets as echoes of thunder rumbled through the dark sky. The space felt more like a dank cave than a conference room.

"Detective?" A young man rapped on the door, then tossed an envelope onto the table. Megan focused on the storm outside and responded with a halfhearted thank you. She picked up the letter as if it were merely an electric bill, until she flipped it over to see the return address: Hudson Psychiatric Center.

"Son of a bitch."

His writing was unmistakable; flamboyant italics as if written with a quill pen. Megan knew Fintan Worth's handwriting all too well. He left a note attached to each kill, with the exception of the last murder. There were two envelopes at that crime scene: one for the victim, the other addressed to Megan. Now, placed before her was the second letter in three months addressed to her from a mad-man. She knew she couldn't ignore his attempt to communicate with her. But there had been two murders she was sure Worth had committed that they couldn't tie him to. Two families had not been given closure. Was this a carrot he would dangle in front of her forever? Opening the letter felt as though she were allowing him back into her psyche, her life—what remained of it.

She tore it open, nearly ripping the stationery.

Dear Detective McGinn,

I hope this note finds you well. I, as you are well aware, am currently residing in Hudson at the psychiatric hospital. The accommodations are within reason for the facility. I'm treated with more regard than the typical resident. I assume much of that is due to my notoriety of late. Judging by the news, my actions have been misconstrued as infamous. Yours, however, have not. It seems you have become quite prominent within the New York City Homicide Division. Your professional advancement was well deserved. By far you have been the only detective—ever—to apply such keen instinctive abilities to what, I think we can both agree, were very few leads in a case such as mine.

It would be insulting to us both if I were to say luck had anything whatsoever to do with your achievement.

From time to time, I recall our last face-to-face commu-nication prior to impenetrable brick walls, electric fences, and plexiglass dividers obstructing conversation. Do you, and I'm sure you must, think back to how you captured me? You and I both know I let you win. I, however, am the only one to know why. I dare say, you've most likely never men-

tioned it to your handsome partner or to anyone else for that matter. Well done, detective.

At any rate, I would find it quite interesting to continue our conversation of that night. Yours is the only name I've placed on my visitor's list, if you feel so inclined.

In closing, I would like to offer my sincere condolences for the loss of your father. I'm sure he was quite proud of your success.

Your tenacity reminded me of a quote from Blaise Pascal: "It is the fight alone that pleases us, not the victory."

I'm curious, detective, what is the next fight on your horizon, and will you be as victorious with it as you were with mine?

Until we meet again,
Yours fondly,
Fintan D. Worth

It's an odd experience how mere words on a paper cast a person's mind to a particular time and place. A love letter whisks your heart into a frenzy just remembering how you felt in that person's presence. A Dear John letter does the same but with much more painful results. Megan's brother took a year off of college to backpack through Europe. Brendan sent a postcard from every place he visited. None ever had more than a handful of words on them; all made Megan dream of the time she would visit those places. What she now held in her hands was a seedy personal reminder of the lengths she had gone to, to catch a killer. And that's how she planned to keep it: personal.

Megan tossed the letter on the conference room table just as Nappa entered.

"What's going on?" He could sense something was up.

"Well," she raised her eyebrows, "partner, that is a loaded question. Read." She handed him the envelope with the letter attached.

"Hudson Psychiatric Center. You've *got* to be kidding me."

Megan watched his facial expressions as Nappa read Fintan's correspondence. He was just as, if not more, disgusted than she had been. "What's he talking about 'continue the conversation'? What did the two of you talk about?"

Megan refused eye contact when she answered, "I have no idea what he means. He's nuts."

"Sick bastard. I can't believe he's even allowed to send mail, let alone write to *you* of all people."

Megan took the last sip from her coffee before throwing the empty cup in the trash. "Yeah, well, there's not much we can do about it."

"You okay?"

"Fine."

Fucked up. Insecure. Neurotic. Empty. F. I. N. E.

Lovely.

Megan rubbed her forehead using the base of her palms as if kneading flour into dough. She didn't want to linger on the subject of Fintan Worth any longer. He was in her past, and she was determined to keep him there.

"Crime scene photos." Nappa handed Megan the folder, then added, "Just got word from Rasmussen—he and Palumbo are coming up now with the video from the building's security camera."

"Have they looked at it?" Megan half-heartedly wondered, knowing it wouldn't make a difference if they had or not. It was about what *she* might find on it.

"I don't think so."

Megan opened the folder containing the crime scene photos. She hadn't expected the first picture to be that of McAllister's sutured vagina.

"Christ," she tossed the picture over to Nappa shaking her head. "What goes through a human being's mind to do something like this?"

Nappa turned the photo around. Through an exasperated sigh, he said, "I wouldn't call anyone who does this *human*." He pinned it up on the board. Next to it he added the photo of the ring found embedded behind the vaginal suturing.

Megan fastened the last photo in the package flush left: Shannon McAllister's driver's license photo. This particular shot was the most difficult for Megan to view. In it, Shannon was alive. Smiling. Breathing. Real.

Gone.

Palumbo entered the room carrying a padded envelope under one arm while crunching through an excessively large bite of an apple. Both actions stopped short when he was at eye level opposite the worst of the photos. It was one thing to intellectualize the postmortem details, a far cry from having 8x10 color photographs of a dead woman's crotch on a bulletin board. He wiped the side of his mouth before he spoke, yet was unable to look away from the grotesque vision before him. "Hey, we … we have the security tape from the building. Rasmussen is coming up with some of the phone records: cell, apartment. We're working on the warrant for the center the"—Palumbo forced himself to look away—"vic worked at."

"Throw it here," Megan said. Palumbo tossed her the package as Rasmussen walked in with the phone records. Unlike Palumbo, the mounted pictures didn't give rise to a perceptible reaction. It was just how Rasmussen worked. An emotional silicon shield ran from top to bottom of his Nordic being when working any case. Everyone on the job had a different way of dealing with the shocking way human life is mistreated on a daily basis: some joke, some get angry, some shut down. Sometimes it's all three, whatever you need to get through the day. There were days when Megan wondered what vice, if any, Rasmussen fell back on to deal with the atrocities they encountered. She never felt it was her place to ask.

The tape began at one second after midnight. The first few people passing by the camera were stumbling and laughing, mainly couples, or one-night stands. For a brief moment Megan wondered if she and the stockbroker guy from the other night looked as ridiculous as these poor fools had.

Probably so. Whatever.

The visual looked like black lava pouring over the screen, then nothing but static.

"Wait, Christ," Megan snapped.

"I'll fast forward." Nappa skipped over static until a new visual could be found. The timer landed on ten past five in the morning.

"That's over four hours missing. Shit!" Megan began biting her fingernails. "Let's keep going."

The video returned to the original format. Mr. Mendoza was shown entering and leaving the hall a handful of times. A brunette walked out of the building at five twenty. Her hair mussed up in the back and the back of her shirt half tucked into her skirt.

"Walk of shame," Nappa commented passively.

A woman with a ponytail skipped down the stairs, checking her watch before opening the door.

"Wait!" Megan yelled. "Go back, that's Shannon."

All detectives, including Megan noticed her faux pas: calling the vic by the first name made it personal.

Shit.

She attempted a weak pardon for her fervent display, "That's our *vic*." They scrolled back. Shannon Elizabeth McAllister stood in the entranceway of the building she was about to be murdered in, setting the time for her run. The very last jog she would take in her short-lived life.

All four detectives sat anxiously in front of the monitor. Images froze seconds at a time, then again the screen turned to black. Megan was ready to throw the television to the floor when the visual returned. Shannon re-entered the building, "What does the time read in the corner?" Megan moved closer to the screen, "Christ, even that is hard to read."

"Six twenty-six?" Palumbo guessed.

"That makes sense. That's near the time the super, Mr. Mendoza, said he'd spoken with her," Nappa added.

"She's alone." Megan knelt in front of the screen. Every second the video continued felt like cement hardening around her chest. The next shot would be the last on the security video.

"Look. Someone's buzzing into the building."

Nappa, Palumbo, and Rasmussen leaned forward, as if somehow the movement would give them a clearer view. A person dressed in a hooded sweatshirt, back to the camera.

"They're not in full shot," Nappa said.

"He didn't want to be," Megan answered. The video showed one quick motion up to the building's buzzer. "What is that?"

"The shot is so grainy. What is *what*?" Nappa asked.

"*That*." Megan pointed to what looked like a string wrapped around the wrist. "I can't make it out." The video froze before darkness overtook the monitor for a final time. A macabre feeling silenced all four detectives. Megan glanced back at the photos she'd pinned up. Their horrid nature now felt even more gruesome. She pointed at the screen.

"That's our mother fucking unsub."

NINE

As I received the Holy Communion during morning mass, I couldn't help but smile at my accomplishment. I indeed had chosen well. God bless you, Shannon.

———

Megan's eyes remained closed as she turned over. She didn't need to look at her alarm clock—it was always morning when you had insomnia. Thoughts acted like kamikazes hitting her mind. She turned and twisted under the sheets. She usually slept on her side or stomach; for the next few minutes she'd lie on her back, avoiding the realities of the day by focusing, instead, on her body.

Megan was right-handed, but wished she'd been born ambidextrous, at least when her legs were spread. Her left hand flowed through her hair and across her face, lightly touching her lips. Her right hand did the same, just lower.

For the next few minutes, she was able to keep the morning at bay, but her body always ended up feeling better than her mind did when she was done. She turned over, snuggling her head into the pillow when a single tear ran down her cheek. Just one. That's all she allowed before work.

Megan wiped her cheek and stared at the Bloomingdale's bag in the corner of the room. She'd bought her mother a new nightgown weeks ago, but she hadn't yet given it to her. Now, with Pat gone, she couldn't just drop it off with her father at the house in Brooklyn. It was hard to get used to the idea that the house was now empty, and that her mother was living in a nursing home. But since it was so early, Megan knew she had time to take the subway to the Olsen Facility and back before meeting Nappa.

The thought of her mother wearing a generic patient's gown gnawed at her. Her mother would have a fit if she were alert enough to know she weren't looking her best. It wasn't out of vanity; Rose grew up with very little but was taught to respect what she owned, and now her few outfits consisted of nightgowns, slippers, and diapers. Megan wanted her mother to keep what integrity remained. There were times she thought it was out of guilt, but now it was partially due to Shannon's murder. There's a mother-daughter bond, if you were lucky, that reached beyond a mother dishing out guilt and bra advice. To have a woman in your life who understands you just as well as, if not better than you know yourself, was an incredible gift. Megan could tell Mrs. McAllister had had that special bond with Shannon. She envied it.

Megan knew more than ever that her time with Rose was limited, but "forgive and forget" proved more difficult to achieve as she got older. Some wounds take a hell of a lot more than just time to heal, and others would never have the chance. Megan kicked the covers off to attempt a quick shower. The prewar building had prewar plumbing, too; it took more time to wait for the water to heat up than for the actual shower. She passed the few minutes brushing her teeth while simultaneously looking in her closet for something to wear. Catching her reflection in the full-length mirror, she abruptly stopped brushing to critique her morning attire: an oversized NYPD sweatshirt and a pair of bright blue boxer shorts. She shook the tip of the toothbrush at her reflection. "McGinn, *not* a sexy look. This is why your right hand sees more action than you do. Well, most of the time, anyway." The thought of her sex-fest with the stockbroker made her shake her head.

When she opened the bathroom door, a wave of steam greeted her, warming her face and legs. She noticed her bathing suit hanging from a hook on the back of the door. The moisture in the bathroom brought out the chlorine smell still lingering in it, which was surprising given how long it had been since her last gym visit. She used her bath towel to cover the black spaghetti strapped reminder of her lack of motivation. No need to feel more guilt so early in the morning.

She brushed past the shower curtain, climbed into the bathtub, and stood under the showerhead, the stream of hot water directly hitting her face. The vibration of the stream of water against her body was soothing. She could have stayed in there for hours feeling the repetitive force of the water relaxing her muscles. Almost like meditating. But her mind wandered, as it usually did. Thinking about finding her father dead and seeing her mother so disoriented left her heart as bare as her body was now.

She paid the price for lingering under the spray. A sudden shot of cold water sprang Megan from her thoughts. "Fucking hell!" Her upstairs neighbors had turned something on in their bathroom, forcing cold water down to hers—the not-so-luxurious part of living in a prewar building in Manhattan.

After Megan finished her morning routine and ran out the door, she was waiting impatiently for the elevator when she caught a glimpse of her reflection in the hallway mirror. "Oh shit." She'd forgotten to put her favorite necklace on: a delicate silver cross with her birthstone, green peridot, set in the center, given to her by her parents the day she made her first Communion. She'd never forgotten what her father said as he clasped it around her neck.

Megs, I want you to always wear this, especially when your mom and I aren't around to keep an eye on you. That way I'll know the Big Guy is looking out for my girl, keeping you safe, and hopefully out of trouble.

She'd worn the necklace every day since her parents gave it to her. The only time she took it off was when she swam, and at night when she slept.

Megan dropped her stuff down next to the elevator and ran back into her apartment. When she took the necklace off at night, she always hung it on the corner of a framed photo taken the day of her Communion. A day, and a time, when her life felt more secure than it did now. Her gun might protect her, but it was the necklace that made her feel safe, and, now in a roundabout manner, served as the last lifeline she had to her father.

Megan made it back to the elevator just as it reached her floor. She rushed out of the building and headed to the subway station at 96th Street and Lexington. The smell of burnt bagels and bacon emanated from the corner deli across from Megan's building. She joined the countless Upper East Side straphangers as they funneled underground. Clad in business suits, carrying briefcases or shoulder bags, they were armed with their morning coffee, newspaper, or electronic device of choice, walking numbly through life.

Megan made two quick calls from her cell phone as she power walked to the station. She left a brief message for Dr. Max, inquiring as to any more lab results. And she left another for Nappa to confirm where she was meeting him to interview one of Shannon's best friends, the only contact Mrs. McAllister had been able to give them in her state of shock.

Megan entered the Olsen Facility in gust-of-wind fashion until she was stopped short when her jacket's belt got stuck in the door. She yanked at it angrily until she was freed. Two nurses were seated at the front desk. One was a skinny blonde with far too many visible dark roots; the other was on the robust side, with a much prettier, kinder face. Her smile widened when she saw Megan enter.

"Morning." Megan placed a small pink box tied with red and white string on their desk. "A few gourmet cookies for the morning sweet tooth." A little food bribe could go a long way with staff members anywhere, not that Megan needed to bribe these women for better care. The fact that she was a cop and carried a gun certainly made a stronger impression than a box of sweets.

"My mother, Rose McGinn, was admitted yesterday. How was her first night?" Megan asked.

Marcie, the amply proportioned nurse with the kind face, answered, "We didn't meet yesterday. I'm Marcie, your mother's main nurse. She's doing well. She's having a good morning. She got her hair washed and just finished breakfast."

"Good." Megan nodded in relief.

She had already turned to walk down the hall when Marcie added, "Your brother sent a beautiful bouquet of pink roses. I put them in her room earlier."

"Great, thank you." Megan turned and muttered, "Yeah, like she can tell a rose from a fucking wrench at this point."

Megan hesitated at the door to her mother's private room. Rose sat at the window, her hands folded in her lap, tranquilly staring out at the day. Megan felt her heart sink as swiftly as an anchor to the bottom of the ocean, remembering her mother as she once was: a bright, stylish, articulate woman. They may not have had a harmonious mother-daughter relationship much of the time, but Megan gave credit where it was due. She was hard-pressed to recall a moment when Rose left the house not immaculately dressed. To this day Megan clearly remembered the first time her parents went on vacation without her and her brother. Rose wore a perfectly tailored teal suit similar to the one Tippi Hedren wore in the movie *The Birds*. She kissed her children goodbye, pulled on a pair of white gloves, and held Megan's chin up toward her meticulously painted lips. "Be a good girl, Megan. Do everything your aunt says, and please take *one* bath while we're gone," she pleaded with the tomboy of the family before adding strongly, "I'm serious, no messing around, missy. You better be on your best behavior while we're away."

Forgiving the warranted threats, Megan never forgot how beautiful Rose looked that day. But disease has a way of aging the beauty right out of a person, and it had happened to her mother in record time. Face moisturizer and ChapStick replaced the morning regimen of makeup application. A robe, a nightgown, and slippers replaced colorful outfits, and a hospital name tag replaced jewelry as her accessory.

"Morning, Mom. How are you doing?" Megan prayed Rose would recognize her this morning, but the childlike smile she received was proof that confusion dominated Rose's attempt to identify her visitor.

"I'm fine, dear."

"You had your hair washed. It looks good. Did Marcie do it for you?" she asked.

Rose ran her fingers through her bob-length hair. "Marcie? Yes, she's a wonderful girl. She's a good daughter. She takes good care of me. A sweet girl."

So much for prayer.

"Mom, I'm your daughter. Me. Megan. Marcie is your nurse."

"Oh, you're pretty, too," Rose said, looking up at Megan.

Megan sighed, dragging a chair over alongside Rose. She grabbed the brown shopping bag off the bed.

"Did you send me those beautiful flowers?" Rose asked, pointing at the vase.

For a moment, Megan contemplated taking credit for the arrangement: a Band-Aid to cover the wound of not being recognized. Though tempted, she figured the one visit Brendan would make, Rose would have a lucid moment and tell him about all the beautiful flowers Megan had brought her. With a mischievous grin she answered, "No. Brendan sent them to you. He's your son."

"What kind are they?" she asked.

"They're roses, Mom. Pink roses."

"They're pretty," she said.

Megan hadn't been in the room five minutes and she could hear the testiness in her own voice. "He sent them because they're your favorite. You love roses. Your name is Rose."

"I know my name, missy."

"Now I'm talking to my mother!" she said, smacking her thigh. "I'm the only one you take that tone with."

Rose's self-pleasing grin was as brief as her lucid moment reminding her daughter who was in charge.

"Do you want to see what I brought you?" Megan gave Rose her gift. "Do you like them?"

Rose opened the brown bag as if it were the wrong order from a deli. "No." She sounded like a child who was impossible to please.

"Back to black," Megan whispered under her breath. "Mom, you love this color. It's the color you chose on your wedding day for Aunt Maureen's maid-of-honor dress." Megan reached over and picked up one of the many photographs she'd placed around Rose's room. It was her attempt to keep the memories from getting too far away. "See? This is you, Dad, Uncle Mike, and Aunt Maureen. You're wearing blue. You love that color."

Rose's confusion forced Megan into defeat. No longer hoping for a breakthrough today, she folded up the new robe and slippers and stuffed them in the armoire on the other side of the room. A bottle of L'Occitane hand lotion on one of the shelves gave Megan an idea that she hoped would make her visit go by faster. "C'mon, Mom, I'll rub your hands." Not receiving a defiant no was a plus, so she squirted lotion into her palm and began to rub Rose's hands together.

"What's your name again?"

"*Marcie.*" Now Megan sounded like the disgruntled child.

"You're not as fat as Marcie." Her comment made Megan laugh out of the sheer rudeness of it, and the fact it was true.

She turned up the cuffs on Rose's robe, massaging the insides of her arms. She'd forgotten about her scars until the tips of her fingers ran over the pale marks. The jagged line on her left wrist was a little over an inch and a half. The one on her right was longer. It still amazed Megan how much blood came from such small wounds. That memory was embedded in Megan's mind. Luckily for Rose, it was one that was swept away with her illness.

If there were a chance to go back in time and change an event, Megan would have changed the moment she found her mother. Pat had called home to say he was working late. Megan had answered the phone, already devising her lie. She'd had months of practice covering for her mother at that point. Pat wanted to speak to Rose, but Megan said she was napping. There was no need to give the technical term: sleeping one off. Megan would have the glasses cleaned and put away before her father returned home. The empty bottles she would wrap in brown bags and put in the neighbors' garbage cans. Megan remembered there was something different with that particular phone call; the level of concern in Pat's voice was stronger than in the past. He said he'd stay on the line while she went to wake her mother up. Megan tiptoed into her parents' bedroom, something she did a lot after the cocktail hour, which had crept earlier and earlier those few months. The shades were drawn, as they always were. Depressed people prefer the anonymity of nighttime. Less to see, less to be reminded of, less to deal with. Megan went over to the bed only to find it empty. The light in the bathroom filtered through the crack in the door. She could hear water running but no sound of the shower.

"Momma?" The door creaked as she pushed it open. The splatter of red against the white wall looked like a painting by Pollock, but it was no canvas. Blood everywhere.

And that's how she would forever remember the day before her twelfth birthday.

———

"That girl is going to be the death of me," Rose blurted out.

Megan rubbed her forehead as if doing so would wipe the memory away. "What girl, Momma?" She rolled Rose's cuffs back down, covering her wrists.

"That girl is going to be the death of *me*," she repeated.

"I heard what you said, Momma—*what* girl is going to be the death of you?" She wanted to kick herself for asking. She knew what the answer was. "Now would be a good time to say Marcie."

An older man pushing a newspaper/magazine cart leaned his head into Rose's room before passing by.

"Good morning." The man's dentures clicked as he spoke. He had a tall frame and looked far too thin for the brown button-down sweater he wore.

"Hi," Megan said, answering on auto-pilot.

"My name's Howard," he said.

"How are you, Howard?"

"Oh, I'm fine. They keep me busy around here."

Howard must have been what they called cash-and-carry in adult-care facilities. If he had enough money, Megan knew, the care facility would allow a twenty-five-year-old to live there. The nurses yesterday had said Howard had days of forgetfulness but nothing that couldn't be coped with living at home. His sons had more money than time, so they used the excuse that their father was more comfortable at the nursing facility than he would be living with them. Howard was a nice man, apparently, but you needed to always check your change when you bought a newspaper or magazine. His math wasn't what it used to be, or so the nurses had told Megan.

"Are you Rose's daughter?" he asked. He smoothed his sweater over the plaid shirt underneath.

"Yes, I'm Megan McGinn," Megan said, looking back at her mother.

"Your mom is a lovely lady. I hope it's okay. I read to her last night. The first night can be rough. I thought it might help."

Megan smiled. "I think it did. The nurses said she did well."

"Your dad was a lucky man, I have to say."

"Yes, he was. Thank you, Howard." Megan smiled at the thought of her father.

"Can I interest you in a paper?"

"Sure."

"Here you go, and take one of these old magazines. You can have a copy of *The Catholic Times*, too. It's free." He gave her the morning paper along with a three-month-old *Ladies' Home Journal* and *The Catholic Times*.

Megan paid him and then he continued down the hall on his paper route. She began with the morning paper, having absolutely no use for the *Ladies' Home Journal* and no interest in *The Catholic Times*. She sat down on her mother's bed, scanning the news as Rose looked out the window, seemingly content for now. Shannon's murder was, of course, on the front page. There was a small picture of Shannon with the words GIRL MURDERED: UPPER EAST

SIDE in big black letters. She was halfway through the article when her cell phone rang.

"McGinn."

"Hey, it's Nappa. Meet you on Park Avenue and Twenty-Eighth Street in about twenty-five minutes?"

Megan checked her watch and realized she had stayed longer than she'd planned. "Make it thirty-five minutes." Megan hung up without saying goodbye, stuffing the newspapers into her purse.

TEN

Megan met Nappa on Park Avenue South outside the 28th Street subway station. She quickly buttoned the front of her jacket when she emerged from the subway. The wind was much more blustery than it had been earlier in the morning.

Nappa was buying coffees at a deli cart on the corner, his suit jacket lapels turned up to cover the nape of his neck.

"Hey, Nappa, that look went out in the eighties."

He laughed and handed her the cup of coffee. The blue paper cup with gold Greek lettering reading *We Are Happy To Serve You* was a warm welcome to her cold hands.

"I should have worn a real coat—I wasn't thinking when I left my apartment."

"Thanks for the coffee." They walked toward Madison Avenue. "Sorry I'm late. I made a quick run over to see my mom."

"She okay?"

"Everything's fine. I just wanted to drop off a few things for her." Megan quickly changed the subject. "So we're talking to"—she pulled out her small black Moleskin notepad—"Katelyn Moore?"

"Mrs. McAllister said they were the closest out of all of her friends."

"This is the girlfriend from college?"

"Roommate. Hey, did you get Palumbo's message this morning?" he asked.

"Yeah. They went through the whole building and street. I can't believe no one saw or heard anything."

"Nothing. The neighbors all said the same thing—she was a sweet girl, didn't cause any trouble."

"And the super, Mr. Mendoza?"

"Nothing. Rasmussen and Palumbo are going over to the college this morning to speak with her professors and classmates."

"Phone records?"

"Got them. The vic called her parents a few times, ordered food, updated the roaming capabilities on her cell."

"Incoming calls?"

"Four. One from her parents' landline, two came in over a number that doesn't have an account."

"Disposable phone."

Nappa nodded.

"The fourth?"

"You." Megan was reminded she'd called Shannon's cell after leaving Dr. Max's office when the McAllisters identified their daughter's body.

"The vic's cell account is still active, but there's zero activity, and we're still waiting on the clinic."

A dark silence loomed over both detectives. The cell phone wasn't stuck in a cushion of a couch or left in a jacket pocket. They hoped but knew better. These stupid lines of communication have become third arms to our existence: too much information, too easily retrieved, too easily lost, and never too far away.

"I've been going through the vic's datebook. It's a total mess. There are no names or addresses. And she writes initials for I don't know what—meetings? Dates?" Nappa pulled the book out of his coat pocket. "Take a look."

Megan thumbed through the pages. "This doesn't help at all. Why even have a calendar or an address book if you're not going to write in it?" She handed it back to Nappa.

They walked in silence, each wondering where this case was going, how it would end. Homicide detectives came from a place of speculation mixed with a child's hope. A string as thin as the chance the case would end in a happy, shiny place, or at the very least a place filled with justice. *An odd word,* Megan thought: *justice.* There's an aftermath of inequity when that word is heard; a sense of one searching to find the strength to overcome tragedy, a cruelty, a repression, discrimination, a sin. Megan had witnessed most of these. Few threads remained to cling to, yet she, in a deep and private place, tried.

———

Megan was using the coffee more as a hand warmer and less as a caffeine jolt as they walked over to Madison Avenue. "I was thinking I'd like to stop by the crime scene again and take a better look. I want to do another walk-through of her apartment."

"Sounds good," Nappa responded as they entered Katelyn Moore's building.

The pale stone exterior sandwiched between two businesses made the Madison Avenue building seem more commercial than residential. A doorman standing in the alcove to the right of the steps allowed them into the building. Recessed lighting highlighted the splashes of jade in the black marbled tile, but was barely enough to illuminate the narrow hallway to the only elevator in the building. Lemon-scented ammonia filled the air as the building's porter pushed a mop back and forth at the end of the hall.

They boarded the elevator and Megan pressed for the fifth floor. Nappa repeated the action as the doors closed.

"I just pressed it. Why do you *always* do that?"

"Do what?"

"Press the elevator button after I've already pushed it? Jesus Christ."

"I don't know. It's just a habit. Whatever."

"It's not like pressing it a second time is going to get us there any faster. It's not like me pressing the button had a neutral effect on the mechanics of the elevator system and you suddenly had the golden touch. It's not like the stupid light to the fifth floor wasn't already lit."

They both stood, arms folded, staring forward.

"Do you want us both to ring the doorbell, too?"

"I should have taken the stairs," Nappa said, rubbing his forehead.

Megan exited the elevator first and rang the doorbell, daring Nappa with her eyes to ring it again. He hung back about five feet behind her. Then Katelyn Moore answered the door, tissues in hand. Her green eyes were bloodshot and swollen. Her resemblance to Shannon was startling. They shared similar height, body type, coloring. Both wore their hair parted on the same side.

"Katelyn Moore? I'm Detective McGinn, and this is my partner, Detective Nappa."

"Yes, please come in. Call me Kate." She fought back tears, attempting the usual social graces. Kate motioned for them to go into the living room. "Is there anything I can get you? Coffee?"

Both held up their paper cups, signaling they were taken care of.

She gave a meek smile. "Right. I'm sorry. I'm a little foggy this morning. It's been a long night since I got the news about Shannon."

"That's to be expected," Megan said.

Megan took a look around the exceptionally sparse apartment. Boxes lined the floor leading to the sofa, and a bundle of Bubble Wrap lay in the corner. The coffee table had the protective cardboard around the corners. Three large garment boxes were on one side of the room.

"I'm sorry it's such a mess. Please have a seat." Kate moved newspapers and moved boxes off the couch. She positioned herself on one of the boxes to face them.

"In or out?" Nappa asked.

"Just moved in. We haven't gotten a chance to unpack yet. My husband's been traveling for work, and I've just started a new job, so it's been a little hectic. And, well, the obvious."

"We don't want to take up a lot of your time," he said. "We just have a few questions for you."

Megan glanced over at a picture frame placed on one of the unopened boxes next to the sofa. It was obvious who was in the picture: Shannon and Kate were sitting on a beach holding tropical drinks, mugging for the camera. The photo gave away more than just best friends beaching it on holiday.

"The two of you looked a lot alike." Megan placed the frame back. "You must have been mistaken for sisters all the time." She noticed something else in the photo besides their resemblance.

"Yeah, we got that a lot." Kate picked up the photo, losing herself in the memory of the day it was taken. "This was a few months ago. We went away for a long weekend, one of those last-minute deals off the Internet. God, did we have a great time. We were planning another trip next month." Her words were cut short between the tears streaming down her cheeks. "I'm sorry, I just can't believe this. I can't believe this has happened." She began patting her eyes with the crumpled tissues.

"I know this is hard for you, but we need to ask you some questions." Megan paused for her to gain her composure. "When was the last time you spoke to or saw Shannon?"

She cleared her throat. "The last time I spoke with Shannon was four days ago. She called before one of her clients came into the center for a session."

"Clients?" Nappa asked.

"Her patients at the center. She technically doesn't have her master's in social work yet, so she refers to them as her clients. *Referred* to them as clients."

"What did the two of you talk about?" Megan asked.

"It was brief, nothing unusual. We were just making plans to get together again. We meet up a few times a month for sushi."

"Did she mention anything out of the ordinary?" Nappa asked.

"Like what?"

"Have any of her clients been giving her a hard time? Was there anyone harassing her in any way that you knew of? Not just the people she counseled, but anyone at work?"

Katelyn looked confused. "Harassing her? No, not that I know of, I mean, I know she doesn't deal with the most *sound* individuals, but there wasn't anyone threatening her. They depended on her."

"What type of patients—sorry, clients—was she working with?" Megan asked.

"Shannon worked with mentally and emotionally challenged prisoners. They're a part of a work program where they leave during the day and return to the prison at night. That's all I really know about it."

Megan was disgusted how the system leaned toward rehabilitation for people who were repeat offenders. Teenagers had a chance, but almost all the others, right or wrong, were lifers. She'd seen too much to view it in any other light. However, as soon as they heard the words "mentally and emotionally challenged prisoners," Megan and Nappa shared a very concerned look.

"She loved the people she worked with. She spent a lot of time with them."

They both knew that Shannon's work life was definitely an avenue of interest. For right now, they needed to find out more about her personal life.

"What about men in her life? Her parents said she wasn't dating. Do you know if she was seeing anyone?" Nappa asked.

"I don't understand. Why are you asking about boyfriends? I thought this was a break-in. Her father told me she came home when her place was being robbed." She looked back and forth at Megan and Nappa. "Isn't that what happened?"

Nappa chose his words carefully. "At this point we're looking at every angle. Right now we're focusing on the possibility this was someone Ms. McAllister knew."

"That's absurd. I don't believe that. She didn't have any enemies."

"Was she seeing anyone?" Megan asked. "Her mother was adamant that she wasn't."

Katelyn stammered briefly, "She did that speed-dating thing a few times. But that was ages ago."

Megan didn't hide her ignorance. "Speed dating?"

Kate sighed at the fact she was about to have to explain the process. "You have ten minutes to interview one another and then you move to the next table. It's kind of a way to see if there's interest on either part. It's not a big deal. But it's definitely not something her parents, Mr. and Mrs. Westport, Connecticut, would approve of."

"Where was this?" asked Nappa.

"She did it a few times, once in Manhattan and once in Brooklyn. We have a friend who lives there, so Shannon went with her."

"Did anything come of it?" Megan asked.

"I think she went out on a date with one guy—it was a while ago, maybe a year—but nothing came of it. Like I said, she wasn't the type to sleep around."

"Anyone else, anyone at all?" Nappa asked.

"Um, I love Shannon's parents, but, well, they didn't know... um... everything she did. Well, certainly not all parts of her, um, social life."

They could tell Kate was stalling.

"What do you mean, all parts of her social life?" Nappa asked.

"I mean, well…"

Megan could see how uncomfortable Kate was getting, not looking them straight in the eye, rubbing her hands. Exposing your best friend's secrets can bring that out in a woman. Then it hit her.

Megan sighed. "He's married."

Kate lowered her head, rubbing her temples. "One of her professors."

Megan reminded herself once again that Lieutenant Walker was often right. There are selective things daughters share with their mothers.

"I can't remember his exact name, Bower or Brower, something like that. She was working on a research project with him. She was into him, bought the whole 'miserable in his marriage, loves his wife but not in love with her' bullshit routine. I think he was playing her." Katelyn's tone turned from sad to bitter.

"Playing her?"

"Tall, dark, handsome type." She looked over at Nappa. "No offense."

He cocked his head. "None taken."

"He had a lot of young female students fawning over him, a real rock-star type. At least that's what Shannon said."

"Did Shannon fawn over him like his other students?" Megan asked.

Kate cackled at the notion. "Shannon? No. Shannon wasn't the fawning type." They didn't interrupt Kate. She was telling them things about Shannon only her best girlfriends knew. "Listen, you need to know she wasn't that *type* of girl. Shannon didn't go out with married men. This was the first married guy—well, the *only* married guy—she ever went out with. It wasn't her style at all. She didn't search him out. If anything, she was turned off by him at first."

"What changed her mind?" Megan asked.

"It just kind of evolved. At least that's what she said." Kate mockingly held her hands up against her heart. "She thought she fell in love. *I* didn't even know about it until they were seeing each other five, maybe six months."

"Why do you think she waited so long to tell you?" asked Megan.

"I'm married and she knew I wasn't going to give her an easy time of it. I was the voice of reason … reality, really. I would have convinced her to dump him a lot earlier than she did."

"So she broke it off with him?" Nappa asked.

"About two weeks ago. Apparently, he didn't take it well."

"What do you mean?" Megan asked.

Kate's mood moved from broken despair to distinct revulsion for the story she was about to tell. "Shannon called me after she dumped him. She was starting to feel really guilty about the whole situation—wife, kids. She decided no matter how much she felt for him, it was time to cut it off. I think the scenario was getting to her. He was over at her apartment. I guess that's where they would usually hang out. From what she told me, he freaked out when she said she wanted to stop seeing him."

"What did he do?" Nappa asked.

"Shannon said he got extremely angry and started to yell and swear at her. I guess he threw a glass against the wall. She sounded pretty rattled when she called me."

"Did she say she was threatened by him, anything along those lines?"

Megan could see that Kate wanted badly to say yes, but it wasn't the truth. "No. She said he had his meltdown and then left."

"Are you absolutely sure about that?" she asked.

"Yeah."

"Okay." Megan knew to choose her words very carefully. "Other than yourself, who may she have confided in? Who were some of her other girlfriends, or guy friends, for that matter?"

Katelyn's defiant glare was enough to prepare them for her next comment. "I know *everything* there is to know about Shannon. I mean, I'm sorry, but what more can I tell you?" She looked at both of them defensively. "We're best friends."

The leather couch made a rubbing noise as Megan leaned in closer to Katelyn. Her adamant tone was unmistakable. "Katelyn, this isn't about how close the two of you were; this isn't about where you were on the totem pole of friendship with Ms. McAllister. We're trying to find out how and with whom she spent the last few weeks of her life. You weren't with her twenty-four hours a day. No one can be there one hundred percent of the time—for anyone." Megan's mother-daughter guilt trickled through her last comment. "We need your help."

Katelyn rubbed her forehead hard enough to incur a partial face-lift. "I know. I'm sorry. Let me think." She took out another tissue and started to blot underneath each eye. "Well, there's one woman from work. Shannon would go out for drinks with her every so often. She was assigned as Shannon's mentor when she started her internship." She searched for the woman's name. "It's

Linda or Laura, something like that. Her last name was... Christ ... um ... I'm trying to think of it."

"I have a list of initials that we haven't yet been able to match up with anyone from her address book, if that helps." Nappa handed Katelyn the printout he'd compiled.

Katelyn forced a smile. "Jesus, she's been doing that since freshman year. I once tried to read her schedule to meet up with her after class one day. She had AH written on her calendar. So, like a jerk, I walked clear across campus to Anderson Hall, where some of her classes were. She wasn't there. The AH stood for auburn highlights. She was out getting her hair done." Katelyn shook her head at the memory. "Let me take a look." She studied the list. "Here it is, LB, that's it. It's Lauren Bell, or Lauren Beall, something like that, and PG, that has to be our girlfriend in Brooklyn. Her name is Paige Gowan. I can give you her number. But she's in London right now. I called her there this morning to let her know about Shannon. She's going to try to come back for the funeral."

Nappa wrote the names down on the printout.

"Thank you. That helps," Megan added, trying to alleviate her bully-detective status.

"Believe me, I wish I had more information for you. She was my best friend. The kind of friend you think you're going to have your whole life. And now ..."

She began to sob. Her tears virtually leapt from her eyes as if in a race to see which could reach her jaw line first. Most were caught by the crumpled tissues she held tightly; some fell onto her lap, while others made their way to the wooden floor.

Megan knew this was as much as they were going to get from Shannon's best friend this morning. She tapped Nappa's arm, indicating it was time to leave.

"I think we've taken up enough of your time for now. We're going to leave our cards. If you think of anything, please call us. We may need to speak with you again at some point," Megan said.

"That's fine. Whatever I can do to help. I don't know how something like this could happen. You didn't know Shannon. No one was as good as she was. How could someone do this to her? I just don't understand it."

"We'll be in touch."

Katelyn didn't get up to show them out of the apartment. She sat and stared at the picture of her and Shannon.

This time Nappa pressed the elevator button.

"Did you notice the photo? The one of them on vacation?"

"I looked at it."

"The Claddagh ring was on a different hand, and facing the wrong direction."

Nappa shook his head. "She said the vacation was only a few months ago. Maybe that's when the victim had a change of heart and turned it around."

"No, Nappa. The ring was in the position of being taken. Kate said it was just a few weeks ago they broke up, or fought. And then she's found with the ring on the opposite hand, symbolizing she's open to love."

"But she was, McGinn. She dumped the professor, and she must have moved the ring—that's what makes sense."

"If she was hung up on this guy as much as Katelyn said, she wouldn't have done that so soon. At least I couldn't. When my ex-fiancé and I broke up, it took months for me to move my ring. I don't buy it. Give Palumbo and Rasmussen a call. Tell them we'll meet up with them at the college. I think we should have a chat with Professor *Love.*"

"I'll get them on the cell and see where they are."

ELEVEN

MEGAN AND NAPPA WALKED through the outdoor plaza of Columbia University. They were meeting Detectives Palumbo and Rasmussen in front of the Low Memorial Library next to *Alma Mater*, a bronze sculpture by Daniel Chester French, famous for his design of the Abraham Lincoln statue in Washington, D.C. The Low Memorial Library was distinguished as having the largest all-granite dome in the country and was built to resemble a Greek amphitheater. It's also the central social scene for Columbia University students to study, sunbathe, or just hang out before and after classes.

Megan couldn't help but notice the youthful surroundings: fresh faces, collegiate attitudes, fashionista wannabes, fashion disasters only youth could account for. Many were on iPhones, and most had computers in tow.

"Is it me or do some of these students look really young?"

Nappa smiled and looked around at the students in the plaza. "It's not that they look really young, it's that you're getting older."

Megan rolled her eyes. "Yeah, I'm hours away from my first Social Security check. Remember, Nappa, you're older than I am."

"I knew that comment was coming."

It wasn't difficult to spot Palumbo and Rasmussen; both wore dark suits and their posture was as stiff as the statue they stood next to. Detective Rasmussen greeted them by raising his index finger as if motioning for the check in a restaurant.

"Hi guys, what do you have so far?" Megan asked.

Detective Palumbo opened a small notepad as reference. "First off, nothing came through on the database. No cold cases with the MO of the jewelry in the..."

"Crotch," Megan finished flatly.

"Uh, yeah. We were at the victim's building earlier. We went through again to see if any neighbors could offer anything. There's still a handful that we haven't been able to connect with, so we'll go back. No one we've spoken to saw or heard anything out of the ordinary. Most of the stores near her building"—he gestured using his thumb—"the dry cleaner's, the florist, and the hair salon, all closed by eight o'clock. The deli was open, but the owner didn't remember anything peculiar. He did say he remembered seeing her a few days ago when she picked up some groceries."

"Did he remember if she was alone or *anything*?" Megan regretted how testy her question sounded.

"Alone," Rasmussen answered.

"Did you get her class schedule and list of professors?" Megan asked.

Rasmussen handed the list to Megan. She scanned through the names of Shannon's professors, hoping to find anything close to the name "Brower" that Katelyn Moore spoke of. Nappa got Rasmussen and Palumbo up to speed on their talk with Shannon's best friend.

"Here he is, Professor Bauer. Last name spelled B-a-u-e-r." Megan double-checked the list again. It was the only name that came close. "This must be him. Nappa and I will start with Bauer. Why don't you guys go to the counseling office where McAllister interned and see if you can come up with anything there?"

"Got it," Palumbo said.

Rasmussen hadn't taken his sunglasses off, though it was a cloudy day. "We'll be in touch."

Megan gave the paper to Nappa to review. "Definitely him. Let's go."

———

Professor Bauer's secretary sat outside his office at an oversized wooden desk. The turquoise-colored glasses halfway down her nose were attached to a chain resembling rosary beads. Her hair was cut butch short and she wore a dark suit with a thin scarf tied tightly around her neck. Her appearance aged her; so did her stern disposition. She didn't look up as Megan and Nappa entered. She was busy opening envelopes with a letter opener large enough to have decapitated Marie Antoinette.

Megan whispered to Nappa as they approached her, "The happy-go-lucky type. You go for it."

"Hello, I'm Detective Nappa, and this is my partner, Detective McGinn. We're here to speak to Professor Bauer."

They showed her their badges, but she was unimpressed by their credentials, since she didn't even take the time to look up at them.

"Do you have an appointment?" She was as personable as a drill sergeant ordering fifty push-ups.

Megan rolled her eyes. "No."

Nappa looked down at her nameplate. "Ms. Crawford, we don't have an appointment, but it's very important we speak with him." He smiled, attempting to use his charm on her. Getting a cobra to play nice would have been easier.

She finished opening a large envelope and picked up the phone. "Professor Bauer, there are two police detectives here requesting to speak with you. They *do not* have an appointment."

Mrs. Crawford hung up, continuing sorting through the day's mail. "Go in. He has ten minutes until his next meeting."

"Thank you so much, you've been very helpful." Megan looked over at Nappa and within earshot of Ms. Crawford said, "Y'know, I've always felt direct eye contact is crucial in making a good first impression."

Professor Martin Bauer sat all too confidently in his wide-backed red leather chair. His hands were steepled in front of his face, covering a slight grin. His thick, dark hair was swept back underneath the glasses he positioned atop his head. He wore a jacket and tie, but with a more casual effect, not the stodgy professor-with-a-pipe stereotype. His slightly oversized wrinkled white shirt, loose tie, and dark pants looked as though he pulled an all-nighter in a nightclub, instead of grading papers.

This is Professor Love? More like Professor Pompous.

"Yes, come in. And you are?"

"I'm Detective Megan McGinn, and this is my partner, Detective Nappa, NYPD." They both flashed their badges.

"I can only presume why you're here. Sit down." He motioned to two small red leather chairs positioned in front of his desk. Nappa sat, but Megan declined. The demand in his tone was enough for her to ignore him and lean against the armoire in his office.

"Obviously, you're here because of the tragic death of one of my students, Shannon McAllister."

The professor's arrogance could have set Megan off, but she kept her wits about her, for the most part. "It wasn't a tragic death, it was a brutal murder," Megan said.

Let the pissing contest begin.

"That's what I meant." A glare replaced his smug grin and he directed it at Megan.

"Student or lover?" Megan asked without the bat of an eyelash. "Or both?"

"You know it was both or you wouldn't be asking."

"You're married, aren't you?" Megan asked.

He held up his left hand and showed his wedding ring to Megan but replied to Nappa, ignoring Megan completely, "She's *good*, Detective."

Nappa stared Professor Bauer down long enough for him to get the hint there would be no male bonding in the near future.

"*Yes*, I'm married. *Yes*, I had an affair with Shannon. *No*, I did not kill her."

Megan answered without missing a beat, even though his mocking tone made her wince inside. "Great, I guess that'll be all, then."

"You actually think I've gone unaffected by her death? Do you honestly think I can go about my day and not think about how this young woman was brutally murdered?"

"From where I'm standing, you seem to be handling it quite well," Megan responded.

"We don't all wear our feelings on our sleeves, Detective. I was shocked when I found out about Shannon's murder. Shocked and incredibly saddened."

"You seem incredibly saddened," Megan said with as much excitement as someone about to undergo a colonoscopy.

Nappa interceded, "Professor, why don't we start with the last time you saw Ms. McAllister."

Bauer's disdain for Megan was obvious, and it was more than clear it was mutual. He pulled out his daily planner and began sifting through the pages.

"Let's start with professionally seeing her," Nappa added.

"Well, that would be at the end of last week. She was auditing one of my classes, so she would sit in once a week." He glanced through his itinerary and confirmed his statement, then repeated himself. "Yes, the end of last week."

"Did the two of you speak that day?" Nappa asked.

"No. It was a very busy morning. I had two morning classes, a business lunch, and then meetings for the majority of the afternoon."

"Who was the lunch with?" Nappa asked.

"My editor. I've written a book, and I was meeting with her to go over a few business matters."

"Is that a strictly professional relationship, or did you cross the line with her too?" Megan asked.

He leaned back in his leather chair. "I'm not her type. She's attracted more to cold, hostile women who exhibit penis envy. Want her number?"

Megan put one finger up to her temple and mocked, "Note to self: add 'cold, hostile, and exhibits penis envy' to my Match.com profile." She continued to lean against the armoire, her arms crossed, staring him down. Nothing threw Megan off, much less a narcissistic professor. "When was the last time you saw Shannon romantically?"

"That would have been two, maybe three weeks ago." He began tapping the end of a pencil against the legal pad again.

"How long were the two of you seeing one another?" Nappa asked.

"Eight months. Give or take."

"How did it start?" Nappa asked.

"We were working on a research project, spending many late nights together. One thing led to another and we started seeing each other. It's not something I orchestrated or even wanted at first. It just—"

Megan interrupted, "Evolved."

He stared at Megan a moment longer than needed. "Yes."

"Were you in love with her?" Nappa asked.

He sighed and shrugged. "I don't know. Maybe."

Professor Martin Bauer suddenly became more sensitive than when they first entered his office. His answer sounded sincere now, more than previously, anyway.

Megan almost believed he cared for Shannon, almost.

"Not enough to leave your wife for, though, right? What about your wife, Professor?" Megan asked.

"She didn't know anything about us, and she still doesn't," he answered. "Shannon was a very idealistic spirit. She only saw the good and the possibilities in everything. She couldn't see the barriers to our situation."

"Your situation meaning marriage, children, and a whole other life?" Megan asked.

"Make your point." Professor Bauer's patience was thinning.

Doesn't take much to push you very far, huh? Megan wondered if Shannon had pressed any of the same buttons.

"Who broke off the affair?" Nappa asked.

"It was mutual."

"So, both of you decided to end it, and there were no hard feelings, for either of you?"

"Of course not."

"Really?" Megan asked.

"Why don't I cut to the chase, Detectives? You're obviously having problems doing so." With his last comment, he made direct eye contact with Megan. "I'm an adulterer, yes. I'm probably even an asshole," he conceded.

"Probably?" Megan interrupted. She didn't expect an answer.

Professor Bauer scoffed at Megan's dig. "All right, so I'm an asshole. But I am *not* a killer. I could never hurt her. Why don't you ask me where I was the night she was murdered? Isn't that an obvious line of questioning?"

They knew he wouldn't have offered the information if he didn't have a good alibi.

Nappa bit. "Where were you the night before Ms. McAllister was killed?"

His pompous attitude returned. "I was giving a speech at an alumni dinner. Over one hundred people can account for my presence."

"What time did you leave the dinner?" Megan asked.

"Cocktail hour was at seven p.m., dinner at eight p.m., and my wife and I left around eleven p.m. We drove with another couple. We arrived home a little after midnight."

"Actually, Professor, we're more interested in where you were *yesterday* morning."

The question prompted a ricocheted response, "Why?" His tone now turned cautious. "Why yesterday morning?"

"Ms. McAllister was murdered in the morning."

"I see." A hint of perspiration broke free over his brow, "Well, yesterday morning I was driving into the city for class."

"Do you own an E-ZPass?"

"Yes, of course. I do the drive countless times a week."

"Mmm. We'll be checking on that," she said.

"Do whatever you need to do. I have nothing to hide." He tossed his pencil onto the yellow legal pad in front of him.

"You say that now," Megan offered. "But my hunch is you're not telling us everything. So, tell you what, if you decide to put your cock on the block and come clean with whatever it is you're not sharing, call us."

Ms. Crawford entered Professor Bauer's office just when Megan said the word *cock*. Her disgusted gasp prompted them to turn.

"Honey, it's something you could use a lot more of." Megan enjoyed shocking her.

111

"I've never."

"I actually believe that," Megan replied as they walked out.

———

"Professor Bauer...what an asshole. Penis envy my lily-white Irish ass. What a prick."

"No kidding. But you don't like the guy? I couldn't tell. Question: Why didn't you ask about his meltdown with Shannon? The one Katelyn told us about?"

"I wanted to see if he'd lie about anything. He admitted to the affair way too easily."

"You think he's lying about anything else?"

"Time will tell. Listen, why don't we split up? I'll go back to McAllister's apartment and take a look around," Megan said.

"What are you looking for?" Nappa asked.

"I don't know. I just want another run-through."

"Okay. I'll meet up with Rasmussen and Palumbo to see what they have. It might save some time."

"You never know, maybe someone missed something at the apartment. Do you have any idea how many times I've lost my cell when it was on vibrate, only to find it deep down the side of a chair cushion?"

"Yeah, I do. You're always emailing me to call you to see if you can find it," Nappa said sarcastically. "You really ought to get a land line so you can call yourself without getting me involved."

"Thanks for reminding me, Nappa. Maybe I'll do just that."

TWELVE

THE TREES PEEKING OVER the wall on Fifth Avenue were virtually bare of their autumn leaves. The day looked more like an evening in London from the dark skies and the continuous deluge of bad weather as Megan walked toward Shannon's apartment. A gust of frigid wind blowing down the avenue reminded her the days were numbered until the Manhattan drizzle turned to snow.

She turned onto Shannon's block but stopped short a few entrances of her building. An exquisite orchid arrangement caught her eye in the window of a floral shop. Inside stood an older woman behind a table, cutting the base off long, sleek flowers. The woman glanced up and Megan smiled in compliment to her work, an affirmation that beauty still remained in the world. Unsure as to why, she entered. Maybe she just wanted to smell life again.

Megan held out her badge. "I'm Detective McGinn. Do you have a moment?"

The woman nodded. "It's about the girl down the street, isn't it?"

"I'm afraid so."

"Two detectives already came by. I didn't have anything to tell them. The girl—"

Megan felt the need to interrupt and give "the girl" an identity. "Her name was Shannon McAllister."

"Oh. Well, she would come in once in a while, always buying white roses." The woman continued snipping the ends off the arrangement she was working on. "Sweet girl, that Shannon."

"If you think of anything, here's my card." Megan handed it to her, adding, "You do beautiful work." She turned to leave.

"Detective?" The florist handed her a single white rose. "You look like you could use a little beauty in your life."

Megan accepted the rose, nodding in thanks but knowing it would be a long haul before she found beauty in her life again. Outside, the Yorkville neighborhood seemed surprisingly normal; only one day earlier cop cars, news vans, and curious pedestrians lined the street outside Shannon's apartment. Now bits of yellow police tape dangled from the front door. It was back to business as usual.

The front door of the apartment building was wedged open by a stepladder. A large man in a gray jumpsuit with red print reading COLIN'S SECURITY COMPANY stood on the top step. He held a small screwdriver between his teeth as he adjusted the camera to the corner of the entranceway.

Megan maneuvered between the ladder and the door when the guy removed the tool from his mouth. "Hey, you should be careful. A girl got murdered here, ya know."

"Yeah, I heard." She thought about what her lieutenant had said: *I bet they'll fix the camera system now. It's a little too late for Miss McAllister.*

Walker was right, again.

Megan saw the porter in the lobby of the building. He seemed more interested in the song he was listening to on his iPod than her request to open Shannon's apartment. She showed the young man her badge and asked the whereabouts of the super, Mr. Mendoza. Apparently, Mr. Mendoza was off the premises. So the young man followed her up the four flights, unlocked the door, and without removing his headphones said, "It sticks a little."

"Great. Thank you," Megan said, not knowing if he heard her or not.

When she tried to open the door, it didn't just stick a little; it stuck a lot. She leaned into the doorknob and gave the door a quick smack using her shoulder. Shutting it took the same measure. The slamming sound echoed throughout the silent apartment.

The stillness of the room disarmed her. The living room was covered with dusty charcoal brushstrokes, residue from the search for fingerprints. The apartment had been bustling with people one day earlier. Now it was only Megan and her instincts with no distractions. The only noise came from shoes clicking on the wooden floor as she walked over to the couch. Megan stared at the now vacant space on the floor. Magazines and papers were strewn across the floor as before, only now they were next to tape outlining where the dead body had been. She slipped a pair of latex gloves on and sorted through the pile of class work and research papers. Nothing seemed out of the ordinary. She started to feel around the couch, behind all the cushions, but came up with only a candy wrapper and lint.

She went into the kitchen and searched through cabinets and a junk drawer but found nothing.

A loud noise from the street distracted Megan. Car accident? Manhole explosion? She knew it wasn't a gunshot, but she looked out the window anyway. There was a delivery truck across the street idling in front of an electronics store. Whatever it was, the disturbance didn't eliminate the void she felt in Shannon's apartment; the emptiness only intensified. She talked herself through the scene to break the silence.

"You let him in. You knew this guy. I'm sure of it." She rubbed the tips of her fingers together. "He cleaned under your fingernails." The thought immediately made her think of nail polish remover. She went into Shannon's bathroom.

There was more charcoal residue covering the white tiled bathroom. She opened the medicine cabinet. The top shelf had hand and body lotions. The second held a contact lens case, a nail file, a small jar of lip balm, toothpaste, and dental floss. She pushed the white shower curtain to the side. There was nothing in the tub, not even soap. She opened the door to Shannon's bedroom and leaned against the entrance. It was the one room that made her feel as though she were trespassing, especially when the victim was female. She was searching a room where women kept their most personal of items: journals, lingerie, the occasional battery-operated pleasure devices. Megan knew she was only doing her job, but what woman would want to suffer an untimely death and have a total stranger find her vibrator in the lingerie drawer next to the K-Y warming lubricant?

Shannon's bedroom had a sample-showroom Crate and Barrel feel to it. It was decorated in earth tones. The walls were light khaki in color and the trim was painted white. The bedding was a similar color, only lighter and with white piping around the edges. Oversized burgundy pillows were placed at the front of the headboard. Megan sat on the edge of Shannon's bed and gazed around the room. Every young woman had a secret hiding place. Megan thought about where she'd hidden things growing up: a box of Kool 100s in an old pair of tube socks in her top drawer. In her rebellious teenage years, Megan would sneak a cigarette regardless of whether her family was home. Every once in a while she'd hang out her windowsill and smoke. Then, one day her mother decided to do some spring cleaning while Megan was at school. Rose seized the Kool 100s, and Megan found herself grounded for two weeks. Megan's father, an occasional cigar smoker, gave her parole after one week.

Megan went through the dresser drawers, underneath the bed, and through Shannon's desk. She'd hoped something would jump out at her, but nothing did.

"Christ. Give me something to work with here."

She stood in the bedroom looking around at nothing but dead ends. She opened Shannon's closet and started to comb through every inch of it. She opened every pocket of every coat, and every pair of pants. Spare change, and the occasional packet of Listerine strips were the only items she found—not exactly overwhelming clues to Shannon's murder. She sat on the closet floor and opened every shoe box, feeling each pair down to the toe. Exhausted from rifling through a dead girl's things, she put everything back the way she'd found it.

Megan wasn't sure what emotion hijacked her the moment she slammed the closet door shut. Whether it was anger, frustration, or guilt, it didn't matter, but it was strong enough to bring her to her knees and break one of her own rules. She leaned back against the closet door as her eyes welled with tears.

"This one time, McGinn, I'll give you this one time," she said to herself, staring up at Shannon's bedroom ceiling. In between shallow breaths she yelled, "Throw me a bone, will ya, just a little clue to put me in the right direction. Whisper it if you have to, but for fuck sake give me something." Megan started laughing while she wiped the tears away, using her sleeve. "Wow, this is a new low. You're begging a dead girl to help you on the case. That's healthy. Next week you'll be wondering why the Easter Bunny hasn't stopped by for a beer lately."

She closed her eyes and took in a long, deep breath, exhaling it as if she were practicing for a labor contraction. "Get off your ass. Stop acting like such a girlie-girl. Buck up, kiddo, this is only the beginning."

Megan pulled herself up, went into the bathroom, and splashed water on her face. "Okay—get back to work," she said to her reflection in the mirror. She did one last walk-through and then put everything back the way she found it and returned to the living room.

The nagging feeling that she was missing something still ate at her. She was about to call Nappa to see if he'd made any progress when the screen on her cell phone lit up with an unidentified number. She hoped it was someone from the medical examiner's office. She answered abruptly to cover any sound of the meltdown that could be heard in her voice. "McGinn."

Nothing.

"Hello? Hello?"

There was silence, then the line went dead.

Megan closed her cell. A wrong number, no doubt. These touch screen phones were always dialing numbers on their own from the inside of a purse or from someone's back pocket.

She went back to her thoughts of the crime scene. There was nothing in the apartment that gave any indication of Shannon's murderer. It was time to move on. Megan placed the single white rose on the floor where she'd inspected Shannon's dead body. "For you."

She opened the door to Shannon's apartment to leave, and again the door stuck. "Jesus! You had to have let the killer in. He couldn't have opened this fucking door on his own!" She grabbed the knob with both hands and was violently yanking the door open when something fell from above the frame.

The object made little noise when it came down. If it hadn't hit Megan in the cheek, she wouldn't have noticed it. She picked it up, and held it in the light of the hallway. She recognized the shape, but it was slightly different from the crosses she was accustomed to seeing during her days in Catholic school. This one was made of reeds and a cream-colored silk tie fastened in the center. The four arms of the cross were even and the tips turned outward in opposite directions. It was small, delicate. She turned to go back in the apartment to place it on the armoire, but something made her put it in her jacket pocket. She wasn't sure why she was taking it, but that nagging feeling, the one where she couldn't help but sense she was missing something, was now gone.

THIRTEEN

Megan had just returned to the precinct when she passed Lieutenant Walker's office and saw Nappa inside. She lightly knocked and they motioned for her to enter. Based on the look on Walker's face, the telephone conversation she was on was an intense one. She stared sharply at the calendar on her desk and started to turn the pages. Her voice was uncharacteristically soft in answering. Her responses every few seconds consisted of, "Yes sir," and "I understand. Of course sir."

The older woman hung up, spewing a long breath at Megan. "Jesus fucking Christ. Do you know who that was?"

Megan looked at Nappa. "Um . . . no. Should I?"

Walker pointed at the phone with her index finger. "That was the mayor. You know. The mayor I always have lunch with."

"Ah, *that* mayor."

"Yes. *That* mayor," Walker said. She had to get one more dig into Megan before she was willing to move on. "Anyway. *That* mayor is on *this* department's ass. Your victim's father was apparently a strong financial supporter of this administration's campaign. Oh, and that's not all. Do you want to know who else I heard from?" Walker didn't wait for an answer. "A lawyer representing a Professor Martin Bauer. Did you bring up Professor Bauer's …genitalia?"

"Alleged genitalia. I'm not so sure he's packing," Megan answered.

Walker read off one of the pink slips on her desk: "You threatened to put his cock on a block?"

"I never threatened that!" Megan looked at Nappa for support.

"It was a colorful phrase, but no one never threatened his genitalia," Nappa confirmed.

"Alleged genitalia," Megan added.

"I'm curious to know how the word *cock* comes up in an interview, so to speak." Walker crossed her arms, not really expecting nor wanting an explanation. "Just get me up to speed with the McAllister case."

Megan began, "We met with Katelyn Moore this morning. The victim's best friend."

"Was she able to give you anything?"

"You're not going to like it," Nappa said.

The lieutenant looked back and forth between the two detectives. The stressed look returned to her face. "Oh Christ. What?"

Nappa began, "She was having an affair with Professor Bauer."

Walker threw her pen up into the air with enough force that it hit the ceiling. When it landed, it rolled off her desk onto the floor. "Lovely. And by *affair*, I assume he's married."

"Yeah, and he's a pompous jerk," Megan said.

"The guy is definitely full of himself," Nappa explained. "He did admit to the affair, which surprised us, but he also had a good alibi for the night before the murder, which he'd assumed was the time of death. We still have to do some checking on the morning, but I don't think he's our guy."

Walker looked at Megan, wanting her opinion too.

Megan reluctantly answered, "I don't think we should totally rule him out. Nappa's right. His alibi seems good. He was busy the night before and has an E-ZPass that'll track his movements that morning, so I can't see how he would have been able to do it. But I'm not ready to cross his name off the list."

"I take it you took a real liking to this gentleman, McGinn?"

Nappa smiled. "They *really* hit it off."

"I don't know what the girl saw in that man." Megan shook her head in bemusement. "He's the classic midlife-crisis scenario, and I don't think he's even hit midlife yet."

"Okay. What else?" The lieutenant was clearly hungry for answers, something to give her bosses. The victim having an affair with her married professor probably wasn't the information she'd hoped for.

"After meeting with Professor Bauer, I met up with Palumbo and Rasmussen. We spoke with some more people at the university, other students, teachers, but got nothing," Nappa answered.

"What about the mentor Katelyn Moore spoke of?" Megan asked Nappa.

"The school is getting back to me. Her internship isn't at the college. It's up in Harlem. This is interesting, though: the victim worked part-time as a counselor, overseeing mentally challenged prisoners who are a part of a work program where they leave prison, move into a halfway house, go to work in the morning, and return at night."

"Jesus, the girl really was a saint. Maybe one of her clients had a thing for her? I'd get in touch with that mentor," Walker suggested. "McGinn, where were you when Nappa was there?"

"I went back to the victim's apartment. I wanted to do another walk-through."

"Find anything?"

"No, not really."

"What about the lab?"

"We haven't heard anything yet, but we expect something soon."

"Good."

There was a knock at the door, and Detective Rasmussen stuck his head in the room. "McGinn, Dr. Sutherland is on line one and Mrs. McAllister is on line two."

Megan looked over at Nappa and said, "When it rains it pours. I'll take Mrs. McAllister. Why don't you take Sutherland?"

"No problem," Nappa answered.

Lieutenant Walker went back to her paperwork and offered, "Good luck. Keep me updated."

The detectives returned to their respective desks and took their calls. Megan answered, "Detective McGinn."

"Detective McGinn, this is MaryEllen McAllister."

"Yes, Mrs. McAllister, hello."

"I'm terribly sorry to bother you. I'm sure you're very busy, but I just had a quick question." Mrs. McAllister's overly polite demeanor bordered on apologetic, but she still couldn't mask her exhaustion.

"It's not a bother at all, Mrs. McAllister," Megan assured her.

"I'm calling because I was wondering if it's possible for us to get into Shannon's apartment for a few things…" She paused briefly before continuing, "for her funeral."

"Of course. We have everything we need from the apartment."

"I'm coming into the city tomorrow to make arrangements with the funeral home. May I come by and pick up Shannon's personal effects?"

"That's not a problem at all."

"Detective, while I have you on the phone, I was just wondering…"

For a moment Megan regretted not taking Dr. Sutherland's call instead. She knew what the next question was going to be.

"I was wondering if you've been able to find out anything regarding my daughter's case? If you have any leads?"

Megan was not about to give her the only new information they had: their daughter was dating a married man prior to the time she was savagely murdered. Megan knew Mrs. McAllister wasn't aware of Shannon's affair, and she didn't see any reason to pour salt over this poor woman's wound by telling her now. It could wait a day or two.

"I know it hasn't been long since Shannon … passed, but I was just wondering if you had any information."

"No, I'm sorry, not yet." Megan was ashamed of her answer. She wanted to offer some kind of hope that there would be justice waiting for them at the end of this stroll through hell.

"I figured as much, but I thought it wouldn't hurt to ask." Mrs. McAllister tried to hide her feelings of defeat in her answer.

"Actually, while I have you on the phone, do you mind if I say something?"

"Please."

"Mrs. McAllister, I just want you to know we're doing everything within our power to find who did this to your daughter." Megan felt a need to convince Shannon's mother of her commitment. "I…" Megan glanced over at Nappa as she offered Mrs. McAllister reassurance. "We won't stop until we get the person who is responsible for this."

"I know that, Detective. Thank you." The last part of her statement ended with her voice cracking and sniffling heard on the other end of the line.

"One last thing, ma'am. Would you mind bringing the laptop with you when you come in? I'd like to have our technical department take a look at it. If that's not a problem."

"Not at all."

Nappa had gotten off the phone with Dr. Max while Megan continued her conversation with Mrs. McAllister. He sat across from her and offered an empathetic look as he waited for her to finish.

Megan concluded their conversation by giving Mrs. McAllister her cell phone number and office address. She hung up the phone, slumped her exhausted body down into her chair, and slouched over her desk, burrowing her head into her folded arms. Her muffled question was barely audible, "What did Dr. Max have to say?"

"Well, for one thing, she was strangled."

Megan lifted her head up and looked at Nappa with a "you've got to be fucking kidding me" look. "Boy, that Dr. Max knows his stuff, huh?" Megan joked.

Nappa continued, "Her larynx was nearly crushed. This guy really wanted her dead. Other than that, there wasn't a lot."

"Mmm. What about the fibers, anything more on those?"

"No. He said the same as before. They're very common," Nappa answered.

"Did the lab get anything on what was used to clean under her nails?"

"There were traces of acetone, most likely from nail polish remover."

"Did they test the bread from the oven?"

"Plain old Irish Soda bread. About th—"

Megan interrupted, "Did he find *anything*?" She sighed. "Sorry."

Nappa continued, "The thread used is typical thread from any sewing kit, but the knot at the end the unsub made is surgical grade. The kind of knot still has him stumped. He said he'd get back to us."

"Surgical grade," Megan paused, "to basically guarantee *it*"—she motioned with her hand, knowing the word *vagina* would make Nappa uncomfortable—"wouldn't be opened."

"Looks that way." Nappa pushed his desk chair back and ran his hands through his thick black hair. He was just as frustrated as Megan with what few leads they had. Nappa remembered what Megan mentioned in Walker's office of her time in Shannon's apartment. "Hey, what did you mean when you said you didn't find anything at the apartment, *not really*?"

Megan was quickly reminded of the item in her pocket and used a tissue to pull it out. "This fell from the archway when I opened the front door in the McAllister apartment." She pulled out the cross and showed Nappa. "Isn't this a little weird?"

"It's a cross. What's weird about that?" Nappa thought she was reaching.

"The shape. Don't you think this shape is odd? Who puts a cross like this above a door?"

Nappa was unfazed with her discovery. "Well, the victim had a Claddagh ring on. Maybe she was sort of religious?"

Megan dropped her chin down. "Sort of religious? This religious woman dated a married man."

"Now who's being judgmental?" Nappa said.

"I'm not judging. I just think it's weird to have something like this above a doorway."

"Didn't Mrs. McAllister say that the apartment actually belonged to Shannon's grandmother? It's probably hers," Nappa said matter-of-factly.

Megan turned the cross around to look more closely at the shape. "That's true, I hadn't thought about that. But I think I'm going to have the lab look at it anyway and have them run some tests."

"You're an Irish Catholic. Shouldn't you know what kind of cross it is?"

"I'm a recovering lapsed Catholic who didn't pay all that much attention in Sunday school. The Irish side of me hits more bars than churches. Hey, have we heard anything from the tech guys regarding the desktop?"

"Nothing yet."

"Great. Mrs. McAllister said her daughter had a laptop. She left it at their house, and she's bringing it in, in the morning."

Nappa nodded. "It'll take some time for tech to get to it."

"I have a friend who might be able to help us."

"What kind of friend?" Nappa asked.

"The kind of friend that you go see about a dog and six wee pups."

"What?"

"It's something my grandfather would say." Megan laughed.

"When he was avoiding the answer?"

"No, when he didn't want to tell my grandmother he was walking down to the corner pub. Would you have rather me responded with 'None of your damn business'?"

"You wouldn't have said 'damn.' You would have used another word."

"True."

"What about her phone?" he asked.

"I went through the whole apartment again. Nothing."

"I called the number again. Same. Nothing."

Detective Palumbo walked in to hand Megan an envelope. "Finally got the warrant for the center. Only the vic's phone line. Rasmussen is checking out a few more details on the professor's alibi."

"Thanks. How's that coming?" Megan asked, opening the envelope.

"So far it looks legit, and the E-ZPass timing checks out. There are a lot of people that night who verify he was there."

"We figured as much. Oh, by the way. Did either of you try calling me earlier today?" Megan asked.

Both men answered no.

"What about Rasmussen?" Megan asked.

"Not that I know of, and we were together all day," Palumbo answered.

"I got a call when I was at the McAllister apartment. It must have been a wrong number or a butt dial or something. The line went dead shortly after I answered. I didn't recognize the number."

"It wasn't me. Maybe it was an adoring fan from your recent television interview?" Nappa ribbed.

"You're *so* not funny when you try to be, Nappa," Megan said.

"You're just a tough crowd."

"Still not funny. I have an errand to run." She put her jacket on and gathered the case files together.

"Buy him one from me, all right?" Nappa had a soft look in his eyes and offered her a knowing smile.

Megan felt a lump form in her throat. "How did you—"

"You're my partner."

She stared back at him in gratitude, along with a dash of astonishment he'd remembered. She mouthed a silent *thank you*, and went on her way.

———

"Hey, Gint. I brought you something." Megan placed two cans of Guinness beside the freshly covered grave and knelt down. Not that she was waiting for one, but had she received a thank you following her greeting, the Guinness would have been the first thing she'd have gone for.

The air was cold, the ground wet. The mist matted her hair down, long strands clamped over one cheek, making her look more like a disheveled child than a grieving daughter. She bundled her hands in her coat pocket while glancing at the graves scattered nearby. She realized her duties with funeral arrangements had yet to be completed. The headstone would need to be chosen, and paid for by Brendan, of course. A strong surge of wind blew against her back as if forcing her thoughts forward. She stared down at the wet mound of dirt in awe of the fact her father was merely days away from his sixty-eighth birthday when he died.

"Happy Birthday, Gint. You almost made it. Good thing I didn't get you a gift." An uncomfortable laugh was followed with the hope that somewhere in the ethers her father would have found that unseemly comment funny; instead her pain shot out in volcanic anger. "You son of a bitch! You weren't supposed to go yet. *You weren't supposed to leave!*" She grabbed the closest rock in front of her and chucked it, wishing God, disappointment, and pain had physical form so they could feel her wrath.

Her face fell into the palms of her hand as she begged, "Please, God, just bring him back. *Please.* I'll never drink again if you just bring him back. I'll go to church. I'll … I'll … *please.*"

Megan wanted to slump over and hug the earth where her father had just been laid to rest. She wanted just ten more minutes with him, five if that's all that would be allotted. Instead she conceded, "Fine. Fuck you." She wiped the tears from her face with her sleeve and cracked open one of the beers. "I don't have to keep any promises." Her mind went directly to the promise she'd made earlier to Mrs. McAllister. "At least not to *you.*"

Megan chugged the beer, throwing the empty to the ground. Images of Shannon's body, the disgusting things done to her, raced through her head.

"I'm going to get the bastard, Dad. I'll get him."

FOURTEEN

When Megan left the Bronx, it was dusk; it was pitch black when she returned to Manhattan. She sat on the downtown train. It was the local, but it could have been an express for the amount of attention she gave the loud speaker. When she emerged onto Lexington Avenue, she was forty blocks south of her stop. Her miscalculation had nothing to do with her exhaustion or the one Guinness—she'd handled a hell of a lot more on a hell of a lot less. Her focus was on Shannon McAllister, her mother, her father ... her murder.

The chill in the night air accompanied by the drizzle wasn't enough for her to venture back to an empty apartment filled with mounting sympathy cards and regrets. She walked the streets, hoping to see the city as tourists do—a beacon of fast-paced excitement and opportunity. But what she saw were murdered people pulled out of buildings in black body bags. The line outside the Empire State Building was long, even for this hour, but Megan's memory was longer. She was called to a crime scene in the building her first year on the job. A security guard was stabbed in the chest.

Sirens wailed down the street as she turned to walk toward Times Square. Empty white noise to her ears. Megan maneuvered through the crowd as umbrellas slammed into her shoulders. A Starbucks was now at the location where a strip club once was. A hooker was found there one night with a needle sticking out of her arm from an overdose. There would be no grande lattes in her future.

Megan found herself in Midtown heading to the Upper East Side. She waited at the crosswalk, staring into the window of a restaurant. People laughing, clanking glasses of wine, enjoying overpriced food. The last time she was in a restaurant like that, a chef had stabbed the owner with a butcher knife. Slashed him right through the gut. That was the extent of Megan's fine dining experience.

Megan crossed at 59th Street on a green light when a yellow cab screeched to a halt. His horn and angry foreign words yanked her back from trolling the list of homicides she'd worked to the fact she was nearly mowed down in front of Bloomingdale's—which was not the way she wanted to go out.

The night's drizzle was now turning into a full-on bitter cold rain. Her own image caught her eye at the corner electronics store. The store was closed, but the televisions for sale in the window remained on. It was the late news. Eight televisions cast the same story: her interview leaving Shannon McAllister's apartment. Between the sound of the rain hitting the pavement and her focus on the muted newscast, she didn't hear her phone right away. She flipped open her cell. No answer, only a dead line. She glanced at the same unknown number she'd seen earlier that day.

"What the hell?"

She rang back and heard Shannon McAllister's voicemail. *Motherfucker.*

Megan stared at her own countenance on the screen. Her facial expression was tired, whipped. Now, standing in the storm, saturated through and through, she felt a fire ignited by a killer's simple gesture that no amount of rain could douse.

She stared down at the cell phone, knowing she wouldn't receive a call from that number again.

"I am no one's bitch. I will *not* be fucked with."

FIFTEEN

MEGAN HAD PASSED DRENCHED a half hour previously. Her kaleidoscope of moods would not tolerate sitting alone in an empty apartment for long, though. She pressed the outdoor buzzer to the entrance of the Carnegie Hill Swim Club. Glancing up into the security camera, she thought for a brief moment how ironic it was that her gym had a better security system than most apartment buildings in Manhattan. Being buzzed in through two doors and swiping a gym card for admittance made entrance to the Pentagon seem less troublesome than gaining access to the semiposh Upper East Side swim club.

Manny, the attendant on duty, sat at the desk reading an outdated issue of *Sports Illustrated* when Megan walked in. She swiped her membership card through the monitor, and her photo appeared on screen as well as the date and time of her last workout.

Manny was a big guy with dark, curly hair. He had a year-round tan and muscles that Megan was sure were aided by performance-enhancing drugs.

He glanced up at the screen. "Been a while, huh?"

"Yeah, thanks for noticing, Manny."

He grinned, handed her a towel. "Have a good workout."

"Could I have two towels, please? I'm swimming tonight."

"You look like you already have been. Oh, just so you know the lifeguard is on his break, so you'll need to wait until he gets back. Gym policy."

"Sure. I'm steaming first, anyway," she lied. *Policy* was not a word she felt a close kinship with, and the local swim club was no exception.

Two women were getting dressed when Megan entered the ladies locker room. The smell of baby powder mixed with an overpowering perfume filled the air. She stripped off her clothes, put on her bathing suit, stuffed her belongings into one of the lockers, and hoped she was able to remember the combination to her lock by the time she returned.

Megan set her swim paraphernalia—towel, goggles, swim cap, and earplugs—on the counter while she showered down. Her flip-flops made slapping noises as she walked into the shower stall. She was one flight down from the pool, but the scent of chlorine already had its calming effect on her. When she made it to pool level, she was surprised and relieved to see she had it all to herself. She walked over to the aerobics room door and glanced in. The lifeguard was busy chatting up a short, young blonde. He was definitely still on his break, and Megan wasn't about to wait for him.

One side of the room had floor-to-ceiling windows with glass doors opening to a landscaped courtyard, now empty with autumn's arrival. Sycamore trees and wooden sculptures lined the fenced-in area. The view from the pool made Megan feel like she was in a wooded backyard rather than a hard city. As daylight began to fade, the underwater pool lights turned on automatically.

As Megan placed her towel on one of the lounge chairs, she realized she'd forgotten to remove her jewelry while in the locker room. She took off her watch and crucifix and placed them underneath the towel. She tugged at the backside of her swimsuit in an attempt to cover more of her ass, then set her goggles, swim cap, and earplugs on the adobe-colored tile and stood at the pool's edge to warm up. She rotated her arms forward and backward, loosening up her shoulders. She twisted her back left and right, all the while listening to popping noises as she moved. She bent forward, touching her palms down on the cold floor to stretch the backs of her legs. Sitting down on the edge of the pool, she dangled her feet in the water and was greeted with a mild shock to her flesh. "Christ, what is this, the Polar Bear Swim Club?"

The pool's glimmering light reflected off her pale face. It would have had a hypnotic effect if not for the last few days she'd experienced. The quiet only offered space in her mind to wander back to the crime scene: remembering Shannon's lifeless stare, the moment in Dr. Sutherland's office when he'd recounted his examination. The mental images weaving through her mind became more uncomfortable than the water temperature. She quickly inserted her earplugs, stuffed her hair into the swim cap, and suctioned the goggles to her face. The dark-shaded lenses made it difficult to see anything outside of the water, so she used the underwater lights as her guide when she plunged in. Using all her lower body strength, she pushed off the wall to begin her first lap. Months ago the first ten laps had been simple, a mere warmup for the following twenty. Today her body was deadweight as she tried to maneuver down the lane. The only noise she heard was the pounding of her heart as she cleared the first lap and wondered if it had been a good idea to start swimming without the lifeguard present. By the fourth, she began to assume a decent pace. Long rhythmic strokes moved her from one end of the pool to the other. She soon found her groove and quickly reverted to her old pattern: front crawl, backstroke, sidestroke. Repeat.

She stopped after eight laps, grabbed the edge of the pool, and pulled herself up to again stretch the backs of her legs. The pause was more to catch her breath than ease her tight muscles. She drew in a deep breath and continued. If Megan had hoped to find a meditative state during her swim, she would have been better off going to an ashram.

———

The movement was instantaneous. Megan saw a shadow shift in front of her lane. She stopped mid-length in the pool and yanked her goggles off her head. "Hello?" She turned full circle in the water. In between heavy breaths, she yelled out, "Is anyone there?" The echo of the water slapping against the pool's side paled in comparison with the sound of her heart pounding in her chest. "Is anyone there?"

Behind one of the columns the lifeguard appeared, the sound of the door closing behind him. "Hey, are you okay?"

Megan didn't answer right away. She knew the movement had come from the front of the lane, not from where the lifeguard entered.

"Yeah." She swam over to the ladder and pulled herself out of the pool, leaving her few moments of relaxation behind her. Cold air attacked her wet body. She beelined herself over to the lounge chair and quickly wrapped herself in the towel. "Did you see anyone else in here?"

The lifeguard shook his head no.

She continued to look around the room as she dried herself off. "Maybe it was my imagination."

Maybe.

She ran the towel through her soaked hair, shaking her head to one side trying to release water lodged in her ear despite the earplug. She stared down at the chair. Her watch now lay facedown. Megan always placed her watch face up, so the crystal wouldn't get scratched. She cautiously picked it up by the band as if it would snap at her fingers. There was no sign of her necklace. She shook her towel, hoping the piece had gotten tangled and would fall out. "Hey," she shouted over to the lifeguard, "did you see a necklace around here? It's a silver cross with a green stone in the center."

He said he hadn't but offered to help her in the fruitless search.

"Are you sure you didn't see anyone come in while I was swimming?"

"No, no one. Just you and me." The lifeguard checked around the chair where Megan had placed her things. "There's a heating duct behind the chair. Maybe it slipped down?"

She moved the chair back. "I hadn't noticed that. Damn it."

―――

Megan left the gym smelling like chlorine, her wet hair pulled back into a ponytail. She didn't care. She didn't stick around to take a steam or a shower, she just wanted out. She was oblivious to the chilly air hitting her as she walked up the hill to her apartment.

Her thoughts only one hour ago were about Shannon, the murder scene, the thin line of leads. Now her mind sprinted from the recent unidentifiable hang-ups to her missing necklace. She dug deep into her gym bag to find her keys and walked into her apartment to the sound of her cell phone beeping. She knew she'd been preoccupied earlier when she left for the gym, but Megan was never without her cell and was surprised she'd left it behind. The phone's screen read *3 voicemail messages, 1 text message*. The first message was from the lab. They didn't come up with anything on the reed cross she'd sent in for testing.

"Figures," she muttered.

They said to call back if she had questions.

The second voicemail was from Uncle Mike, checking in.

The third message was from her brother, but she didn't wait to listen to it all the way through. Megan closed the phone, forgetting to check the text message. As soon as she placed it on the kitchen counter, it vibrated, reminding her the text had yet to be opened. When she pressed the button to open the message, her seven-hundred-square-foot apartment suddenly felt miles away. She turned, bent over the counter, and evacuated everything from the pit of her stomach down into the sink.

The message read: HOW WAS YOUR SWIM?

So much for wanting to feel like your old self for a few hours, she thought. She knew she didn't need to call the number where the text originated—it had been etched in her mind—but she also knew she had to, just to be sure. And the response: Shannon McAllister's outgoing message.

SIXTEEN

I TOSSED BOTH HALVES of the phone into the East River while thinking there was something about Detective McGinn I found familiar. And then I made the connection.

———

Megan slid down to the floor against one of the kitchen cabinets, but not without first lighting a cigarette. Her cell phone rang again.

"Restricted." She stared at the phone as it continued to ring, wondering if she should answer it. She pressed the green call button and slowly put the phone up to her ear. She didn't hear anything on the other end and waited a few seconds before speaking.

Nothing.

"Who the fuck is this?"

"Hey, kiddo—hello to you too."

"Fucking hell, Brendan. You scared the shit out of me." Megan covered her heart with a shaking hand, as if that would slow its pace. "Where are you calling from? The phone doesn't register a number."

"I'm still at work in one of the conference rooms," he said. "You sound like shit."

Megan said, "Thanks," followed by a long drag off the cigarette.

"Smoking again, I hear."

She rolled her eyes. "Hey, trust me, it could be worse." She tried to think back if she still had any pot left in her bedroom from the night the stockbroker slept over, although she'd already decided it was going to be an Ambien evening.

"Have you been to see Mom?"

"Yeah. She seems to have settled into the nursing home, but her condition is status quo."

"Did she get the flowers I sent?" Brendan asked.

"Yes. And why did you send her flowers when you know she has no clue?"

"It made me feel good and it gives her something nice to stare at. Doesn't matter if she knows who they're from, does it?"

Megan couldn't argue with that. Guilt has a way of blackmailing you into doing anything to rid yourself of even the smallest amount of shame.

"We need to go over a few things about the house. I want to get it up for sale in the next couple of months, so we really need to start going through their things, maybe think about an estate sale before the weather gets too bad."

"First of all, you don't mean *we*, you mean *me*. I'm working a case; how the fuck do you think I'm going to be able to handle the house all by myself?"

"Aunt Maureen and Uncle Mike will help out, and I promised I'd come back."

"You better keep that promise and not be a douche bag, Brendan."

"I think I read a greeting card with the same sentiment," he laughed, which made Megan laugh in return. He always could cut through her dark moods better than almost anyone else, with the exception of their father. "I've been going through dad's will. It's all pretty standard. I'm always handling the business end of things while you play one of Charlie's Angels."

"Very funny."

She heard a rustling at her door.

What the fuck? The doorman didn't call up?

She closed the phone with the force of a brick smashing through a Tiffany glass window. She reached for her gun next.

SEVENTEEN

"Fucking hell." After checking the peephole, Megan opened the door to a slightly stunned Nappa.

"Don't shoot, I brought food."

"Why didn't the security guard call me?"

Nappa shrugged. "He saw my badge and gun, and I guess just assumed."

"What an ass."

Nappa pretended to turn around to leave. "I can take this food elsewhere."

"I didn't mean you. Get in here." Megan double locked the door, and then checked it a third time.

"Why are you answering the door with your gun drawn, McGinn?"

She shook her head. "I just was ..." She was about to tell Nappa about the text she'd just received, but for some reason held back. Partly out of pride, partly out of not wanting to come off as a puking, smoking, trigger-happy hysteric.

"Just so you know, I would have shot you if you weren't bearing food."

"Well, that's good to know. It's not particularly comforting, but it's good to know," Nappa answered warily.

Megan took the bag from Nappa's hands. "Thai? Why are you at my apartment with my favorite food?" She asked with raised eyebrows and a suddenly ravenous appetite.

"I was in the area." An expressionless stare followed.

"No, you weren't," Megan returned with the same poker-face.

"No, I wasn't. I brought wine. Is white okay?"

Instead of protesting the change of subject, she kowtowed to her empty stomach. "Of course. If it's not in a box, the opener is over there." Megan nodded toward one of the kitchen drawers.

Nappa stood staring down his partner as he opened the bottle of wine and let her fidgety behavior speak the volumes she was unable or unwilling to.

"Are you okay?"

"What do you mean?" She pulled plates and utensils out of drawers as if they were weeds invading her blue-ribbon vegetable garden.

"You're flying around the kitchen like Julia Child on crack."

She waved him off. "Yeah, I'm fine … I just had a conversation with Brendan." Shit, she'd have to call him back soon too.

He studied her a moment. He knew a long line at Starbucks could put Megan in this kind of mood, so he decided to let it be. "Well, here." He handed her a glass of wine. "Maybe this will help."

"Thanks. And thank you for the food. Go in the living room. I'll plate us up."

He took his glass and did as ordered. "Ah, look, my favorite photo," Nappa said. He looked back and forth between Megan and the photograph. "I still can't believe this is you," he said, removing it from the armoire.

"I was a little pudgy when I was a kid." She smiled, grateful for a light moment.

The photo was taken when Megan was ten. She and Brendan were sitting outside. He had his arm around his baby sister. Megan's mouth was covered with chocolate ice cream. Based on her Buddha belly, ice cream was consumed often. Though the picture wasn't terribly flattering for her, Megan loved the expressions on their faces.

"McGinn, pudgy is one thing. This is..." Nappa searched for the most politically correct description.

"Baby fat?" Megan interjected.

"You were no oil painting. Unless there was a call for cherub models, that is."

"Okay, so I was a little on the round side." Megan brought all the food into the living room. She moved the photographs and files to one side of the coffee table to make room for their dinner.

"I mean, look at you now. I would never have guessed you were such a fatty growing up."

"Look at me now? What is that, a back-handed compliment?"

"Well, you don't crack mirrors anymore." He tried to steer the conversation away from his flattery. "Can I get a copy of this, one for my wallet or maybe an eight-by-ten? Even better—poster-size?"

"Very funny." She handed him his dinner. "Hey, something happ—"

"I need to cut to the chase before we start work." Nappa's tone was suddenly very official. "Are you up for this case? You have had a hard time of it. A really hard time. You haven't even had time to mourn your dad."

"Wait, hold on." Megan pointed her wine glass in his direction. "*You* were the one to call me with the McAllister scene. You!"

"I know, I feel responsible. As your partner, I need to check in."

"No. You mean Walker needs to check in, and she asked *you* to see if I'm good for it."

"Look. You've had to deal with your father passing, taking care of your mom. It's been a whirlwind."

"She's in a nursing home now, Nappa. That doesn't really qualify me as caring for her."

"McGinn, what else were you supposed to do? You work twelve-, sometimes fourteen-hour days. There's nothing to feel guilty about. She's in an excellent facility. You couldn't have done it all on your own."

Megan knew Nappa was right. But that didn't make it any easier. Things started to go wrong for Rose around her sixtieth birthday. The small incidents soon magnified into much larger situations —leaving things on the stove or in the oven, which could have led to fires if Pat hadn't gotten home in time. It wasn't so much her forgetfulness that had Pat concerned but the change in her personality and her personal habits. Then it *all* began to change. Her thoughts became jumbled. She'd have emotional flare-ups for the smallest reasons. She started leaving the house disheveled—hair messy, no makeup, her clothes wrinkled. It became too much for Megan's father to deal with privately. They saw countless doctors and had scores of tests done. The professionals referred to it as an early onset of dementia or Alzheimer's. While her father was alive, he vowed to take care of her, and he did. But with Pat gone now, there was little she or Brendan could do but place her in the finest facility they could find. It was the hardest decision she ever had to make, but it was what was best for their mother, and that's all that mattered. Megan knew it would be a long time before she could accept that fact.

"I don't think anyone could hold up to that kind of pressure as well as you have. And now this case comes up."

"Forget about that. Tell me the truth: Do *you* think I should be on this case?"

"I think you can handle anything that comes your way, but when you lose it with our lieutenant, I get worried."

"Nappa, what do you want? You want me to apologize again?" She took a chug of her wine.

"No." His voice deepened. "I want to know you can handle this. Both you and I know this is only the beginning."

In that moment she knew she couldn't share the information about the text; she'd be taken off the case immediately, and she couldn't let that happen. "Yes. Got it?"

"Okay, okay." They sat for the next few minutes eating in an uncomfortable silence. "Sorry," Nappa offered.

"Shut up, Nappa." Megan then nabbed a dumpling off his plate. "Hand me the remote."

She turned on the CD player.

"Neil Diamond? You listen to Neil Diamond. You *like* Neil Diamond?"

"No, I *love* Neil Diamond. He's a god. I have every one of his albums, or CDs, whatever you want to call them now."

"Okay, let me get this straight. Not only do you listen to, love, and think Neil Diamond is a god—which, by the way, is more than just a little scary to me—you own every single album?"

"Yep. I've seen him twelve times in concert. Sometimes I even wear my Neil Diamond concert T-shirts to bed, not that you needed that information." Megan sipped from her wineglass before belting out a line from the song, at an unbearable volume. "Sweeeeet Caroline..."

"Well, now I know why you're single. Neil Diamond T-shirts to bed, not sexy."

"Fuck off, Nappa!" Megan laughed at his shot.

"Yes, the Neil Diamond obsession and the mouth on you, that explains why you're single."

———

Over the course of the next few hours, they went through more wine as they worked on piecing together a case that had very few pieces to work with.

"I can't figure out how he did *so* much and left only two fibers behind." Megan sighed. She went through some of the less-graphic crime-scene photographs. "Maybe we're wrong about this." She handed Nappa the photo of how Shannon was found. "He could have just put her in this position for the hell of it."

Nappa looked at the photo from every angle. "But the suturing. That wasn't just for the hell of it."

Megan was tired and stiff from sitting on the wooden floor. She moved to the couch next to Nappa. "I can't look at that photo one more time tonight." A photo of a sewn-tight vagina didn't mix well with Thai food. She turned the picture over and looked at Nappa. "So why are *you* single?"

"What?" He threw his head back on the couch, laughing at the odd timing of her question. "We move from talking about vaginas to my love life."

"What, the two don't go together?"

"Not currently."

"I know what you mean."

"Yeah, our work doesn't bode well for lasting relationships."

"I have a feeling you are a man with a few secrets, Sam Nappa."

Nappa did have his secrets, and he knew he'd had enough wine to unwisely divulge some of them, so he switched gears and asked the questions instead of answering them. "You know, I've never asked—I assumed, but I never came out and asked—what made you become a cop?"

"Excellent ploy, Nappa, redirecting the conversation back to me."

"No, seriously, I'm curious." Nappa's interest was sincere, but also a successful strategic move.

"What did you assume the reason was?"

"I figured because your father was a cop, he'd influenced you."

"I prefer to look at it as *inspired* rather than influenced. *Influenced* feels ugly to me, like he pressured me. I was never pressured to become a cop, though I did enjoy how it sent my mother through the roof." She smiled. "My mother would have definitely preferred a stockbroker or lawyer. A home in Westchester, two grandchildren, a golden retriever, and me volunteering for the Junior League."

"Sure, I could see that." Nappa conveyed his sarcasm with an eye-popping expression. He refilled their glasses before sitting back on the couch. The few times Nappa had met Rose before her health had gotten really bad recently, he took joy in watching the one person who could get under Megan's skin. But he also saw the love they had for one other. It was as deep as the Mariana Trench, and just like it, you couldn't touch the bottom, but you always knew it was there.

"So, because my mom wanted me to do all those things, that's exactly what I didn't do. As for my dad, well, you've heard all the stories about how great a detective he was. I don't think I'll reach that level, but ..."

"You're wrong. You'll probably never see it, but you're wrong. You're a great detective."

"Thanks." She could feel her face redden.

"Oh my God. Detective Megan *The Meganator* McGinn is blushing."

"It's the wine." She sipped from her glass, feeling her face turn even hotter.

He shook his head and whispered, "I don't think so." He lightly stroked Megan's cheek. She closed her eyes trying hard to remember the last time she'd felt a man's gentle touch. Sex had been recent, and rough, but a soft caress—that hadn't happened for a very long time. She put her hand up to his, about to push it away; instead she leaned into him, allowing their lips to touch. It was a light, tender kiss until Megan ran her fingers through his black hair, pulling him closer. Their tongues met as she moved back on the couch, pulling him on top of her. His deep kisses moved from her lips down her neck. He stopped, straddled her while taking off his shirt, then removed hers button by button. He rubbed his palms over her chest, slowly moving each bra strap down her shoulders before unfastening it, tossing it to the floor. His mouth moved over each breast, sampling the taste and feel of her nipples in his mouth, softly between his teeth. She moved his hand toward her pants. He started to unbutton her jeans when their cell phones rang. He collapsed his head into her bosom in frustration.

"Shit." Megan buried her face into his hair. "*Shit.*" The phones continued to ring. "We have to get that." Megan moved photos, files, searching for her cell. Nappa checked his jacket. Nothing. He let it go to voicemail by the time Megan located hers.

"It's Rasmussen." She answered, doing her best to calm her breathing, "McGinn."

Megan knew fate had stepped in, but she was currently of the opinion that fate was a real bitch. She listened to the details from Rasmussen. "Yeah. Uh-huh."

Nappa put his shirt back on and picked up Megan's bra. He stood behind her, brushed her hair to the side, slowly slipped the straps up each arm, moving the cups under her breasts, which moments ago he'd tasted.

"What's the address?" she asked. His soft fingers fastened each hook with delicate precision. His touch sent shocks up and down her body. "Hang on a second." When she paused the conversation with Rasmussen, Nappa placed his forehead on her shoulder, his arm around her. She fell back into his touch, knowing that this could never happen again.

He kissed her neck, then released his hold on her.

Her tone turned overtly official. "The address?"

"Young. Female. Upper East Side. Hundred-and-Eighth Street and Fifth." She snapped the phone shut and quickly pulled her shirt back on. "Let's go."

EIGHTEEN

THE NEXT MURDER SCENE had the impressive Fifth Avenue address, but the neighborhood bordered Spanish Harlem, and at night, it also bordered safety. It was dangerous to go too far away from the avenue after dark, and even more dangerous to be in the area of Central Park that faced the building. On occasion, a floater would be found in the center of the Harlem Meer, the pond just inside the northeast corner of the park. A mugging or random stabbing was usually to blame, and there was certainly enough to consider that particular area of the Upper East Side less than safe. They'd ruled out a connection to their earlier unsolved homicide, but another murder so soon after Shannon's would make the headlines.

Detectives Palumbo and Rasmussen were waiting outside the apartment when Megan and Nappa got off the elevator.

"There you are." Palumbo closed his cell phone when he saw Nappa accompany Megan off the elevator.

"Hey, guys." Megan was anxious to get into the apartment. "What do we have here?"

"Young, probably in her twenties. Caucasian, female," Detective Palumbo answered.

Megan didn't wait to hear the remaining information. She walked into the two-bedroom apartment, assuming the body was going to be in the living room. A member of the forensics team alerted her, "Detective, she's in the other room. The bedroom down the hall."

"Thanks," she said.

The young woman's dead body lay naked with her face turned to the side. She had two nipple piercings and a tattoo of a rose on her lower abdomen. A sheet covered the rest of her. In the ashtray next to the bed was a half-smoked joint and next to that were two lines of cocaine on a small mirror.

"Detective, this is getting to be a habit. We've seen one another twice this week," Assistant Medical Examiner Jonesy said.

"Well, I guess that means neither of us has a life because we're always working," Megan replied.

Jonesy pointed his black pen down at the naked dead woman before him. "Well, we have more of a life than she does now."

"Looks like she was partying it up before she went."

"She went out with a bang, a puff, and a snort. I've seen worse," he said.

"Christ. Aren't you too young to be this jaded?" Megan turned the woman's head to check the marks on her neck.

"She was strangled with this." He pointed to the side of the bed. A long black scarf was crumpled up next to the bed.

"Sex games?" Megan asked.

"Yeah. She lost to autoerotic asphyxiation." He continued making notes on a legal pad as he answered her questions.

"Who found her?" Megan asked.

"Roommate." He flashed a look toward the door, indicating the roommate was down the hall.

"Where is she?" Megan asked.

"That would be a *he*, and he's down the hall." Jonesy flashed a skeptical look.

Nappa walked in, looked over the scene, and commented, "Well, this is certainly a different setting from the last one."

"I'd say so. The roommate is down the hall."

"I was just with him. Palumbo and Rasmussen are speaking to him right now. They're trying to find information on next of kin."

"What do we know about her?" Megan asked.

"Her name is Eve Scott. She's from Park Ridge, New Jersey, but she's lived here for the last five years with the roommate," Nappa explained.

"Did she have a boyfriend that the roommate knew of?" Megan asked, sounding more like Jonesy in her tone. She began looking through some of the dead girl's personal things.

"The roommate said they come and go at different times. He wasn't up on her personal life." Nappa looked around the bedroom. The drugs and a scarf were on the floor next to the bed.

Jonesy piped in, "That's an understatement: *come and go.* Specifically, she went when she came."

Megan and Nappa looked at each other in slight awe of the cynical comment. "Jesus, can you be more specific?" Megan sarcastically asked.

"She died as she orgasmed. The scarf was too tight," he said.

"Yeah, I understood that part, Jonesy. I was kidding."

"I've seen this before. A lack of oxygen makes the orgasm stronger, more intense, something along those lines." Jonesy hadn't looked up once from his note taking as he spoke.

Nappa glanced at Megan and grinned. "Jonesy would know."

Megan leaned into Jonesy, making sure none of the other crime-scene investigators were currently in the room. "We need to ask you something. Has her vaginal canal been sewn shut?"

That question prompted Jonesy's first glance up from the pad he'd been writing on. "You're fucking kidding me."

Both detectives remained silent.

"Okayyyyyy." Jonesy lifted the bedsheet. Given the victim was spread-eagled underneath, it wasn't too difficult to give them an answer. "No. And I do not want to know why you asked me that."

Megan's attention was drawn to an item on Eve Scott's desk. "Jesus."

"What?" Nappa asked.

She used her pen to lift the key chain off the desk. An identification card in a plastic cover hung from the end. "Look."

"Oh great," Nappa said.

It was a Columbia University student ID.

———

The crowd that had gathered outside the dead woman's building began to scramble for cover when lightning flashed and thunder rumbled. Long, needlelike spears of rain broke over the pavement. "Let's sit this out a little bit. What do you say, Nappa?"

They sat down on the faux-leather sofa in the lobby, their backs facing the street and the press. "I don't think the two are connected, but I'm worried about the fact two women from the same university have been killed in the same week." Megan shook her head. "The media will ride this one hard."

"Of course they will. Gotta sell papers. Gotta get ratings." Nappa stared down at the floor. "I think we should talk about what happened earlier."

"Sam…We will, but not now." She raised her eyebrows. "The last few days have been a lot to take in. Can we just put *it* on ice for now?" She put her hands up in prayer. "Please."

He smiled. "Yeah, I would say there's a few bigger things going on. Ice is fine for now."

"Thanks."

They sat in silence thinking of what had taken place on Megan's couch. Megan cleared her throat moving closer to Nappa, "There's something I think I need to explain," she raised her eyebrows with a slight grin. "Earlier at my place when we were…"

"Researching the case?"

"Yeah, then. You touched a part of my lower neck." Megan pointed to the covered scar. "I got this when I was seventeen. I visited a friend at her college upstate. We were at a keg party at one of the fraternities. Well, four beers later—hey, I was a lightweight then." She stopped and stared out at the storm. "My girlfriend hooked up with some college hockey player and decided to stay at the frat house. She gave me the keys to her place and I started walking home. More like stumbled, I guess. Some guy took me from behind by my neck. He pulled me into this vacant house. It was disgusting. He was disgusting. There was garbage everywhere. Broken dolls, really sick shit." Megan ran her hand through her hair looking up at the ceiling to gain composure. "He started to drag me up the stairs. Smashing my head down on each one. I thank God to this day I never lost consciousness. But then, he pulled out a knife." She closed her eyes, picturing the knife. She'd never seen a knife so big, so close to her eyes before. "He started to run it across my chest."

She looked over at Nappa. He remained silent.

"I don't remember much after that. I don't know how I got away, but I did. Never called the police, underage drinking and all."

"You were a young girl, you didn't know any better."

"But you see, I was the lucky one; McAllister wasn't. If this guy is anything like what I think he is, he's lining up his next victim. We *have* to find him. I can't let another woman go through something like what McAllister went through."

"And what you almost went through." Nappa looked at Megan with even more respect than he already had for her. "I thought you were a pit bull cop to prove a woman could be great at the job. Turns out you're a survivor."

"That's funny, I never thought of myself as a victim."

NINETEEN

THE RAIN CONTINUED TO pour down, holding them hostage in Eve Scott's apartment lobby. "God, I can't wait to get out of here." Megan stood and grabbed her bag without realizing it wasn't fully zipped. All the contents emptied out. Keys, pens, makeup, Moleskine notepads, a three-day-old banana, and *The Catholic Times* fell onto the lobby floor.

"Now, that's interesting." Nappa picked up the newspaper. "I thought you said your were a lapsed Catholic."

"Nappa, I didn't buy this. When I went to visit my mother yesterday, the old guy pushing the newspaper/magazine cart gave it to me."

"As a hint?"

"Funny."

Another shock of lightning and thunder smashed over the sky. The lobby felt as if it were moving through a car wash; the rain pounded down without break.

"Looks like we have time. Let's take a look." Nappa started to flip through the free newspaper. "Bingo this Saturday?"

"I'm busy." Megan smiled.

"Father Joseph McCann is being honored."

"Pedophile party?"

"McGinn, please. Now we've hit the mother lode: the obits."

"Um, what do we need to read *that* section for?"

"It's next to the personals—"

"Nappa, close your mouth when you read. You look like you should be playing a banjo on a porch somewhere." Megan grabbed the paper.

"Second column, middle of the page."

It was a small paragraph: *Shannon M. You Have Been Returned.* The date of Shannon's murder was written underneath the heading. She turned to the front page of the newspaper to check the date. "Nappa, this paper is for this week. This can't be right. It can't be the same Shannon M."

But neither detective believed in coincidences. Megan turned the paper back and forth from the obituary section to the publication date on the front of the newspaper.

"If this is what we think it is, the killer submitted it to the paper nearly one week before he killed her. Motherfucker," Megan said.

"When should we call the lieutenant?"

Just as he asked the question, Megan's cell phone rang. She glanced down at the caller ID. "Looks like right now."

"McGinn," Megan answered.

"Please tell me this murder is in no way connected to the McAllister case." Walker had a way of getting to the point when exasperated.

"I don't think it is."

"Thank God."

Been a lot of thought of the Holy Father in the last few minutes. "But..."

"But what?"

"This vic was a student at Columbia. We found her university ID among her things."

"She couldn't have gone to NYU?" Walker griped.

"If it helps, the crime scenes are in complete contradiction. On this one there was rough sex, drugs involved, and she was strangled with a scarf, not by hand."

"I'm not sure that's going to help, but it's something. Was her snatch sewn shut?" Walker did have a way with words sometimes.

"No."

"Good. Mrs. McAllister is coming to the office in the morning for her daughter's personal effects. You know she'll probably have questions. Are you prepared?"

"I spoke with her earlier. I told her I'd be there."

"Good." The lieutenant hung up without a goodbye.

Megan looked at Nappa. "Just when we were really starting to connect, she ends the call."

"You didn't mention the paper."

"No. Let's check it out before we bring it up as a lead."

"You're meeting with Mrs. McAllister tomorrow. I'll check it out first thing."

They both sat quietly staring out onto Fifth Avenue. "I guess it's time to face the other part of the storm," Megan said, motioning toward the camera crews and the reporters clustered around the building.

"I'll keep it brief," Nappa insisted.

Lightning flashed again, followed by a smash of thunder strong enough to send a slight vibration through the room.

"No time like the present," Megan added.

TWENTY

As I sit in this overpriced coffee house, people come and go, many with the newspaper shoved under one arm as they pour cream and sugar into their fancy drinks. I can't help but feel a coy smile brewing between my lips—I'm enamored by the morning's headline.

———

The big black letters of the morning paper could hardly be missed as Megan walked past the kiosk on her way to work: THE TAILOR STRIKES. It stopped her in her tracks.

"What the fuck?"

The article bared all the information of the suturing of Shannon McAllister's genitalia. There was no mention of the gold ring. She flipped open her cell and dialed Nappa.

He answered immediately, "I know. I saw it."

"Who the hell could have leaked this?"

"I don't know. I don't know."

"I'm on my way in now. Call Dr. Max; this had to have come from his office."

"Already done. I'm waiting to hear back from him."

"What the fuck is wrong with the media? 'The Tailor'?"

"No mention of the ring, thank God."

"I doubt the McAllisters are thinking that right now."

"You're still meeting with her this morning?" Nappa asked.

"After I pay Professor Bauer a visit."

"Not without me you're not."

Megan looked up and down the avenue, wondering if there were hidden cameras, as if this was some kind of punk gone awry. "What the fuck? Excuse me?" She was stunned at the chauvinistic tone Nappa used and had very little temperament for that kind of attitude. She followed her grandfather's advice: *Megsy, don't take guff from anyone. Ever.* "Hold on just one fucking second, Nappa!"

"No! You hold on! I'm going with you, *partner.*"

"What, you think I can't handle going head to head with this asshole?"

"It has nothing to do with you personally."

"The *hell* it doesn't." Megan began to punch the air with her index finger as she prepared to lay into Nappa, and it wasn't the kind of lay they came close to experiencing the night previously. "Nappa, let's be clear about this. *You* are the one who said I needed this case. *You* were the one who practically *begged* me to be on this case. *This* case! Well, I am! And, I'm also *lead* detective. Got that? *You*"—the air was now Swiss cheese—"are going to check out the newspaper; Rasmussen and Palumbo are working the case from last night to see if there are any more connections between the vics. So that, *partner*, is that! I'm calling on the prick professor."

Goodbyes come in many forms; within the context of this conversation, it was wrapped in a bow of hang-ups. She slapped her cell shut three consecutive times.

———

Megan stormed into Professor Bauer's office. Unfortunately, there were no recipients for the sword-wielding mood she was hoping to inflict. It was empty and his pit bull secretary was on break. Megan took it upon herself to check his schedule and discovered he was teaching a class at the moment. She had to ask directions from a student, but she found it and the professor with little difficulty.

She entered Professor Bauer's lecture as he was knee-deep in enthrallment with the sound of his own voice. Of course, the first two rows of students were all women, staring starry-eyed at their teacher. Megan leaned against the wall, purposely opening her coat, displaying her badge and gun to be seen by all. The students noticed her and her credentials immediately. It wasn't until their whispers and awkward glances distracted Professor Bauer that he realized he had a visitor.

"Well, class, it seems we have a guest. Have you decided to expand on your community-college education, dear?"

Megan smiled at his snide remark. "I've thought about it, but for now I'm more interested in finding Shannon McAllister's killer. Which is why I'm here. But don't let me interrupt. Please, continue."

Rage filled Bauer's face as he stared Megan down, but she refused to look away. Hyde had to turn back into Dr. Jekyll to deal with his students. "I think that will be all for today. Remember to read the assigned chapters for our next class. Thank you, and have a good week."

The gossipy murmurs began as the class slowly shuffled out of the room. Professor Bauer slammed the door behind the last student leaving. He forcefully stuffed papers into his briefcase. "This is bordering on harassment, Detective."

"I don't think asking you questions borders on harassment."

"You come in here while I'm teaching, interrupt my class, take time away from my students' education. Then—"

"You know what, Bauer? I've had enough. During our last discussion—"

"That was hardly a discussion, it was an interrogation."

"I don't give a shit if you call it a discussion, an interrogation, or a verbal colonoscopy. Call it whatever you want. I'm here because I want to know how two women in less than one week are murdered and you are connected to both of them."

"What are you talking about?" The crease between his eyebrows deepened. "Whoa, whoa, you think I'm some how connected to the girl I read about this morning?"

His arrogant laugh made Megan grin. She was getting to him, and they both knew it.

"What are the chances when I go back through Eve Scott's university files, she would have had a lecture, a class," Megan raised a palm, "maybe even been seen with you socially?" She stood closer, her words turned into a whisper, "Y'know, for *tutoring*?"

He placed his work papers much more thoughtfully into his leather case before adjusting his glasses and stepping toward Megan, forcing her back against the wall.

"Detective, where's your knight in shining armor? Your partner?"

"He's hooked to my holster and filled to capacity with rounds. Want to meet him?" She used her forefingers to nudge Bauer back. "You're invading my personal space." She was so close, she could smell the light scent of alcohol on his breath.

"I'll invade more than that if you keep pressuring me."

"Threatening an officer, now that's not nice."

The door flung open and a young woman with black hair sashayed in. "Marty, I can't make it until—"

Bauer recoiled. The tension didn't fall short on his current conquest.

"Am I interrupting?"

Megan ignored her, focusing instead on the professor. "Until our next *discussion.*" Megan walked toward the door. "See you again, real soon."

"Not without my lawyer," he said as she left the room.

Megan mocked the young woman's girly tone. "But Marty, I didn't think you had anything to hide?"

TWENTY-ONE

MEGAN ARRIVED AT THE office wanting to meet with her boss as soon as possible. The door to Walker's office was closed, but she was clearly there, given the level of noise emanating from within.

"Is she in there regarding this?" Megan showed Joanne, Walker's assistant, her copy of the morning headlines.

"Her phone hasn't stopped ringing." Joanne was always two steps ahead and was rarely flustered by Walker's demanding personality. She had tight blond curls and hazel eyes and was blessed with full lips that 99 percent of the time had a smile exposing the slight gap in her front teeth. But not this morning.

"Who is she on with?"

"The mayor, and he's pissed."

"It's not like *we* leaked it. Jesus." Megan handed the paper to Joanne. "Do me a favor. Mrs. McAllister is coming in this morning. You see any of these hanging around, get rid of them."

Joanne nodded. "You got it."

"Thanks." Megan nodded in the direction of the conference room. "I'll be in there. Are Palumbo and Rasmussen in yet?"

Joanne shrugged.

"Find them, now." Megan felt bad about the tone she used. "Thanks, Joanne."

Megan spent the next half hour processing Shannon's personal items, as few as there were. The lab wanted to continue running tests on the clothing Shannon wore during the attack. Only the jewelry remained: Shannon's watch and the Claddagh ring.

Walker rapped on the door and leaned her head into the conference room. "You have some time?"

"Of course. Obviously you've seen the paper."

"Jesus Christ, how did that get out?" Walker asked.

"Not from this end, I can tell you that much." Megan wasn't being defensive, just honest, and Walker knew that.

"No, no, that's not what I meant. I *know* that. I should have prepared for a leak with a situation like this. I've been on the phone with the mayor, chief of police, and Mr. McAllister's lawyer. It's a mess."

"Well, for what it's worth, you look great. You didn't have to go to all that trouble for a meeting with little old me."

Walker wore a red suit with a cream-colored silk blouse and a gold necklace with matching gold earrings. It was an outfit that looked more like something a woman doing high tea on Madison Avenue would wear, rather than a woman in her fifties who carried a firearm.

"I didn't. My daughter asked me to speak in front of her women's studies class today. So I'll be sneaking out of here around lunchtime."

"Which daughter, Sophia or Serena?"

"Sophia."

"A women's studies class? How old is she now?"

"Sixteen."

Megan released a playful groan. "Sixteen? I remember when she just got her braces. I'm feeling very old right now."

"Please, you and me both. She's already talking about which colleges she wants to apply to." Walker was stressed and cut the chitchat. "Is Nappa in?" She joined Megan at the table.

"No, he's checking on a lead. That's one of the things I wanted to talk to you about. I wanted to get you up to speed on a few things."

Megan pushed *The Catholic Times* across the table for Walker to inspect. "Read the highlighted section."

Walker had to put her glasses on to read the small print. "What the hell…?" She flipped to the front of the newspaper, just as Megan had when she first read it. "What's the date on this?"

"One week prior," Megan answered.

Walker smacked the paper down on the tabletop. "Nappa is checking on this right now?"

"Yes."

"It says, 'You've been returned.' What do you think that means?"

"I'm not sure."

"How in hell did you come to find this?" Walker asked.

"I was visiting my mom at the nursing home. The man who delivers the newspapers and magazines gave it to me to read. I ended up throwing it in my purse. I didn't even realize I had it. Nappa found it when we were waiting out the rainstorm at the sex-gone-bad crime scene."

There was a light knock at the door, and Joanne peeked through the small opening she allowed for herself. In a slight whisper she said, "Excuse me, Mrs. McAllister is here. I have her waiting in your office."

"Mr. and Mrs. McAllister?" Walker inquired.

"No, just Mrs. McAllister. She came alone."

In circumstances like this, usually the parents of the victim are seldom apart.

"We'll be right there," Walker answered.

"Everything is done. I did it myself." Megan took the paperwork out of the envelope. "We need her signature on a few of the forms, that's about all."

"Good. Let's get this over with."

"McGinn," Palumbo interrupted as she and Walker walked over to meet Mrs. McAllister. "You're going to want to hear this."

Megan turned to see Eve Scott's roommate seated at Palumbo's desk with two men wearing suits. One of the men had a briefcase on his lap, while the other stood behind the young man; neither looked pleased to be there.

"Who is that?" Walker asked.

"The roommate of the girl who was murdered last night," Megan answered.

"With his father, and his father's attorney," Palumbo added.

"Christ, don't tell me ..." Megan rubbed her head and looked toward Walker's office. She could see Mrs. McAllister seated across from Walker's desk.

"Yep. He wants to give a full confession," Palumbo said.

The three looked at one another. All sharing the same wishful thought: Wouldn't it be great if every case could be solved this way?

171

"Where's Rasmussen?" Megan asked.

"He should be here any minute."

"Good. I'm not sure how long I'm going to be." Megan clutched the envelope of Shannon's personal items and nodded in the direction of Walker's office. "Start when Rasmussen gets in, and then I want to meet with both of you, got it?"

"Got it," Palumbo answered.

"Can there be any more surprises today?" Megan whispered to Walker.

"Be careful what you wish for, Detective."

Shannon's mother sat across from Walker's desk. Her hands held the end of the seat cushion. It seemed to be the only thing steadying her. Her hair was pushed back behind her ears, emphasizing her pale, gaunt face. When Megan and Walker entered the office, Mrs. McAllister turned, offering a small smile. She was a painfully polite woman even in the depths of her grief. "Detective McGinn, Lieutenant Walker, good morning. It's nice to see you again." Of course, it was anything but. Mrs. McAllister stood, holding her hand out to greet them. Her grasp was weak—more a gentle squeeze than a handshake.

"Please, have a seat. Did my assistant offer you any coffee or a glass of water?" Walker asked.

"Oh, yes, she did. I'm fine, thank you." She sat back down as she clutched her purse. She eyed the envelope Megan held but didn't inquire. "Detective, here's Shannon's laptop, as you requested." She handed Megan a black computer bag.

"Thank you for remembering that. I'll return it to you as soon as I can." Megan set the case on Walker's desk.

"Unfortunately, my husband wasn't able to make it in today. He wasn't feeling up to it. My sister is meeting me at Shannon's apartment. It's still okay for me to go there, isn't it?"

Megan nodded. "Yes, we have everything we need. It's not a problem."

Walker approached the indelicate morning news, "Mrs. McAllister, regarding the information in this morning's newspaper, I'd like to—"

Mrs. McAllister shook her head, politely skirting the painful topic. "Shannon has a beautiful dress at the apartment. It's lilac, with tiny white flowers on it." Through an uncomfortable smile, she continued, "She said it brought out her eyes, and hid her child-bearing hips. Shannon was always so hard on herself." Mrs. McAllister stared off into space, recounting the last time she saw Shannon wearing it. "She bought it for my husband's corporate spring outing. It's a beautiful dress."

Both Megan and Walker offered a solemn nod, silently acknowledging that the topic of the leaked information was off the table for Mrs. McAllister.

"The funeral home should be working with the coroner's office for you. If there's a problem, we can make a few phone calls," Walker offered.

"Thank you. We're having the main service at St. Thomas More here in the city, and then a more intimate gathering near our home in Connecticut. Most of her friends are down here, so we felt it made sense."

"St. Thomas More is near where I live. It's a beautiful church," Megan said.

Walker glanced as if she were thinking, *First she's reading* The Catholic Times *and now she's familiar with a church. The surprises are neverending.*

"Shannon loved that church. It's where she would go for service and for Ash Wednesday. We went to St. Thomas More a few months ago when Katelyn, Shannon's best friend, was married there." She paused a moment, cracked a smile, and threw out a nervous laugh. "It astonishes me. Never in a million years did I think a few months ago that I'd be arranging my baby girl's funeral at the same church."

Walker pulled a box of tissues out of her desk drawer and offered it Mrs. McAllister.

"Oh no, thank you." She had a travel pack of tissues in the side compartment of her purse; she took them out and held them up for viewing. "I come equipped. Hey, never leave home without them, especially when your daughter's been murdered." Tears dropped down her now flushed face. "I have no idea what just made me say something like that. I'm so sorry. It's so unlike me."

Megan tried to give a comforting smile and said, "It's your coping mechanism. There's nothing to be embarrassed or feel badly about. Everyone deals with it differently. There's no wrong or right way."

"Thank you, Detective." Mrs. McAllister cleared her throat and continued, "Well, I guess you have Shannon's things?"

"Mrs. McAllister, I first want to say how profoundly sorry we are that someone spoke to the press regarding your daughter's case. It's certainly not something this office condones," Walker said.

"I just don't understand people. My daughter will now be remembered as one of The Tailor's victims. Doesn't that matter to anyone?"

"Yes. It matters to us." Megan squeezed Mrs. McAllister's hand. "It matters to us."

She responded with a silent nod.

Megan handed her the envelope as well as a few forms. "We'll need you to look at all the items and then sign off on them."

Shannon's mother stared at the unopened envelope, unable to respond to Megan's request.

"Mrs. McAllister? Are you okay?" Walker asked.

She stammered, "Do I have to look at them right now? Couldn't I just sign the forms?"

Megan looked at Walker for guidance. Typically, she would have no problem bending the rules—she did it most of the time anyway—but in front of her superior, she had to hold out.

Walker nodded. "That's fine. You can just sign the forms."

Mrs. McAllister scribbled her name where Megan indicated. "And you'll let me know of any developments with her case?"

"Absolutely," Walker answered.

"And, Detective, I've been trying to put a more comprehensive list together of Shannon's friends, previous jobs, things like that. I'll get that to you as soon as I can."

"Thank you. That will be a big help," Megan said.

Mrs. McAllister rose from her chair again, thanking both Megan and Walker for all their hard work.

Walker looked unsure of her next move. She seemed to need to offer something to Shannon's mother. "Mrs. McAllister?"

"Please, call me MaryEllen."

"MaryEllen, it won't always be like this. It won't always be this hard for you."

Shannon's mother stopped and gave a smile of appreciation for Walker's attempts to console her. "Yes. Yes, it will." She walked out of the office, shutting the door behind her.

"That was a stupid thing for me to say. Damn it. She's picking up her slain daughter's personal effects and I'm telling her it won't always be this hard. What was I thinking?"

Megan folded her arms and stared at the floor. "It wasn't a stupid thing to say. It was the truth. This will be the hardest time that woman will ever see. There's no arguing that, but time does something to the pain. It changes it somehow. You cope and find a place to put it so you can keep going. At least that's what I've heard, and damn, it better be true."

Walker realized Megan was speaking more of her dealing with the loss of her father than Mrs. McAllister losing Shannon. "Trust me, it's true. Hardest day of my life was losing my mother, but over the years I've moved past the trauma and I'm left with good memories and the sadness that she's no longer around for me to share things with. You'll see."

"Yep. I have to get back to the conference room. There's a lot more work to do."

Walker took twelve message slips out from her inbox and pretended to be reviewing them when she said, "McGinn?"

Megan turned around. "Yeah?"

"Thanks for being here this morning for this. You're good with them, you know?"

"Good with who?"

"The victims' families."

Megan smiled. "Thanks."

TWENTY-TWO

MEGAN SECLUDED HERSELF IN the conference room. It wasn't even noon, but she felt like the day had already kicked her in the ass. Mounting piles of papers and files covered the table reminding her of her college years. Back then her desk was piled high with textbooks, term papers, and the usual accoutrements: a pack of NoDoz, a six-pack of Mountain Dew, and the ultranutritious Snickers bar. These days, her inner drive replaced the NoDoz, coffee with creamer and three Splendas replaced the Mountain Dew, and chewing the end of a ballpoint pen while she read through files made up her morning nutrition. Term papers and textbooks were now replaced by ME reports, photos of a dead woman, and countless unanswered questions she was no closer to answering than she'd been four hours earlier.

Megan once again felt the same sense of intrusion opening Shannon's laptop as she had while taking the second walk through her apartment, examining her personal items in the dresser and closet. The desktop picture was of a lake at sunset. A small place in

Megan's heart held out hope that perhaps this—a picture Shannon viewed regularly—was the image greeting her when she succumbed to her killer's power. It probably wasn't, but it was something nice to wish for. She hit two clicks and was confronted with password protection.

"Of course. What did you have, naked pictures of your married lover? Of yourself or the two of you together?" Megan was fatigued. Her energy was low, her temper short, and her patience even shorter when there was a knock at the door.

"What?" Megan's tone was as sharp as the pain searing through her temples, which she began to massage.

Detective Rasmussen entered, unfazed by Megan's less-than-enthusiastic response. "That cheerful facade you're putting on is working wonders." He placed on the desk a large green folder thick with papers.

Megan acknowledged her brusque tone. "Sorry about that. I just met with the vic's mother. Fuck all. What's this?"

"Phone records from her work." Rasmussen removed his jacket, rolled back his sleeves, and began to go through the file, dividing the stack between the two of them.

Megan's jaw dropped. "That's not the last twenty-four hours of her life, is it?"

"If we were talking about my ex-wife, yes—but in this case, it's the victim's records from the last month. It was a bitch, but we finally got them. What do you want to look at first?"

"Let's start with her last twenty-four hours and work back. Maybe one of the bat-shit-crazy *clients* she dealt with had some type of crush or was pissed off at her for something."

"It sounds like someone is due for a sensitivity training," Rasmussen said dryly.

Megan grinned at receiving the kind of humor she was accustomed to doling out, but chose not to respond.

Rasmussen unpacked the brown paper bag. He took out a bottle of water, a bag of potato chips, and a large sandwich wrapped in white paper. He passed half the sandwich over to Megan on a napkin. "Eat this."

"What is it?"

"Eat it." Rasmussen wasn't one for long-winded commentary.

"I'm not hungry." She started to push the sandwich back over to him.

"Eat it." Rasmussen's Nordic background showed through with a tall frame and fair features and an occasionally icy demeanor. Some people were put off by his no-bullshit style. Megan respected it, even admired his bluntness at times.

Megan passed the copy of the memorial in *The Catholic Times* over to him. "Read this." She took a bite of the sandwich and moaned, "There's no mayonnaise on this? Jeez, how can you eat turkey without any mayo? God."

Rasmussen took a bite of his sandwich and tossed a small packet of mayonnaise across the table at Megan while he read the highlighted area. He squinted down at the paper as if he didn't trust the information his eyes fed him. His expression wasn't the *oh shit* reaction Walker gave Megan earlier, but a look of disgust.

"Nappa is checking on it now. He should be back soon." Megan plunged back into her doctored turkey sandwich, taking an oversized bite out of the middle. A dollop of mayonnaise and residual bread crumbs flanked the sides of her mouth as she chewed.

Rasmussen shook his head and tossed a pile of napkins over to her.

Megan garbled a thank you for the napkins, but made no attempt to use them.

"If you keep eating like that, I'll arrest you for assault," Rasmussen said.

"Assault on a turkey sandwich?"

"Assault on dining etiquette."

A piece of lettuce fell out of the corner of Megan's mouth as she responded, "I have perfect Catholic-schoolgirl manners. I just didn't realize how hungry I was. By the way, what's up with the Eve Scott case? I saw Palumbo earlier when the roommate came in. He said the guy was going to confess."

"He is one sick twist. When I was his age, I couldn't even think of anything so demented: handcuffs, sadomasochistic, tie-'em-up, tie-'em-down bullshit. Can't anyone just have normal sex anymore?"

A spasm of coughs ensued after Rasmussen's comment. Megan tried to swallow her stunned reaction along with the piece of sandwich stuck in her windpipe.

"You okay?"

She coughed a few more times. Her eyes began to water as she tried to clear her throat. "Yeah, I'm fine." She pointed down at the paper, avoiding direct eye contact with Rasmussen.

Please, Christ, change the subject.

"If this is what you think it is, well, I don't have to tell you—not good, McGinn," he said.

"So, Eve Scott's roommate, he's getting charged?"

"Yep. It was a sex-act-gone-bad scenario."

Megan helped herself to the bag of potato chips. "That's what I thought." The casual conversation to anyone else's ears would have sounded hard and detached, especially over a turkey sandwich and baked Lay's potato chips.

"Where's Palumbo?"

"He's processing Mr. Sexton. He'll be in a little while."

"Who?"

"The weirdo-sex guy from Eve Scott's case," Rasmussen answered.

"You've got to be kidding me. His last name is *Sex*ton?" They both grinned at the irony of it. "Oh man. That's fucked up. Funny, but fucked up," Megan said.

"You must admit it's weird that two vics in one week both attended the same college," Rasmussen commented.

"Nothing seems weird to me anymore on this job." Megan picked up the empty brown paper bag. "Didn't you get a pickle?"

"Yes."

"May I have it?" Megan asked.

"No." He chomped the end off the kosher dill.

"You talk too much, Rasmussen."

"Uh-huh."

Megan devoured the remainder of her lunch. The fatigue and headache she'd experienced earlier started to wane. She felt more focused and energized. She crumpled the leftover napkins and empty lunch bag into a ball and, mimicking a basketball player attempting a three-point shot, tossed the refuse across the room, hitting the trash can in the corner. She parodied the roar of sports fans and motioned a fake high five in Rasmussen's direction.

Rasmussen stared blankly at Megan and then continued reviewing the phone records. Another hour passed before Nappa returned.

Megan knew by his frazzled look that the news wasn't good. She put their earlier conversation aside for now. "Don't tell me, Nappa, good news?"

"Top-notch system they have over there at *The Catholic Times.* They're a real aggressive organization. I got his name, phone number, address, case solved." Nappa pulled up a chair, throwing his jacket over the back. Nappa rarely displayed any level of frustration regarding the progression of a case. This was one of his first.

Megan and Rasmussen glanced at each other, neither daring to interrupt his minor rant.

"Basically, anyone can walk in, fill out a form such as this." He held up a transparent Pendaflex file containing a yellow form. "And they don't require anything more than payment. Cash, check, or credit card is acceptable."

Megan held the plastic sheet up toward the light to see what could be read. The yellow piece of paper had the name of the newspaper at the top, a space for the written memorial to be printed, and the amount due at the bottom. *Shannon M. You have been returned* was clearly written out. The payment section was just as legible, but the line for signature had what looked like three *M*s in succession. "Wow, our first clue. His name is Mmm." She handed the evidence over to Rasmussen. "I didn't expect the guy to write out his name and phone number, did you? He's a sick bastard, but not stupid," she said.

"Neither did I, but I thought there might be more. I'll send it in for prints anyway." He sounded temporarily defeated. Nappa leafed through one of the piles of papers. "What's up on this end?"

Detective Palumbo entered the conference room on the tail end of Nappa's question and they brought Nappa up to speed on the Eve Scott case.

"There was no connection between the roommate and McAllister, right?" Megan asked. Palumbo and Rasmussen both said no. "Well, it would've been nice if he'd confessed earlier before the papers ran with the assumption that the deaths were connected." Megan stared up at the picture of Shannon's sutured vagina, disgusted by the headline in the paper but also inspired in a peculiar way.

Nappa could tell the wheels in her mind were turning. "What are you thinking?"

She smacked her palm down on the table, "The Tailor, that's what the papers have deemed our unsub." She pointed at the photo pinned to the board. "What if this is some kind of clothing stitch? Or needlepoint or, I don't know what the fuck, I never took home economics. Palumbo, Rasmussen, I want you to take this pic and go to as many dry cleaners and tailors on the Upper East Side as you can find. Ask them if they recognize this exact stitch. Dr. Max hasn't come up with anything on it yet, maybe we will?"

Wide open-mouthed gaps emerged from all three men.

Palumbo pointed at the picture. "McGinn, *this* picture? Don't you think it might be a bit unsettling for someone not on the job to see this? Christ, I nearly lost my breakfast when I saw it."

In Megan's frenzy, she'd not thought of that. "Good point. Go downstairs and have one of the sketch artists draw the stitch and take that with you. It will be less shocking for the people you speak with."

Palumbo and Rasmussen glanced at one another with brows raised as they exited the room. Rasmussen said, "Hope whoever sketches this hasn't had lunch yet."

Nappa sat down in silence, staring at Megan.

"You think I'm reaching," she said.

He shook his head. "Not necessarily. Reaching is a part of our job. What's been going on here?" Nappa pointed at the piles of paper on the conference room table.

"Rasmussen and I were going through the phone records, cross-checking it with her datebook, trying to put together a timeline of her last weeks, days, hours. She basically worked, went to school, volunteered for what seems like every charitable organization in Manhattan, and talked with her girlfriends a lot. I think we need to go back to her work again and try to talk to more people who saw her the last few days. There are a few names in her datebook—actually let me rephrase that, not names, *initials*—on certain dates that so far no phone numbers connect with. We know LB is McAllister's mentor, Lauren Bell. I've put a call in to her and she's expecting us later this afternoon. Now, it's hard to even read McAllister's handwriting, but we know PG is Paige Gowan and, as Katelyn Moore said, she isn't due back in the city for a few days, but I've left word for her to contact me ASAP. Now, SIN, BD, BE, MW ... equals NFC."

"NFC?"

"No Fucking Clue."

"What's that?" Nappa motioned to the computer case Mrs. McAllister brought in.

"The vic's laptop. She'd forgotten it at her parents' house the last time she went home. I'm going to have my friend check it out."

"Your mystery friend," Nappa confirmed.

"I checked with the tech guys, and they've only just started on the desktop. I'm just taking a shortcut, that's all. Cashing in on a favor, so to speak," Megan said.

"What kind of favor?" Nappa asked.

"My usual—oral sex for cash, what else?" she answered.

"Oh, what a relief. I thought it might be a moral or ethical conflict. But since it's just head for cash, that's fine," he deadpanned.

A single knock at the door was followed by Joanne leaning into the conference room. "Megan, this just came in for you." Joanne handed Megan a small, square package wrapped in brown paper.

"From who?"

"There's no return address." Joanne raised her eyebrows. "Downstairs sent it up, sorry, that's all I know."

"Throw it here." Joanne gently tossed it across the conference room table. Megan held it up to her ear and shook it, whispering to Nappa, "Your apology for earlier?"

Nappa's look of concern overrode her humor. He shook his head in protest. "That's not from me."

A travel-size sewing kit fell out of the bottom of the box. "What in the hell?" A note was taped to it.

Sew, sew sorry for your loss.

TWENTY-THREE

MEGAN RIFLED THROUGH AN old issue of *Psychology Today* while she and Nappa waited to meet with Shannon's mentor, Lauren Bell. The assistant told them she was in the middle of a group session and couldn't be interrupted, but would be free in twenty minutes. They opted to wait in the lobby. Megan threw the magazine back on the table, missing it completely.

"I'm so fucked off. This unsub is playing with us. First of all, the balls it took to kill during the day," Megan tugged at Nappa's jacket to gain eye-to-eye contact, "and now mocking us with a sewing kit?"

Nappa sat forward, demanding her full attention. "That's what you're worried about, being mocked? McGinn, the package was sent to *you* directly. The killer is following *your* life. Offering condolences for *your* loss."

"I know, Nappa. I know." She rested her head against the wall, closed her eyes, and took a deep breath. "We both know forensics will come up with absolutely nothing. There's not going to be any prints." Megan squirmed in her chair, anxious for Lauren Bell to make her appearance. "We have to get on these tech guys. I want that section of the security video enhanced, Nappa. I know I saw something around the wrist."

"I saw the same video; I couldn't make anything out," Nappa sighed.

"Well, I did. It was a small...something."

"Let's go back a bit today. What did Bauer say this morning when you paid him a visit?"

Megan rolled her eyes. "If this is about our conversation, get over it."

"No, this is about keeping one another up to speed so we can get a break in this case."

Megan felt more than just a pinch of remorse for withholding the fact that she'd received a call from Shannon's phone. Now it was too little, too late. The phone was surely out of commission by now. "If we continue to speak to one another like this in a therapist's office, they'll think we're here for marriage counseling."

"Fat chance."

The next few minutes were spent in silence before Megan went into guarded detail about her meeting with Bauer, ending with, "It probably would have been a good idea for both of us to have gone." Swallowing her pride proved more uncomfortable than when she bought her first home pregnancy test. Megan picked up the magazine she'd thrown moments earlier, now taking a more serious read through.

"Anything interesting?" Nappa asked.

"Well"—she turned a few pages of the magazine—"there's a self-test, 'Do I Need Therapy?'"

"Yes," Nappa said.

Megan rolled her eyes. "There's an article on obsessive-compulsive disorders, one on how to add humor to your day, and ways to increase communication in your relationships at work."

"I wasn't listening. What did you say?"

"I'm communicating one thought right now. Would you like me to share it?" She smiled. "Actually there's an interesting article about antisocial personality disorder." Megan opened to the page. "'Also known as sociopathic or psychopathic personality and often leads to conflict with society as a consequence of amoral, unethical behavior.'"

"Trying to analyze the killer?"

"No. I guess there's a part of me that still can't believe what people are capable of. Even after all of the horrible things we've seen, I'm still amazed at . . ." There were too many words to choose from to describe the total disregard for human life they'd witnessed.

"The depravity of it all?"

"Yeah. Pretty much."

"Well, that's good in a way."

"It is?" Megan asked.

"Yeah. It means your heart hasn't turned to stone. The day you walk into a crime scene and feel nothing—and I mean *nothing*, no anger, no disgust, no reaction whatsoever—well, that's a very sad day. That's the day to hand in your badge. At least that's what I think."

"I guess so." Megan placed the magazine back onto the coffee table. This time it made it to the top of the other outdated office subscriptions. "Can I see a copy of the calendar and the initials again?"

Megan looked over the paperwork again just as a roomful of people flowed out of a corner office.

"Hopefully Ms. Bell can shed some light on some of these dates and initials. I feel like I'm trying to put together a thousand-piece jigsaw puzzle and the box came with nine hundred and ninety-nine pieces. And no picture on the cover."

Lauren Bell was the last person to exit the corner office. "Detectives?"

Her waifish build and pale skin made her look about fifty even though they knew she was in her early forties. She had chestnut-colored hair pulled back into a tight bun. She was extremely thin, conservatively dressed in a black turtleneck and wool slacks. She had the same bereaved look on her face as Shannon's other friends had, but hers had an air of annoyance mixed in.

"Follow me."

Her military tone made Megan think she was about to scream "Drop and give me twenty!" but she figured when you're working with the kinds of people Lauren Bell was—prisoners with psychological issues—you had to have balls of steel, even if Mother Nature didn't give you a set of your own.

They followed her into her office. Once she closed the door, she seemed less uptight. "Sorry. The last two hours have been rather stressful. Comes with the territory, I guess. Please have a seat."

"Ms. Bell, we'd like to ask you a few questions about Shannon McAllister," Megan said.

"However I can help. Absolutely."

"You were Shannon's mentor for school?" Nappa asked.

"Not so much mentor as field instructor. When Shannon first started the internship program, I was assigned to her," she said.

"She worked with psychologically challenged prisoners, is that correct?" Megan asked.

"Not exactly. Shannon counseled people who live in a halfway house and are preparing to reenter the community through a work release program. While some of the counselors here deal with only mental illness, Shannon mainly dealt with clients who were dually diagnosed with both mental illness and substance abuse."

"You're saying that these clients—mentally ill, substance-abusing ex-felons—leave to go to work every day and willingly return to what is effectively house arrest at night?" Megan asked.

"Yes. They're wards of the state until the time comes when they're fully released, and then post-therapeutic and substance-abuse counseling are maintained. Each client is fitted with an electronic monitoring bracelet attached to their ankle. It tracks their location. If they deviate outside the accepted area, we're alerted immediately."

"Uh-huh." Megan's sour response was noted by Lauren Bell.

"Detective, the recidivism rate for the people in this program is extremely low."

"Can we get back to the internship program for a moment?" Nappa interrupted. "What exactly does it entail? What kind of interaction did Ms. McAllister have with her clients?"

"For her internship she has individual sessions with six clients every week, what you would probably think of as one-on-one counseling. Once a week she leads a twelve-member group session. I would meet with Shannon one day a week for two hours. We discuss everything that came up for her that week: questions about the agency, clients, if she needed me to do a consult. Things like that."

"Did she ever mention any problems with any of her clients, maybe someone who had an issue with her? Possibly threatened her?"

Lauren shook her head no. "She was extremely good at her work, and extremely committed to it. When I heard the news about Shannon, I immediately checked to see that all her clients were accounted for on that day, and they were. I checked with each of their bosses. They were on time to work, and all returned to the facility by the required six o'clock check-in. It's a very tight program. It has to be."

"I'm sure you'll understand that we'll have to check on that ourselves," Megan added, even though they'd confirmed Shannon had an evening class the night before she was murdered, well past the time her clients were required to return. Megan wasn't up for a discussion about the efficiency of the program. She switched gears. "Did you and Shannon socialize outside of work?"

"We'd become friends. Once or twice a month we'd go out for drinks. She'd come over to my apartment and babysit my son once in a while." She leaned on her desk and rubbed the back of her neck. "I haven't told him yet—my son—about Shannon. I guess I can't believe this has happened. I'm in classic denial."

"The last time you saw Ms. McAllister was ...?" Nappa asked.

"We had drinks about two weeks ago, and I was due to see her for the supervisory session"—she paused—"the day she was ..."

"What did you talk about the last time you saw her?" Megan asked.

"You know, that was the thing—Shannon is one of those people who nine times out of ten is upbeat and positive and just full of energy."

"But not that night," Nappa confirmed.

"That night she was in a small funk. Nothing heavy, she just seemed to have a lot on her mind. I think she knew she was spreading herself too thin between classes, homework, her clients, and some of the volunteer work she'd been doing."

"Where was she doing the volunteer work?" Nappa asked.

"I know she'd put in some hours at the ASPCA, walking dogs, I think. And I believe she was helping a friend out at some clinic, but I'm not sure. For a blood drive or flu shots—I know it was something medical, but I can't remember what exactly."

Megan handed her the photocopy of Shannon's datebook and had her review the initials. "Do you know what some of these initials and dates could be?"

Lauren donned a pair of tortoiseshell-framed reading glasses. "You have no idea how many times I tried to get her to organize herself better. I even bought her one of those Franklin planners—baby steps before using the calendar on her cell phone. I doubt she ever took it out of the box." She opened her own planner to double-check the entries. "Okay, obviously, I'm LB, this is the two-hour meeting we had weekly." She indicated with her pen. "Now, GS has to be 'group session.' They were every Tuesday night from six o'clock to eight." She opened a folder on her desk. Megan was able to see *McAllister* handwritten on the tab.

Lauren corresponded the papers in the folder with the Xeroxed copy of Shannon's calendar. "No. None of her clients have these initials." She handed Megan back the paper.

"Do you know if she was seeing anyone? Did she mention anyone special in her life?"

"Shannon and I were colleague-oriented friends, not girlfriend types. We talked about work and everything associated with work. But to answer your question, I can't imagine she was seeing anyone. And if she was, she wasn't able to see him often with how busy her schedule was."

"Let me ask you something. When you heard about her murder, what was your first thought? By that, I mean did anyone in particular come to mind that you thought may have done this?" Megan asked.

Lauren bit the side of her lip, staring at both detectives. She was teetering on a confession.

"Ms. Bell, we already know," Nappa said.

A long sigh was followed by an apology. "I'm sorry. Shannon told me about Professor Bauer when I confided in her that my husband had left me and our son for one of his students. He taught an ethics class in Queens." She cocked an eyebrow. "Some ethics, huh? Well, anyway, I think Shannon felt a huge amount of guilt and probably shame for what she'd gotten into. She said she didn't want to do to another woman what Carl and his student had done to me." She sat back in her chair. "Shannon was like that. She took responsibility for her choices. What made her go out with a married man? It was probably due to her youth, and inexperience. But more importantly, what made her end it? Her character."

193

"So, Professor Bauer's was the first name that popped into your mind when you heard the news?" Megan asked.

"His was the *only* name that came into my head when I heard the news."

TWENTY-FOUR

"WE'VE CHECKED HIS ALIBI more than once. There's no way it's Bauer," Nappa said.

"I know. I know it's not him." Megan stretched her neck while the elevator from Dr. Bell's office was about to open on the lobby floor. Megan's cell went off. "McGinn." It was Palumbo on the other end.

"What's the status on the sketch of the stitch?" Megan looked over at Nappa shaking her head, "Well, just keep going until—" She stopped midstride. "You're fucking kidding me. We'll be right there."

"What?"

"No luck on the stitch. Palumbo wants us back at the station immediately. Get this, there's some detective from out of town that has information regarding the McAllister case," Megan said as if she'd finished running a 10k.

"Holy shit."

As soon as they got into the station house, Megan and Nappa rushed into the conference room. Palumbo and Rasmussen were seated, taking notes from the detective.

Palumbo stood when they entered and made the introductions. "Detective McGinn, Detective Nappa, this is Detective Gold."

Megan recognized the demeanor. The man was on the job. He had as grim a countenance as Megan and Nappa carried since the case started. He was dressed in blue jeans, new white sneakers, and a thin crewneck sweatshirt.

They shook hands and then Detective Gold showed his identification. Judging by his white hair and smoker's deep wrinkles, Megan could tell he'd been on the job a while and assumed he was near retirement.

Rasmussen, in his low-pitched tone said, "Detective, if you wouldn't mind repeating your information to Detectives McGinn and Nappa."

"Of course. My wife and I are here on vacation. I work on the force in upstate New York. Elmira, to be exact." He rubbed the stubble on his cheeks. "Well, we've been here two days, and I've been following the news on the McAllister case. I damn near fell over when I saw the paper this morning. It must have been nearly ten, maybe twelve or more years ago. We had a case. Erin Quinlan. She was a nursing student, a freshman. One semester in and she was found murdered at her family's summer home. The timeline we came up with, we figured she'd been killed on the last day before winter break. When I read about the..." He paused, embarrassed to say this in front of a woman. "About her privates being sewn shut, well, I was dumbstruck."

"And you think your case has a connection to our victim?" Megan asked.

"Let me tell you a few things about your case." He held up each digit on his right hand as he listed the information on the Quinlan case. "Not one print was found. The scene completely stripped clean. She was placed on her side, *neatly*. And by that, I mean positioned, like a child sleeping." He paused, not for drama's sake, but his gut knew the piece of information he was about to share was right on the money. "Your vic had a piece of jewelry inserted inside her before she was sewn up."

All four detectives stared at Detective Gold, knowing full well the papers hadn't broken that news about the case.

"Quinlan had a ring, specifically a nurse's graduation ring, inside her."

Megan whispered, "Jesus."

"I'm right, aren't I?"

"Wait. I'm confused about something. We checked all the databases for any similar case and came up with nothing. Why didn't the Quinlan case show up?"

"We didn't add that particular information to the files because we were afraid it would leak out. It's a small town. News like this would have created total hysteria."

Megan sighed. "Well, ours had a gold wedding band."

"Did you make a connection with the ring?" Nappa asked.

"It came from Saint Joseph's Nursing School," Gold said.

"Was that the school your vic attended?" Megan asked.

"Yep, but the ring was not hers, and it was old, very old. We checked with the school and they said the design wasn't familiar to them. There are about ten Saint Joseph's just in the Northeast alone, not including the rest of the country. Gave us nothing."

"Saint Joseph's is in Elmira?" Nappa asked.

"One of them," Detective Gold confirmed.

"Any more murders similar to the Quinlan case take place after that?" Megan asked.

Detective Gold shook his head no. "We added it to the cold cases, but I think it's safe to say where the scumbag is living now."

"We're going to need your files, see everything you have," Megan said.

"No problem." He pulled out his cell.

She glanced over at Palumbo and Rasmussen. "Help him with anything he needs."

Megan jerked to a stop. "Wait, Detective Gold, I assume you have photos of the ring that was removed from your vic?"

"Of course, and it's in lock-up with the cold case file. Why do you ask?"

"Can you have your people email it over to Detective Rasmussen?"

Everyone knew Rasmussen was more tech savvy than Palumbo, so this was no insult to him.

"Absolutely, but why?"

"I have an idea." Megan motioned to Rasmussen, "Give him your email address and then bring your laptop into the conference room." Megan looked in Palumbo's direction. "You're good here?"

"No problem."

Nappa followed Megan into the conference room, soon trailed by Rasmussen, laptop in tow.

"Clue me in, McGinn." Nappa was anxious to hear of another possible break in the case.

She sat on the conference room table, dangling her legs and smacking her boots together in excitement. "Let's see if we can bait him."

"Bait him?" Nappa asked.

"What if we put a picture of that *very* ring," Megan pointed toward Detective Gold at Palumbo's desk, "the ring he found in *his* vic's case up on Craigslist or eBay? He said the ring is very old. The unsub may want it back." Megan climbed off the table. "Look, so far we can't match either piece of jewelry to either vic, so this jewelry means something very special to the piece of shit who's doing this. He won't want anyone else to have what was his."

Rasmussen's grin was silent applause to Megan's idea.

Nappa began nodding with as much enthusiasm as Megan displayed moments earlier. "I'm following. I'm following."

"Rasmussen, do you have any accounts on either sites?"

He leaned his head to the side. "I don't buy used."

Megan raised her hands. "Sorry, didn't mean to offend. I want every detail of that ring from Gold's file, every ounce of description, and add the photo. Make sure your user name has a religious tone to it. The unsub put the ad in *The Catholic Times,* so there's our angle."

"Then what?" Nappa asked.

"Then we wait."

———

It took some time for Gold's people to unearth the cold case file, but they eventually forwarded all the information.

Megan and Nappa thanked Detective Gold personally before he left.

Detective Gold said his goodbyes, adding, "I wish you better luck than what I had on this one. It haunts me every day."

We're going to need it, Megan thought.

TWENTY-FIVE

The phone rang as Megan prepared her best Dr. Hannibal Lecter impersonation. She was hoping the noise of the Park Avenue traffic wouldn't drown out her voice.

"Clarice Snowden," the woman answered.

"Good evening, Clarice, have the lambs stopped screaming?" She followed it with a sinister laugh.

"You know the next time I see you you're going to owe me money for that comment, right?" Clarice Snowden worked in the CITU, the Computer Investigations Technical Unit. She spent her days monitoring bank accounts of millionaires, identifying pyramid schemes, anything with a financial edge that could be considered a felony using a computer.

"What do you charge now for *Silence of the Lambs* jokes?"

"One dollar, but since you added that bad laugh, I'm charging you two. Bring cash the next time you visit my office."

"Which brings me to the reason for my call," Megan said.

"Anything for you, my dear."

"Can I come in really early tomorrow morning to drop a laptop off to you? I think it could be important."

"You know I'm here by six."

"Well, I won't be there *that* early."

"I'll see you when you get here, and bring two dollars."

Megan made the fast, slurping-type sound that Hannibal Lecter made to Clarice Starling in the movie after he told her about eating one of his victim's liver with fava beans and a nice Chianti.

"I just bumped you up to three dollars."

"See you tomorrow." Megan grinned as she hung up.

————

Megan had better odds of winning the lottery than getting a full night's sleep that evening. Every hour on the hour, she double-checked the bolt on the door, even though she knew she'd locked it immediately upon arriving home. The few moments of sleep she was able to get were plagued by nightmares. The image of her swimming laps and then a man's hand holding her head down underwater awakened her more than once. After the third nightmare, it became futile to attempt more sleep. She got up, made some coffee, and sat curled up on the couch staring at the text she'd received.

How was your swim?

She was angry with herself for feeling scared during the night. Fear of anything besides commitment didn't sit well with Megan. It was more comfortable for her to replace fear with anger, which she did well.

"You sick fuck. What are you up to?" she whispered.

Megan hadn't planned on getting to Clarice Snowden's office so early—neither had Clarice, based on the shocked look on her face when Megan walked in—but the four walls of her apartment felt like they were closing in on her, so she decided to go see her old friend, who hopefully could help her.

Clarice Snowden was a stylish woman of a certain age. The thing was, no one ever knew Clarice's real age, and no one would ever hear it from Clarice. She had smooth brown skin and was a total fashionista. She had the latest bag, hairdo, and wardrobe. She originally came from Charleston, South Carolina, and had been living in New York for over fifteen years, but she never lost that soft Southern lilt in her voice. She'd just recently signed off on her second divorce. Marriage for Clarice was like a pair of new shoes that just wouldn't give, no matter how often or how long you wore them; it always felt too snug. Megan and Clarice had met at an NYPD holiday party three years earlier and had hit it off immediately.

When Megan entered her office, she adjusted her leopard-print eyeglass frames and said, "Do my eyes deceive me or is this Detective Megan McGinn in person? And before seven o'clock?"

"Good morning, Miss Clarice."

"Not one more step until you pay up, sister."

Megan slipped three dollars into a jar with the label "Pay Up If You Didn't Shut Up" for all the *Silence of the Lambs* jokes she'd heard over the years.

"Now, Ms. Snowden, where is all my hard-earned money going this week?"

"Next week's mani-pedi. If you say it a few more times, I can throw in an eyebrow wax."

"I like how you work." Megan took a seat, placing the laptop on the corner of Clarice's desk.

"That, I assume, is for me." Clarice took the laptop out of the bag.

"Yep. Whatever you can find. I have no idea what's in there, but my gut says to check it out. Computer Crimes Squad has the victim's desktop, but we're waiting on them and I doubt they're going to find anything anyway."

"Those guys are busy night and day with child predators and porn sites."

"I very much appreciate this, my friend."

"It's the least I can do after you set me up on that incredible blind date last month."

"Hey, how's that going?" Megan asked.

"Very well." Dating the wrong men stopped being Clarice's problem after her second divorce. She juggled, on average, three men at a time. The latest addition was a man Megan had met in Tribeca. He owned the restaurant she was eating in and they struck up a conversation, which was when Megan decided to play matchmaker. Right now Clarice was seeing the restaurant owner, a doctor on the verge of retiring—a plastic surgeon, no less—and a professor of African-American studies who had a faint resemblance to Sidney Poitier, handsome as hell.

"Clarice, how do you do it? Juggle all these men?" Megan asked.

"What do you mean?"

"Doesn't it get confusing after a while?"

She looked at Megan like she was crazy. "Sweetie, listen, learn, live it: men do this all the time. They juggle women—hey, once in a while they throw a man in the mix, too! I'm just enjoying my piece of the pie before I don't have teeth anymore to chew with."

"You are one in a million, Clarice. One in a million."

"I know it. By the way, when are you coming over for Sunday dinner again? Your scrawny pale body could use some food."

"Everyone wants to feed me these days. I could get used to it."

Six months earlier Megan went to Sunday service with Clarice and her family when they came for a visit. Megan had the spirit move her and she must have gained five pounds from the dinner Clarice's mother cooked that day: Southern-fried chicken smothered with gravy, ribs, potato salad, greens, corn bread, peach cobbler, and the best iced tea she'd ever drank in her life.

"Oh, how I remember those ribs to this day. The meat just fell right off the bone. That meal was better than sex," Megan said wistfully.

Clarice lifted her glasses. "Darlin', you're dating the wrong men. Talk to me. You didn't come over to listen to me gossip about my men."

"No, I came over to check out your new Coach bag." Megan noticed the new camel-skin tote on the chair next to Clarice's desk. She lifted it up with two fingers.

"Some women go for younger men ... I go for older and richer."

Clarice's men doted on her, and she was worth every penny.

"Damn, you should teach seminars. Unfortunately, I can't stay long. My partner is picking me up in a while. We have to head out to Connecticut on business. I promise, next time a longer visit."

"I'll start on this and let you know what I find. Before you go, do I need to ask about a subpoena? Or are we…?"

"Yes, we're fast-tracking this. Keep it on the down-low. If you find anything of relevance, I'll go back and get the paperwork."

"That's all I needed to know."

"Thank you. Seriously, I really appreciate this." Megan got up to leave, but not before Clarice got one more question in.

"Hey, sister. How are you holding up?"

Clarice lost her father a year earlier to lung cancer. She understood Megan's loss quite well.

"One day at a time. One motherfucking day at a time."

Clarice nodded solemnly. "Stay strong, sweets."

———

Megan got back to her apartment before Nappa arrived, and was able to kick back a glass of orange juice and a piece of toast before he called to say he was downstairs waiting for her. "I'll be down in a minute." She ran into the bathroom, brushed her teeth, and popped her daily birth control pill. Given she was up most of the night, it hadn't felt like a new day and she'd nearly forgotten to take it. She threw back the small white pill and her mind went instantly to Shannon.

Nappa was waiting on the corner of Lexington. Megan jumped in the passenger side of the car, but before shutting the door, she asked, "Can I drive?"

He peeled out into the street before laying into Megan. "I have one pretty fucking interesting question to ask you."

Megan furled her eyebrows and gave Nappa back the same amount of attitude. "What's wrong with you?"

"Just the fact that my *partner* doesn't trust me enough to tell me that she received a phone call from the victim's cell phone."

Megan cringed at her faux pas, remembering that call would be listed on Shannon's phone records. She held her palms up. "Wait a minute. Just wait a minute. I was going to tell you the—"

"You were going to tell me? Bullshit!"

Megan was more accustomed to using expletives than hearing them from Nappa. "First of all, yes. Yes, I was going to tell you when you were over at my house, but then you gave me the whole are-you-up-for-this-case-or-not ball-of-shit discussion. If I'd told you I was worried, you'd have pussyfooted it back to Walker and had me taken off the case."

Nappa ran a red light. "Have I ever—have I *ever*—shown you that that is the kind of cop, or for that matter the kind of man, I am? Have I? Answer the goddamn question!"

Megan held on to the dashboard. "Slow the fucking car down. We're going to Connecticut, not the fucking moon." Megan took a deep breath. "No. That was wrong. I didn't think it through. I was a little rattled for one thing."

It was time for Nappa to gain back his composure. "Rattled. Why? What happened?"

"Remember I told you that I'd gone to the gym before you came over? I tried to get a swim in."

"Yeah, and?"

"When I got home, my phone beeped. It wasn't a call; it was a text."

"From our victim's phone."

"Yeah." Megan's voice quieted. "The text read, 'How was your swim?'"

Nappa pulled the car over. Any anger rifling through his body moments before now turned to deep concern. "Jesus, Megan."

Nappa never called her by her first name. It felt odd for her to hear it now. "Yeah, I know." She pointed toward the road. "C'mon, start driving. We don't want to hit traffic." He did as she requested, and they both sat in silence for the next few minutes. "Nappa, I know I fought being on this case, but I don't want off it now."

Nappa stared up at the red traffic light. "I know. I know." He started shaking his head. "McGinn, this takes things up to a whole different level. You keep everything straight with me, and we'll both watch your back. Got it?"

"Got it." She stared out the window, thinking of the wrong turn she'd made by not telling Nappa. "I should have told you. I'm sorry."

He released a heavy sigh. "Yeah, no shit."

Megan dialed Rasmussen. "Anything on the ring, any hits?" She motioned Nappa to drive faster. "As soon as you get anything, call me." She was about to hang up, not realizing Rasmussen was about to give her other information, but it turned out to be no information at all. "I wasn't expecting anything to be found, but thanks anyway. Have Palumbo put some pressure on the lab regarding the cross." She ran her hands through her hair. "No prints on the sewing kit."

After a while the vibe in the car between the two detectives returned to normal. Megan remembered what she was going to ask Nappa before their argument began. "Nappa, do you remember if any birth control was found in McAllister's apartment?"

"Birth control?"

"Yeah. Anything—pills, condoms, a diaphragm?"

Nappa needed a moment to think about Megan's question. "There were two expired prescription bottles in the trash, and I think a bottle of ibuprofen in the medicine cabinet."

Megan stared out onto the Manhattan streets. They were finally making some headway moving crosstown.

"Why do you ask?" he asked.

"Most women keep their birth control in their bathroom or bedroom. She didn't have any. Her medicine cabinet looked as though it had been gone through."

"How can you tell? There was barely anything in it."

"Exactly. What human being has a nearly empty medicine cabinet? What if the killer took her birth control?"

"Why would he do that?"

"*Shannon M. You've Been Returned.* He didn't give her a one-way ticket to the Bahamas. He killed her. He sent her to heaven— at least that's where I'm assuming she ended up, not to get all philosophical or anything."

"Please, it's going to be a long drive if you get philosophical."

"Seriously, think about it. We knew she was having sex. I don't know many women, well, at least in their thirties, who don't use *some* kind of birth control. She wasn't using a diaphragm. Sutherland would have found it."

"Unless the killer removed it before doing everything else he did to her."

"I'm going to call Palumbo and have him get McAllister's gynecologist's records," Megan said.

"Why, how will that help?"

"The memorial in *The Catholic Times*. Sewing her snatch up. Maybe it's some holy thing. Catholics are supposed to be anti-birth control."

"I'm not sure where you're going with it, but at least you've *told me* what your plans are."

Megan glanced over. "Done and dusted, Nappa. Move on."

It should have been a one-hour drive from Manhattan to the McAllisters' home, but the delay leaving the city and construction on the highway pushed their arrival in Westport closer to lunchtime.

Bold autumn colors highlighted the wooded road leading into town. The surroundings quickly changed when they drove down the main street in Westport. A chauffeured limo pulled up next to the NYPD department's seven-year-old Toyota Camry. Cars such as Jaguars, Bentleys, and Aston Martins were parked at the street meters. Quaint shops that could go head-to-head with any store on Madison or Park Avenue occupied the main street. The bistros were closer to five-star dining in New York, despite referred to as *charming luncheonettes* in the small Connecticut town.

"This is so Norman Rockwell," Megan said.

"Yeah, on antidepressants and Viagra."

"Ouch. What's wrong, Nappa? Are you feeling insecure driving the Camry amongst these swanky automobiles?"

"Next time we're getting a nicer car. Maybe something confiscated from a drug dealer."

"On our department's budget, we're lucky we aren't coming up here on mopeds."

A horseshoe-shaped driveway led up to the McAllisters' Mediterranean-style home. It was hidden behind weeping willows and overgrown spruce trees on a hill. The outside of the house looked as though it had been deserted. Life had stopped for the McAllisters. Autumn leaves raked into piles sat in pockets overshadowing the lawn, each with a brown bag next to it, while newspapers in clear plastic bags multiplied at the bottom of the driveway.

They both got out of the car, taking in the scent of a woodburning fireplace. "You don't find a smell like this often on the Upper East Side," Nappa said.

"Nope." Megan was hesitant to say anything more. The atmosphere was intensely quiet. She guessed the inside of the McAllister home wasn't much different.

A short white gate opened into the backyard of the house. They could see Mrs. McAllister was seated at a table, alone and obviously unaware of her visitors. Nappa rapped on the gate, but it went unnoticed, so they let themselves in.

The backyard patio had been ignored lately as much as the front yard. In the corner was a grill the size of a Jacuzzi. It was closed and had been bombarded by fallen autumn leaves. The swimming pool faced a similar fate. The water was dark, nearing a moss green color. Leaves and bits of shrubbery floated on the surface. Amazing what just a few days' neglect could do.

Shannon's mother sat at a white iron table, staring into a large black leather book. She held it with reverence as she slowly moved her hands over each page.

Megan felt she was intruding on a private moment. "Mrs. McAllister?"

Shannon's mother jolted in Megan's direction, trying to hold back her surprise. "Detectives, hello. I'm sorry, I didn't hear you drive up." She placed the photo album on the table and adjusted the tan wrap draped around her shoulders.

They couldn't help but notice the setting on the table: two glasses of wine poured—only one had been drunk from—and a small plate of hors d'oeuvres in the middle. The tray held an arrangement of cheese, crackers, Greek olives, and marinated red peppers accompanied by a French baguette; the food looked as though it hadn't been touched.

"We're sorry to interrupt," Nappa offered.

"No, no, not at all." She looked up at the detectives, who were obviously curious, and then back down to the table. "Oh, this? I know it's silly without Shannon here. This was our bonding time together. She'd come home for a visit and we'd have an outdoor lunch together. More like a gossip session for just the girls. It became a tradition for us whenever she was able to make it home for a weekend."

"I don't think it's silly at all," Megan assured her.

"Please have a seat."

Nappa pointed toward the photo album. "May I?"

"Of course, that's just one of the many family albums we have. This is mainly of Shannon when she was a baby."

Nappa glanced through it. Pictures of Shannon spanned from the first few hours of her life to when she appeared to be three or four years old. Shannon's first bath, first steps, first words, all dated under each photograph in the album.

"Is Mr. McAllister here as well?" Megan asked.

"Yes, John is inside. It's getting a bit chilly out here. We should probably go in."

"It might be easier to speak with the both of you at the same time." Nappa closed the photo album.

They followed Mrs. McAllister through a set of French doors into the main living room. The room, painted a cool blue, had an airy feel to it. White columned bookshelves lined much of the room, while the blond wooden floors were covered with earth-toned area rugs.

Instead of the countless flower arrangements that were dispersed throughout the room, Megan smelled cigarettes. John, Shannon's father, sat chain-smoking as the phone rang continually.

"John? John? Are you going to get that?" Mrs. McAllister excused herself. "I'll be back in just a moment."

Mr. McAllister sat in a chair, drink in hand, staring aimlessly into the fireplace. He looked as though he'd aged ten years since Megan and Nappa had met him in the morgue. His drink was full and the look on his face was hard, a man consumed with more anger than sorrow. His tall frame slouched to one side. He swirled the glass, the ice cubes clanking against whatever alcohol it was; Megan assumed it was vodka and not mineral water, given the flushed look on his face. Crackling noises from the fire filled the silence.

"Mr. McAllister?" Nappa needed to say it twice to get his attention.

John McAllister looked up, surprised by their presence. "I'm sorry, Detectives, I didn't hear you come in. Please take a seat. Can I fix you a drink?" He got up to refresh his own, which was already three-quarters full.

They both declined a midday cocktail.

"So, what brings you all the way up to Westport from Manhattan?" Mr. McAllister asked.

Mrs. McAllister had returned to the living room while her husband was pouring himself a second round—or possibly a third, it was hard to tell.

"John, I told you they were coming."

He looked quizzically at her. "I don't remember."

She glanced down at his drink before she commented, "I wonder why."

Mr. McAllister answered without embarrassment or hesitation. "It's after twelve o'clock somewhere, MaryEllen."

Megan and Nappa were slightly uncomfortable by the exchange, so they got straight to the point.

"Mrs. McAllister—"

She interrupted, "Excuse me, but, Detectives, you were awfully vague in your phone call regarding your visit." She glanced around them. "You're not returning Shannon's laptop, obviously."

"No ma'am. I expect to get that back to you within another week, if not sooner," Megan answered.

"Then you must have some information?"

"Mrs. McAllister, I know this is hard for you, but I need you to take another look at the gold ring our medical examiner found. Could she have been wearing it the last time you saw Shannon? It's very subtle, maybe you could have missed it?"

This was one of the reasons the detectives took the drive out to Westport, but they felt the McAllister's deserved the other information in person.

"Absolutely not. The last time I saw her—"

Mr. McAllister interrupted, "The last time *we* saw her."

"The last time *we* saw her was last week when she came up to the house for a few days to get out of the city and relax. She wasn't wearing this. She didn't like gold, or, as I said before, long necklaces or turtlenecks for that matter. She said she always felt choked by them."

The irony of that statement was obvious.

"Jesus Christ, MaryEllen! Did you need to say it that way?"

"It's the truth, John. You know she never liked anything tight around her neck: necklaces, sweaters. She never wore scarves."

He lit another cigarette and shook his head in disgust, then guzzled half his drink.

"And this I know I've never seen before." Mrs. McAllister handed Megan back the ring, never taking even a hint of a glance at it. She suddenly sounded drained as she said, "I'm sure."

Mr. McAllister took the other route, his speech slurred slightly, his tone demanding. "What do you have on our daughter's case?" He turned to look up at them. "Do you know who I am? Do you have any idea the powerful friends I have? And who in the fuck leaked that shit out about my baby girl?"

"John!" Mrs. McAllister was embarrassed by her husband's display. "I'm sorry, Detectives."

They nodded in full understanding of his anger. "We've been talking to her friends and coworkers, but we haven't had any strong leads as of yet," Nappa answered. "And we're tracking down the source of the leak."

"I know we asked you this before, but do you know if Shannon was dating anyone over the last few months or had a close male friend perhaps?" Megan asked.

Without hesitation Mrs. McAllister answered, "No, she wasn't seeing anyone romantically. I would have known. She did have a few male friends, strictly platonic."

"Did she ever mention a Professor Bauer to you?" Megan asked.

"A few times. She was working on a project with him. I think it lasted a few months. The project, I mean; she wasn't seeing him or anything like that."

Megan and Nappa glanced at each other, but neither spoke.

Mr. McAllister was a smart man and not in the kind of denial Mrs. McAllister was in. "Why do you ask about this Professor Bauer? Is there something you want to tell us? Do you know something we don't?"

Megan and Nappa looked at each other again. Mr. McAllister repeated the question.

"Well, sir, it seems that Shannon may have been having a relationship with Professor Bauer," Nappa said.

"What do you mean, a *relationship*?" Mrs. McAllister said.

"They were … dating," Megan added, in as delicate a manner as she could. Megan knew the calm was over, and the storm was about to hit.

"Impossible!" Mrs. McAllister pointed at her chest. "Shannon would have shared that with me. I don't believe that."

Mr. McAllister took the lead as the reasonable one in the conversation. "So, is this gentleman a suspect? Is that what you're telling us?"

"Not at this time, sir. He has an alibi," Megan answered.

Mrs. McAllister erupted, "Then why bring him up? Why tell us this?"

"We wondered if there could have been anyone, anyone else, that Shannon may have mentioned that perhaps you may have thought of as platonic but…"

"But wasn't?" Mr. McAllister added.

"Yes sir," Nappa said.

Mr. McAllister put a hand on his wife's shoulder. "It doesn't mean the two of you weren't close, MaryEllen. You had the closest mother-daughter relationship I've ever seen. Remember how much you tried to keep from your mother when we were dating?" he said in as comforting a way as possible.

She shook her head in agreement and wiped away her tears. "There was one boy over the summer that she got to be good friends with. His name was Matt. She spoke of him a lot. They worked at Camp Sparta together. I think I still have the camp's contact sheet in the office. I'll look for it."

Mr. McAllister watched his wife leave the living room in search of the information. She looked broken by the news that her only child hadn't shared every intimate detail with her. "Detectives, do either of you have children?" he asked.

They both answered no.

For the first time since they'd met Mr. McAllister, he shared a small smile. "It's the greatest day of your life. This little being enters your world and turns it completely upside down. You love every minute of it, but at the same time you wonder if you'll ever get through the diaper changes, the late-night feedings, the birthday parties, the chicken pox, the first crush." Shannon's father seemed much more lucid now as he recounted the early years with his daughter. "All you can think about is what an awesome responsibility it is to care for this helpless being. Then, one day, and it happens almost overnight, she's riding her bike without training wheels, and before you know it, you're teaching her how to drive a car. She's become a young woman, and you begin to breathe a little easier. You think, great, we made it—it's smooth sailing from here on out. We did our job and now she can go out and make a life for herself. Then you start thinking and waiting for all the paybacks for all your hard work: walking her down the aisle on her wedding, the day she makes you a grandparent. It all seems to fall into place. It's the natural order of things." He paused and stared into the fireplace. The flames jumped and spewed almost in reaction to his emotion. "Then one morning the phone rings and you're given news your darkest nightmare could never have predicted. One sentence, of one phone call, and all those dreams you had for your child, all those moments you were looking forward to—they're gone. Forever. And they're gone because of the one thing you couldn't do."

"What's that, sir?" Nappa earnestly asked.

"Keep them safe from the world you brought them into."

Megan and Nappa knew there was nothing for them to say. They couldn't even begin to understand the level of loss.

"I'm going to see if I can help Mrs. McAllister with anything." Megan excused herself from the living room and found her way to the office.

She found Mrs. McAllister leaning over the desk so heavily it looked as though she were trying to keep it from blowing away. Megan lightly knocked and walked in. The room was small and dark. Deep cherry wood shelves lined the back wall behind the desk. Framed diplomas filled the first shelf. An encyclopedia set filled the rest. Family photos, golf trophies, and a desk lamp lined the windowsill. Megan noticed the faint smell of pipe tobacco when she entered. "Mrs. McAllister?"

She didn't look up. She pretended she was still searching for the contact sheet, but it was right in front of her. "Found it. And please, call me MaryEllen." She turned on the fax machine. "I can make a copy of it for you, it'll just take a few moments."

"Thank you." Megan looked around the room, trying to think of the most delicate way of asking the next question.

"Detective McGinn?" she asked.

"Please, call me Megan."

"Megan. What is it you'd like to ask me that you can't ask me in front of my husband?"

"Well…"

Mrs. McAllister's small smile contradicted her pink, swollen eyes. "Believe me, nothing you ask could come close to the pain of receiving the phone call I did a few days ago. If it will help find the son of a bitch who did this to my baby, you can ask me anything."

"Was Shannon on any medications?"

"Yes. She occasionally took Tylenol with codeine for a back injury when it'd flare up, but that wasn't often."

Megan waited.

"And birth control. She was on the pill. Mr. McAllister is somewhat conservative, so we kept that one to ourselves. Shannon started taking it to help clear up her skin, reduce her cramps, regulate her cycle, that sort of thing."

Right, and most nose jobs are done to correct a deviated septum, Megan thought to herself.

She handed Megan a sheet of paper. "Here's the contact list. He's the only Matt." Mrs. McAllister sat down at the desk. "He's married, isn't he?"

"I'm sorry, who?" Megan was perplexed.

"The professor Shannon was dating. He's married, isn't he?"

"Yes. Yes, he's married. I wanted you to know in case that comes out in the papers. I wanted you to know first."

She nodded. "I'll tell my husband later, in private, if you don't mind. If you could give me a minute, I'll be back in the living room in a moment."

"Of course. And thank you for this." Megan folded the contact sheet, placing it in her pocket. She couldn't leave the room without saying something to help ease Mrs. McAllister's disappointment.

"MaryEllen, I know this is none of my business, and I don't know if this will help anything. My mother and I weren't as close as you and Shannon, but I can tell you, sometimes daughters keep things from their mothers because we think it will hurt them, or worse, they'd be ashamed of us. So, please, whatever Shannon did or didn't tell you about her life, it doesn't take away from your bond. It never will."

Mrs. McAllister gave Megan a small smile. "Thank you. I'll be out in a minute."

Megan rejoined Nappa and Mr. McAllister in the living room; Mrs. McAllister followed a few minutes later.

"Also, there's one more thing. We've been going through Shannon's day planner and she would write initials in on certain dates. I assumed it was whomever she was meeting up with on that day. There are a number of initials that we haven't been able to find corresponding names to, even with her phone records." Megan showed her the list of initials. "Do any of these ring a bell for you?"

Mr. and Mrs. McAllister looked at the list and then at each other. They shook their heads no in response to the question.

"Well, if you think of anyone, please call."

"Of course, and you'll keep us updated on any progress?" Mrs. McAllister asked. She looked more together now than she had in the office.

"Absolutely." The fire made an exceptionally loud snap, grabbing Megan's attention. She glanced up at the mantel above. A card propped up against the wall caught her eye. It was different from the other sympathy cards around the room. Megan walked over. "May I?"

"Of course." The McAllisters continued their conversation with Nappa.

Megan stood speechless staring at the card. A small cross composed of dried reeds, similar to the one that fell from above Shannon's doorway, was attached to the front of the card. Megan avoided handling it as much as possible and used her fingernail to open it slightly. There was a printed poem, but no signature.

Megan interrupted the conversation, "Excuse me, Mrs. McAllister? May I ask you a question?"

"Yes?"

"When did you receive this card?"

"Which one?"

"This one. The one with a cross on the cover."

The question caught Nappa's attention immediately.

"I believe that came this morning or maybe it was yesterday, I can't be sure. We've had neighbors and friends helping out quite a bit, and I haven't opened any of the cards."

"Do you still have the envelope it came in?" Megan asked.

"Oh, no, I'm sure it was thrown out."

"Do you know who sent it?"

"No, but we've been getting a lot of cards, especially after … well … after Shannon was in the newspapers."

"Would you mind if I borrowed this?" Megan asked.

"May I ask why?" Mrs. McAllister asked.

"I'm just curious about something. I'll get it back to you."

"That's fine."

Megan took it delicately by one corner, placing it in her coat pocket.

TWENTY-SIX

"THESE TWO CROSSES ARE no coincidence, Nappa." Megan took the condolence card out of her jacket. "I'm dropping this off to forensics when we get back into the city."

"I agree, and I thank you for sharing." Sarcasm noted, he continued, "Here's an idea, why not call Aunt Maureen and ask her what it may mean, the reeds? If anyone would know, she would, or you could be up-to-date and search the Internet using my iPhone."

She looked askance at his smartphone. "I'd rather deal with a human being until I can get home to my computer." Megan called the Murphys.

"Aunt Maureen, hi, it's me."

"Ah, Megs, good to hear from you. How are you doing? We saw the papers. What a terrible thing done to that girl."

"I know, I know." She changed tone. "I'm hoping you can help me with something."

"Me? Your uncle Mike is in watching TV. Want me to get him?"

"No, I need your help. You're much more Irish Catholic than I've ever been."

"You don't have to say that twice. Give it a go."

"I'm holding a cross that—"

"You should have told me to take a seat first, Meggie. That news alone could make me faint." Aunt Maureen would do what she could to lighten the mood for her goddaughter.

"Nice, Aunt Maureen, very nice. Anyway, I'm holding a cross, and it's oddly shaped. It's made of some type of dried grass. The middle is a woven square, and the four radials are tied at the ends with the same type of grass."

"Dear, what you're holding there is a Saint Bridget's cross."

"Hold on, Aunt Maureen, I'm putting you on speaker for Nappa to listen in on. You said it's a Saint Bridget's cross? Um... she's..."

"You've heard of Saint Patrick? I *know* you've celebrated him," Aunt Maureen laughed.

"Of course. I'm just trying to remember. Saint Bridget was the saint of..." Megan's attempt to answer was on the verge of crash-and-burn territory. A question on astrophysics or global economics would have taken less time to answer. "Saint Bridget is one of the biggies, right?"

"Biggies. Yes, that's how our Lord and Savior described them: *biggies*. They're also called *saints*. Saint Bridget is one of the patron saints of Ireland. Haven't you ever seen our Saint Bridget's cross?"

"What? No. Where is it?"

"Above the entranceway."

"No shit?"

"Megan Alanna McGinn!"

Megan cringed. "Sorry."

"Thank you. What I know of Bridget is that she was a nun. Her mission was to relieve misery and hardship of the poor. The cross protects the house from evil, fire, you know. I'd have to look her up again for more information."

"You've been a big help, Aunt Maureen."

"Oh, and it's not made of grass, exactly, but reeds, directly from Ireland, if you're that much of a fanatic."

"That's enough to start on. We'll see you as soon as we can."

"I hope you mean you *and* Mr. Samson Nappa."

"Love you, bye." Megan politely ignored her question.

The rest of the drive was spent in silence. Meeting with the McAllisters had been draining. Megan stared out the passenger-side window ashamed at the thoughts running through her mind. She thought back to Mrs. McAllister's story about Shannon's birth control, how they kept that from Mr. McAllister. She envied their close relationship. She and Rose didn't share the level of intimacy needed for keeping secrets. Megan and her father, on the other hand, had plenty.

Every so often Pat would stop by Megan's school and take her out for lunch. It was usually after closing a difficult case that required long hours and a lot of time away from home. He'd lie to the nuns, saying Megan had forgotten a scheduled doctor's appointment. They'd go to a diner or, if it was nice, split a sandwich outside at a park. It wasn't often, but when Megan got called down to the principal's office without cause, she knew her father would be waiting for her.

The memory of their playing hooky together brought a smile to her face, until she went to hold the cross that no longer hung around her neck.

TWENTY-SEVEN

THE SMELL OF BURNING incense filled the air in St. Thomas More Church. Megan arrived a few minutes before the service began. She tiptoed over to the wooden pews so the clicking of her heels wouldn't echo throughout the church.

Oh, Christ, Megan thought. Right before she was about to sit, she turned back toward the entrance to dip her finger into the cup of holy water she'd inadvertently passed. After performing the sign of the cross at bionic speed, she returned to her seat in the back of the church.

St. Thomas More was quaint and surprisingly understated for a Catholic church. Double wooden doors opened to earth-toned tiles that continued from the foyer all the way up to the pulpit. Cement walls divided into archways distinguished each section of pews. Large lanterns suspended from the ceiling on black iron rods replaced the overstated chandeliers typical in Catholic churches. An enlarged color photo of Shannon was placed on an easel near the pulpit and was surrounded by multiple arrangements of white roses. Megan assumed it was Shannon's favorite flower due to the sheer number of them. As expected, the church overflowed with family, friends, and coworkers. Untimely deaths brought people out in droves.

Megan double-checked that she'd switched her cell phone to vibrate mode before the service began. She placed it back in her coat when she felt something in the side pocket. She'd forgotten the last time she'd worn that particular jacket was mere days ago, a lifetime away. She'd thought it was a business card. Embossed black letters at the top read, *In Loving Memory of Patrick McGinn.*

Megan's stomach tightened when she turned the card around and realized she was holding her father's mass card in her palm. The memory of her father's funeral would forever be etched in her mind as deeply as the pain of missing him would remain carved within her heart. She'd read from a book of Irish prayers at her father's funeral. It had been one of his favorite blessings. She knew it word for word and repeated it softly to herself as she traced over his name with her finger.

> *May the road rise up to meet you.*
> *May the wind always be at your back.*
> *May the sun shine warm upon your face,*
> *and rains fall soft upon your fields.*
> *And until we meet again,*

"May God hold you in the palm of his hand," Megan whispered the last sentence to herself as she returned the card to her coat pocket. She swallowed and took a deep breath, hoping the service would soon get under way.

The wooden doors opened and closed again moments before the priest approached the pulpit. The parishioner's entrance went unnoticed by Megan and the other attendees in St. Thomas More Church.

Nappa entered the pew Megan was seated in and sat beside her. She whispered the same question he was about to ask her. "Anyone here pique your interest?" She continued to glance around the room, eliminating all the females and elderly in view, focusing on the men in the church. There were quite a few young men attending the service, but no one that struck a chord with Megan.

"Not really. I had no idea such a small church could accommodate so many people," Nappa said.

The priest began cleaning the chalice and silently repeating prayers before sprinkling the incense. Megan always hated the smell of incense; not for any religious reason, she just found the odor harsh. The service continued when Father Gallagher asked everyone to kneel for prayer. Megan knelt forward, bowing her head on top of her clasped hands. Shannon McAllister's crime-scene photos darted through her mind. Bended knees. Fingers intertwined close to her face. A tsunami overcoming a village would have been less powerful than the connection she just made. "Jesus Christ!"

Nappa placed one hand on his forehead, lowering his head even farther in prayer, a vain attempt to block out the gasps and stares Megan's declaration for the Son of God received from nearby mourners.

She nudged Nappa. "Nappa." He didn't look up. "Nappa!"

"Shhh. We're at a funeral."

She whispered loudly, "She wasn't sleeping."

"What? Who wasn't sleeping?"

"McAllister, in the crime-scene photos. She was *praying*." Megan made eye contact to how she and Nappa were positioned. "Her body was placed in prayer."

Nappa took in Megan's discovery, and then whispered, "Jesus Christ."

She was relieved when her phone started vibrating. It was Rasmussen. She nudged Nappa's arm, showing him the call coming in. They quietly walked out of the church to take it. "Hey, it's me." Rasmussen's next sentence made Megan stop in her tracks, and Nappa followed suit. "Really, uh … huh."

Nappa waited patiently for Megan to finish. She'd never have been able to return the same courtesy if Nappa had gotten the call. A few "what's" and a "tell me, what'd he say," along with a tug on Nappa's arm would have been more probable.

"Excellent. Nappa and I were just at the service. We're leaving now and should be back in about twenty minutes." She slapped the phone closed and pointed a finger at Nappa. "One print came off the receipt from *The Catholic Times*."

"You're kidding."

"I have a helluva sense of humor, but no, I'm not kidding. No matches have been made yet, but—"

"If there are any," Nappa interrupted.

Usually Megan was the pessimist and Nappa the optimist, but she needed to feel like the case was moving forward, especially after attending a victim's funeral. Still, she knew Nappa had a point. "I know, but at least it's something."

"True."

"We don't meet up with Matt Garrison until later this afternoon. Let's get back to the office. I want to do some more research on Saint Bridget and the crosses."

Megan's cell rang again, "McGinn." She waited, "Wait, I'm sorry I don't understand. Why did you have to go into my apartment?" She spun in Nappa's direction, "Don't touch anything! Nothing! Do you hear me!"

Megan emulated the video game Frogger as she ran through the traffic on Park Avenue, barely avoiding being flattened by yellow taxis and New York City buses. "Fuck! Fuck!"

"McGinn, wait!" Nappa raced after her. He was only able to grab every third word from Megan as she sprinted down 93rd Street.

Oven? Burning?

She made it to her building just as Nappa caught up with her. Megan had her gun drawn as she exited the elevator. Alberto, the building's super, jaw dropped as he lifted his hands in the air in surrender. She mouthed for him to step back. Megan leaned her head in when Alberto whispered, "It's empty."

His observation didn't fill her with ease. She quickly turned into the kitchen, aiming her gun toward the blind corner between her refrigerator and the open stove. She traced back her steps and inspected the bathroom, bedroom, and closet. When she acknowledged to herself all was clear, Nappa cautiously approached the living room.

"Empty."

They walked into Megan's kitchen, where the obvious baker's aroma stemmed from, their guns not as postured as before. She used her sleeve to open the oven door. An aluminum bread pan was centered in the middle rack, its contents partially burned.

"Irish soda bread," Megan said.

TWENTY-EIGHT

MEGAN SAT IN THE stairwell while colleagues, some familiar, some strangers, tracked through her apartment, excavating her personal space searching for prints, fibers—whatever would lead them to the person responsible for breaking into the lead detective's Carnegie Hill apartment.

Nappa stepped out of Megan's apartment into the hallway. They looked at one another, silently acknowledging the same notion: *this is a different experience than last time we were here together.*

"The doorman was on break. There's one apartment moving out today, so movers were using the service entrance, allowing direct access to the basement. Anyone could have come and gone without—"

"Being detected," Megan interrupted. The look in her eyes wasn't filled with fear, or anger, but stout resolve. She remembered the declaration she'd made standing in the rain staring at her own image on the television. *I am no one's bitch.*

"We need you to do a walk-through to see if anything was stolen."

"Who is *we*? I'm still a part of the *we*, aren't I?"

"Let's do the walk-through."

"Nappa, what the hell?"

"Let's just do this and then deal with the next steps."

She walked through her own crime scene, each step elevating her determination to hunt instead of being hunted. "I don't see anything out of place."

"Are you sure?" Nappa asked.

"As far as I can tell."

"Your super's changing the locks. Is he good—do you trust him?"

Megan waived his concerns away. "He's great. I've helped some of his family out of a few jams, a nephew with parole officer issues. He has my back."

"So do I," Nappa replied.

Megan glanced up at him. "Good, 'cause someone has their eye on it." Megan never admitted it to anyone, but every so often she wished someone other than herself had her back. Her father did, as much as he could, but it wasn't a foolproof plan. Rose had demanded most of his attention when she'd become ill. Megan knew he was there in spirit, now more so than ever. But ever since finding her mother in the tub that one afternoon when she was young, she slept with one eye open, always waiting for the other shoe to drop. A killer breaking into her apartment sure sounded like a thud. She knew she couldn't stay in her own home that night, so it looked like she was going to have to acquiesce to her brother's request out of default: stay at her parents' house. It's not as if she'd be getting much sleep tonight anyway.

TWENTY-NINE

MEGAN SAT IN TOMMY's Pub, one block down from the home she grew up in. Her father and the owner, Mr. Wilson, shared many a pint over the years. Megan inherited her father's respect from people on the job but also from the locals, Mr. Wilson being one of them, and she adored him.

He didn't utter a word when she first walked in. She sat at the end of the bar and he had the waitress bring over a shot and a beer, all the while he was viewing a sports channel. Irish culture is many things, but intrusive isn't one of them—at least not until the third shot.

Mr. Wilson was one of the kindest men of her father's friends Megan could think of, other than Uncle Mike, of course.

Salt of the earth, Pat McGinn would say, and it was true.

"Sweet girl, how ya' holding up?" Mr. Wilson clinked his glass with hers. "Beautiful funeral, and a lovely wake, he had."

Megan nodded. "The one party you can never show up for." Her laugh was as inappropriate as most endearing comments were in regards to unprepared deaths.

"I've been reading the papers." He poured her another shot.

"Yeah." She threw it back, ignoring his inquiry. "Well, I'm off to start sorting through Mom and Dad's house tonight." She smiled, they tapped shot glasses, and kicked back another.

"To you and yours, my luv."

As Megan was leaving, she noticed that Mr. Wilson had attached a laminated copy of Pat McGinn's obituary to the back of the bar wall, and that was that.

Done and dusted, as her father always said.

She cried walking the one block to the house.

Megan felt she was trespassing for some odd reason as she entered the house, maybe because it felt so empty, deserted, and, worst of all, lonely. She went into the kitchen for a glass of water and sat down at the kitchen table. She recounted the countless family dinners the table held for the McGinn family: everyone talking, no one listening, but continuous banter nonetheless. It made her smile, until the silence crept back in and the thoughts returned of a murderer intruding on her personal space. Her sanctuary.

Son of a bitch.

She set the glass in the sink and headed upstairs to her parents' bedroom. She looked at her father's closet. She wasn't ready for his personal things, their memories. She decided to start with her mother's closet, since Rose would have no use for those clothes any longer. Megan ran her hand across the row of dresses. The smell of her mother's perfume was ever present. Megan pushed the rack to the back and was shocked to find the dress Rose wore the day she tried to kill herself hanging in the back, dried blood covering it.

"Momma. Why? Why would you keep this?" For years Megan could never recall what happened after she opened the bathroom door that day. She sat down on the bed holding the dress in her lap, unlocking the memory she worked so hard to bury.

She'd run to her mother on the bathroom floor screaming for her.

Rose was going in and out of consciousness. "It's all just too much. It's all just too much."

Megan in her hysteria remembered her father was waiting on the phone. She ran over to the receiver screaming, "Daddy! Daddy! Momma's cut herself! She's cut herself!" She remembered how her voice was trembling, but nothing compared to the shaking of her hands. "Daddy, come home! Daddy, come home!"

Megan recalled hearing, "Oh God," then Pat telling her to get towels and wrap them around the wounds. Clear as crystal Megan now remembered: *Tight, honey, really tight.*

"Okay, Daddy." Megan had dropped the phone and ran into the bathroom, slipping on some of Rose's blood. She got to her knees and did what her father instructed her to do; she tied the towels as tight as an almost-twelve-year-old could. Megan sat in the bathroom and started to hyperventilate, staring at her mother. Megan couldn't remember how long it was, but the first one to arrive, she finally recalled, was Mr. Wilson. He grabbed her and put her on Pat and Rose's bed. In a matter of minutes, flashing lights were outside of the house. Mrs. Wilson ran into the bedroom then, clutching Megan and rushing her down the stairs and out of the house. Megan saw her father running toward the front door.

"Daddy! Daddy!"

Mrs. Wilson held her tight. "Everything's going to be okay, Megan. Your dad's checking on your mom. It was just an accident."

It was just an accident.

Megan now rolled the dress into a ball and curled up on the bed, tears streaming down the side of her face. "An *accident* with a razor on both wrists. Yeah, right."

As Mrs. Wilson hustled Megan out of the house, Megan remembered looking back at the bags of her birthday ornaments sitting on the dining room table, knowing they would never be used, not that year. And Megan never trusted another birthday to be celebrated ever again.

That day marked the moment Rose distanced herself from Megan. Maybe out of guilt, maybe out of shame. No matter the reason, theirs would never be the model of a close mother-daughter relationship, like Shannon and her mother shared.

Megan remembered when Rose came home from the hospital her first words were, "You better have been taking good care of your father, missy."

It had been arm's length love from that day on.

Megan's cell rang in the silence, forcing her up. She wiped her face and cleared her throat. "Nappa, what's up?"

"I just wanted to check on you, see that you're okay."

"Yeah, great."

"Are you sure? You sound different."

"No, just a little tired. So, what's happening?"

"The cross on the McAllister's sympathy card? Two drops of blood were found. Very small drops, and rare, AB negative."

Megan transitioned from pained childhood mode to detective status. "You're kidding. Did anything match up in the computers? The Red Cross keeps records of people who've donated blood, especially if they have a rare blood type. Have you checked with them?"

"In the process of checking with hospitals and the Red Cross— and that's only *if* the unsub has donated."

"Or had surgery somewhere."

"Well, I just thought I'd let you know. Are you sure you're okay?"

"Nappa, I'm fine. Seriously. It's just been a long day. I assume nothing was found in my apartment?"

Nappa paused. "Nothing."

"I didn't expect there to be."

They hung up and within minutes Megan was fast asleep, hoping there wouldn't be any nightmares like the one she'd lived through today, or like the horror she'd endured years ago with her mother.

THIRTY

ALL FOUR DETECTIVES RECONVENED at the precinct the next morning. Megan didn't want to speak about the most obvious story: the killer had been in her home. She could feel lingering looks when she walked through the office. The whispers were silenced when she slammed the conference room door.

"The lieutenant's door is closed. Am I waiting for a meeting?" she asked Nappa.

"Joanne said she'll be free in a few minutes. She'll find us."

"Whatever." She rolled up her sleeves. "Okay, let's keep going. Lauren Bell, the vic's mentor, said McAllister had volunteered at something medical for a friend, flu shots, or something, right?"

"The list that Mrs. McAllister gave us is only of the counselors—no medical people or other staff are on it," Nappa said.

Megan had had Shannon's month-to-month calendar from her datebook enlarged and pinned to the bulletin board in the conference room. "BD. Medical. BD," Megan repeated. "Blood drive." She tapped the board before circling the date with the red marker.

"The mentor mentioned a blood drive. I bet BD is for blood drive. It's not a person—BD was what she was doing that day, not who she was seeing. Let's check the people volunteering that day and donating, *especially* donating. If that rare blood type shows up, I want that person brought in."

"Where is the file we have on McAllister's volunteer work?" Nappa asked.

"You mean the list of agencies and organizations. I left that one on my desk. I'll be right back." Megan went out to her desk, shuffling papers around to look for the folder.

"You fucking bitch!"

When someone yells obscenities in a police precinct, what usually follows isn't an FTD floral arrangement. A man's foot made contact with Megan's lower back before anyone, including Megan, could react.

"*Martin!*" yelled Professor Bauer's attorney.

He swung her around by grabbing her jacket when his fist made contact with her jaw. Blood flowed like wild rapids through her mouth.

Surrounding detectives jumped on Bauer faster than women at a Prada outlet pouncing on the last size-eight heels on clearance, but not before Megan was catapulted forward, jamming her abdomen into the corner of the desk. The pain seared through her midsection. She turned to see who had the black belt in drop-kicking, and saw Palumbo slamming Professor Bauer's face to the floor.

"I'll get you for this, you fucking miserable bitch!"

Palumbo jammed his knee into the middle of Bauer's back, but that didn't stop Bauer from continuing his rant. "Because of you, the university has put me on a temporary leave of absence. You fucking bitch!"

"Martin!" his lawyer yelled again.

By the time the second "fucking bitch" was spewed, Nappa was out of the conference room trying to help Megan, just as Walker opened her door.

"What in hell is going on out here?" Walker screamed.

Megan was doubled over grabbing her abdomen, but managed to grunt, "Lieutenant, meet Professor Love. He's the one on the floor." She glanced behind, rubbing her lower back, blood-soaked drool seeping from the corner of her mouth. "I think he has a crush on me."

"You're ruining my career, you bitch!" Bauer yelled up from his headlock.

"Palumbo! Rasmussen! I want him out of here right now!" Walker yelled.

"You're arresting him? For what?!" the lawyer yelled back.

"Assaulting a New York City police officer," she screamed back. "That's a Class B felony, up to nine years in prison. I want him out! Now!"

Palumbo hoisted Bauer off the floor, holding the back of his neck, pinning Bauer's left arm behind him.

"You're going to break my fucking arm, you animal!"

"My client is going to sue this office for police brutality, the excessive use of physical force, and—"

"Shut up," Rasmussen said calmly to both men while he cuffed Bauer.

"Now I'm adding verbal assault to the charge as well."

"Shut up!" Palumbo and Rasmussen yelled in unison as they marched Professor Bauer out of the room.

"McGinn, Nappa—in my office!"

Megan grimaced in pain with each tender step as Nappa tried to act as a human buttress on one side. *I sure could have used that about sixty seconds ago.*

"Sit down," Walker ordered as she poured a glass of water for her.

Megan took a sip and then crouched over, putting her head into her lap. "So, how's your day?" she muttered.

Walker ignored the dry wit. "Are you okay? Do you want me to call an ambulance?"

Megan looked up. "Oh yes, please, because being assaulted at my own desk isn't embarrassing enough."

"What the hell was that?" Walker asked.

"I stopped by during one of his lectures," Megan answered.

"Why? I thought his alibi checked out?" Walker questioned. She handed Megan a tissue for her mouth.

Megan maneuvered her jaw, blotting the corners. "Everyone we've been speaking with said Bauer was the first person that came to mind when they heard the news about McAllister. I just wanted to put a little fire under him."

"Where were you?" Walker asked Nappa.

"Checking out *The Catholic Times.*" He fumed at Megan, obviously recalling the conversation where he demanded she not go to see Bauer alone. She couldn't tell if he was angrier at her for going and putting herself in the position she was now in—bloody, pained, and still stubborn as hell—or at himself for acting like an overbearing parent.

Joanne interrupted with a knock on the door. "You might want to turn the news on." She looked over at Megan. "Need a few ibuprofen?"

Megan nodded.

Breaking news flashed over the screen. Ashley Peters stood outside Professor Bauer's office building with a two-line comment about Professor Bauer being put on temporary leave based on his alleged involvement with the investigation of murdered student Shannon McAllister.

"I guess now you know why you have a size-eleven shoe print lodged in your spine." Walker frowned.

"C'mon, I didn't have anything to do with that leak." Megan nodded over at the television. "You know me better than that. That broad probably paid some college student for the information."

Walker knew Megan had nothing to do with what they just witnessed on the news. But it had *damage control* written all over it in order to avoid a lawsuit. "Are you sure you're okay?" she asked again.

"Yeah, my children may be born with a Florsheim shoe imprinted on their foreheads, but I'm fine." She rubbed her side. "I'll let you know when he's been processed. The interview should be interesting."

"Call the bomb squad for some protective gear," Walker added.

"For Bauer or me?" Megan asked.

Walker's phone began to ring off the hook. They took it as their cue to leave.

"McGinn, Nappa, when you're done speaking with Bauer, get back in here. We are far from done."

THIRTY-ONE

I HADN'T EXPECTED THE detective's apartment to feel so comfortable. It was quite unremarkable, really. Homey, a comforting retreat. I wonder if she'll feel that way now when she heads off to sleep. It finally dawned on me when I sat on her bed who she reminded me of. Funny, how sometimes it's right in front of your face and you never see it. Just like when I was in front of her face, just a few feet away. She didn't sense a thing. That's power.

———

Professor Martin Bauer sat next to his lawyer at one end of the table, Megan and Nappa down at the other. All four looked exhausted, especially Bauer. Based on his bruising, Palumbo hadn't lost touch with his college days on the wrestling team.

"Professor Bauer would like to offer his sincerest apologies for his earlier outburst." The lawyer nudged him. "Go ahead, Martin."

Bauer had every color of the rainbow marked on his face: remnants of a bloody nose, a black eye, a fat lip, and a bump on his forehead that had a fascinating greenish-yellow hue to it.

"Due to unwarranted stress of late, I am profoundly sorry for my earlier outburst."

Henry VIII discussing lasting marriage would have sounded more sincere.

Bite me, Megan thought, but she was smart enough not to say it while the voice recorders were running.

"First of all, I want it noted that Professor Bauer is fully cooperating with your investigation." The lawyer got his two cents in.

"Noted. Go on," Nappa answered.

"It's true. I didn't handle Shannon breaking up with me well. I … I didn't hurt her. I loved her." Bauer was no longer the cocky collegiate faculty member they'd met days earlier. Before, he sat behind an antique desk, with an impressive title at one of the country's top universities. Now he sat slouched at a scarred Formica table, beaten physically and mentally by the loss of something all the impressive diplomas and titles couldn't give him: a young woman's love.

"I saw her outside that day having lunch with that … *boy*." He trailed his thumbnail up and down the scores embedded into the table as he spoke. "I got so angry when I saw them together. And then I waited for her to come by my office as I'd asked her to. When she didn't show up, I was infuriated."

"What boy?" Megan asked through a swollen lip.

"I don't know," he answered, "but she looked happy, happier than I ever made her."

"You don't have a name?" Nappa asked.

"I never saw him before." His voice cracked. "Nothing had been the same since we stopped seeing one another." Bauer maintained a fixed stare down at a coffee-cup stain on the table. "Shannon was right—in the beginning it was a meaningless fling to me, but the more time I spent with her, the more I knew that it had become something more substantial."

"But it was too late," Megan said.

He nodded.

"You wanted your young, vibrant mistress. You wanted your wife and kids, and your perfect life in Westchester. You wanted to have your cake and eat it too," Nappa said, sounding a bit more like Megan in his cynicism.

"I had a plan. I was going to leave her—my wife. I just never had the chance to tell Shannon. She ended things, and, well, I should have acted sooner. She wouldn't listen to a word I had to say. I felt like my voice had been taken away."

Christ, I wish I had a dollar for every time a woman felt like that, Megan thought.

"She had a way of making you feel like everything you wanted to do was possible, and every part of who you are was right and good. I didn't want to give that up. I just couldn't see myself not having *some* type of relationship with her. There was a huge emotional deficit in my life without her in it."

Megan wasn't about to let the conversation turn into a Lifetime Channel movie. "She made you feel less like the asshole that you are."

"Out of line, Detective!" the lawyer interrupted, slamming his palm down on the desk.

"No, Lawrence, it's okay." This was the first time Bauer looked over at Megan during the interview. "Detective McGinn's right." He knew whom at the table he needed to convince of his innocence, and it was the woman he'd drop-kicked earlier. "I didn't kill her, Detective McGinn. I…did…not…kill…Shannon…Mc-Allister."

Megan gingerly rose from her chair, ambling toward the door. "I know. You're just a dick."

THIRTY-TWO

"Was it worth it?" Nappa asked.

Megan knew what he was getting at. She pulled rank on him and got her ass and face kicked in over an innocent man—an asshole, but nonetheless an innocent man.

"Does it matter?" She folded more ice in a towel to hold up to her face.

Walker's bellow reminded her of the nuns at Catholic school on the playground: "McGinn! Now!"

"I know what this is about. Go with it," Megan said.

"Shut the door," Walker demanded. "We're issuing a formal apology to the professor and clearing his name in the press. We're also dropping the charges for assaulting you."

"As long as he doesn't sue the department," Megan added.

"It's not personal. It's called politics, and it's called business."

"I'll remember that when my dentist is resetting my jaw."

"On to the next topic." Walker didn't bother taking a seat; she was in power mode. "Detective, it's been made known to me that the break-in at your apartment was not the first contact the killer made in reaching out to you. Don't bother figuring out your reply. The sewing kit? I know about that, and I know about the call and text sent to your phone."

Neither Megan nor Nappa were surprised.

"I'm putting you on paid leave. You have a lot of time coming to you, and I'm strongly suggesting you take it."

"That's bullshit!" She slammed the ice pack on Walker's desk. "The killer is making contact with me, and you're saying I should take a vacation? We can use this to our advantage! Put me in the line of fire, and we'll catch him. We can draw him out!"

Walker ignored Megan's attempts to negotiate. "Nappa, I'm putting Rasmussen on with you. I'll make sure Palumbo is covered."

"Wait! Wait one Goddamn minute! This is not happening. You can't do this!"

Rasmussen knocked on the door. "McGinn, we got a hit on Craigslist on the Elmira vic, Erin Quinlan's ring. You're not going to believe who answered it."

Fuck.

Megan swung around to Walker, "Lieutenant, please give me this one, this could be our guy. At least let me finish this day out and then I'll take a vacation. Just give me today."

Walker stared Megan down. She didn't look like she was going to cave.

"Pearl." Megan never addressed her boss by her first name. "*Please.*"

Walker glanced at Nappa, and he nodded in testament to Megan's plea. He was in his partner's corner.

Walker threw Megan's folder on her desk. "The paperwork will take the rest of the afternoon. That's all you get. Your vacation starts tomorrow."

Before leaving Walker's office, Megan turned back. "Thank you. I mean that."

"Get out of my office."

"Talk to me," Megan said as she, Nappa, and Palumbo circled Rasmussen's desk.

"One hit. He didn't even bargain on the price."

"Who is he? I thought this stuff is anonymous, I mean you're supposed to ship it to him, right?"

"I had Computer Crimes Squad trace my email and his reply. The offer came from Saint Mary's Byzantine church on Fifteenth and Second Avenue. He's a priest."

Megan broke the silence between the four detectives. "Fuck all. Go get him." She checked her watch. Five hours before *vacation* started. "Be back here in an hour."

"You want us to arrest him?" Palumbo asked.

"No, just tell him we have some questions. Don't give any hint that it has to do with the Quinlan or McAllister cases. Tell him we could use his religious knowledge regarding an ongoing investigation. Go."

THIRTY-THREE

MEGAN AND NAPPA WAITED in the interrogation room. Palumbo had sent a text that he and Rasmussen had picked up the priest and were on their way. When they arrived, the man was nothing what Megan expected. He was young, carried himself in a sheepish fashion. He slouched into the chair, beads of sweat already forming on his face.

"I'm Detective McGinn, this is Detective Nappa. You are?"

He pushed his wire-framed glasses farther up his nose. "I'm … I'm Father John Leary."

"Do you know why you're here?" Megan asked.

"You had questions for me regarding religious information for something?" He rubbed his palms together. "But I don't understand why this conversation couldn't have taken place at my church."

"Father." Megan felt odd calling him *father* given he was more than ten years younger than she. "You tried to buy a nurse's ring on the Internet?"

He was visibly confused as he jetted his attention around the room. "Um, yes, I don't see what that has to do with anything."

"Why did you want the ring?" Nappa asked.

"You didn't even try to negotiate the price, why?" Megan questioned.

"That's what *this* is about? I tried to buy a ring on the Internet?"

"Answer my partner's question: *Why* did you want that particular ring?" Megan demanded.

"Well, I . . . I—"

"Answer the question, Father!" The *tick-tock* of the clock was moving closer to Megan's forced vacation and she wanted answers, fast.

"My grandmother was a nurse. She went to a nursing school in upstate New York, Saint Joseph's, in Syracuse, and it reminded me of her. That's all. It reminded me of the ring she wore when she was alive. I just wanted a . . . a . . ."

"A what?!" Megan yelled.

"Just something to remind me of her! That's all!"

Megan sat back. She knew this man wasn't the unsub. Just to be sure, she tested him, disclosing how the ring came into their possession and the girl who was murdered. He vomited on the table.

"Drive him back to his parish," Megan requested of Palumbo and Rasmussen.

Through a trembling voice, Father Leary wiped his mouth, "Detective McGinn?"

Megan turned before leaving the interrogation room.

"I'll pray for you."

A low humph emerged. "Too late."

Megan cleared what she needed from her desk. Walker continued to eye her from her office. She didn't make a big exit, only stopping by the conference room where Nappa, Palumbo, and Rasmussen were assembled. "Gentlemen, till we meet again," followed by a whispered, "keep your private cells on."

Rasmussen glanced over at Nappa with a knowing look.

Nappa replied, "Did you expect anything less?"

THIRTY-FOUR

MEGAN WALKED UP THE avenue not feeling today's rain. She was numb with the exception of her throbbing jaw and her lower back. Those hurt like hell. Cigarettes and more ibuprofen were her immediate demands. She stopped at the deli around the corner from her building to buy Parliaments. The meds were in her apartment: booze and painkillers, the evening's appetizers. She stood under the deli's canopy, ripping through the plastic, when a cabbie pulled up illegally parking in front of the kiosk. She lit the cigarette and took a nice, long drag. It gave her a buzz. With the bad weather, there were more than a handful of people vying for a ride. Megan ignored the verbal scuffle between potential passengers, focusing instead on the neon sign above the cab. The green letters in the advertisement were ones she recognized from Shannon's datebook.

Son of a bitch.

She tossed the cigarette into the storm sewer grate. "Fuck all."

When she entered her building, Bernie the doorman approached her, removing his hat. "Miss McGinn, I can't tell you how sorry I am about your apartment. I was the one on duty and I never should have let that happen. I'm real sorry for all of it. I feel totally responsible."

"Bernie, it's not your fault."

"No ... no." He shook his head. "It is my fault. I forgot to lock the door when I went on break." He knocked his temple with his fist. "I have no idea how I could be so careless. I'm *really* sorry, Miss McGinn."

"I know you are. I know. Don't beat yourself up over it, Bernie, okay? Things happen."

"Thanks for being so understanding, Miss McGinn. Thank you."

"No worries, Bernie. Have a good night."

Megan was more interested in getting back into her apartment and online. She didn't carry a grudge toward Bernie. She knew if a perp wants to get into a place, it was going to happen. She wasn't excited about re-entering the latest crime scene, formerly known as her safe home, but it had to be done. She double locked the door, and, in a neurotic moment, turned around to repeat the action.

She jumped on her bed, powered up her laptop, and lit another cigarette while doing a search for SIN. The irony of searching for *sin* made her grin. "That's usually not a problem for me."

The website was first on the results. It opened to a framed outline of the map of Ireland. A leprechaun danced to Irish music and tossed four-leaf clovers into the air. Then in a sweet lilt of an Irish brogue said, "Irish? Single? Lookin' fur luv in the big city?"

"Sweet Jesus." Megan rolled her eyes at the site's introduction. She clicked into a sample offer of men that the site promoted. "This is unbelievable. Christ, my father would have loved some of these guys. I *cannot* mention this site to Aunt Maureen. She'll have my photo posted in a heartbeat."

Shamrocks blinked around a green cupid holding a bow and arrow. The advertisement read *SIN, Single Irish New Yorkers looking for love.* Men of every shape, size, and age range were listed. And they had two things in common: they were Irish and looking.

"I'm willing to bet one of you boys may have dated one recently murdered Shannon McAllister. I'm going to find out who."

You were allowed only limited access to the site unless you joined for a small fee. Megan pulled out her credit card and filled in the information.

"I can't believe I'm doing this." She completed the required questionnaire. "Looking for: a man. Age range. Let's see, Shannon was in her twenties, so I'll say twenties to early thirties. My age: I've heard people say I don't look a day over thirty, so I'll say ... twenty-six. Religion: skip that. Height: average. Body type: curvaceous. Occupation: I'll put down social worker. Smoke?" She took a deep drag. "Nope. Never. Drink: occasionally."

In other words, there really doesn't need to be an occasion.

Once she'd paid and selected a user name and password, she scrolled through women in their twenties searching for men. "God." She read multiple listings. Women looking for their soul mates, women looking for long-term relationships, one woman offering Irish men American citizenship in exchange for marriage. "Desperate, much?" The next one cracked her up. "'I'm your Irish wet dream waiting to cum.' You're a classy gal, sweetie." She found Shannon's listing on the fourth page.

Lovely Irish lass looking for her Irish lad. Her photo was in the corner of the page. It was a simple headshot displaying her big smile. Megan read Shannon's biography. It was generic. Nothing overstated, as she expected it would be.

Megan called Clarice at the office. It went directly into voice-mail, and then she checked her watch. She hadn't realized how late it was, so she planned to call Clarice in the morning to see if she could find anything on Shannon's laptop from the SIN website. There was little doubt in her mind there was a connection.

THIRTY-FIVE

MEGAN'S CELL PHONE WOKE her before the alarm went off. She rolled over and mumbled into the receiver, "McGinn."

"Wake up, sweet cheeks." Clarice accentuated her Southern drawl when she wanted to be cute.

"What time is it?" Megan threw her head under one of the pillows.

"Ten after six."

"You're an evil woman, waking me up at this hour," Megan groaned.

"Do you want the information I found on the laptop?"

"Is it worth waking me up at six o'clock for?"

"Yes," Clarice answered.

"Shoot. No, wait. On second thought, let me guess: she belonged to a computer dating service, appropriately named SIN."

"I won't even ask how you found that out. Anyway, there are a few emails from a Seamus McCann."

"Threatening emails?"

"No, not at all; sweet, actually. How much he enjoyed their dates and so on."

"Is there any information on him?" Megan asked.

"There aren't many emails, but from what I've been able to gather, he's a schoolteacher in Manhattan. I took the liberty of getting into the New York State Department of Education's database to make a match."

"God, you're good," Megan said.

"There is a Seamus McCann registered to teach at a school on the West Side."

Megan wrote down all the information Clarice was able to give her. "You're an absolute diamond, Clarice. I owe you big time," Megan said, yawning into the phone.

"I'll have more for you later this morning. I do have to make it look like I'm earning a paycheck here, though, know what I mean?"

"As far as I'm concerned, you already have."

Megan logged on to the SIN website to look up Seamus McCann. With the exception of *Irish Teddy Bear Looking for a Hug*, he wrote as generic a biography as Shannon had. He was a teacher, he enjoyed sports and going to movies, and he loved Italian food.

———

Seamus McCann was kicking a soccer ball back and forth with a few of his students. He was a lot heavier in person than his photo led one to believe. *That's where the Italian food comes in*, Megan assumed. He was a good-looking guy, but not exactly what she was expecting.

"Mr. McCann?" Megan approached. "I was wondering if I could take a few minutes to ask you some questions."

"I'm sorry?" He looked at her with more concern than defensiveness.

"It's regarding Shannon McAllister."

"Hey, guys—get a few of the others and get a game going. I'll be with you in a minute." He kicked the soccer ball back to his students. "Is it okay if we talk out here? I have to be on the premises with them."

"Sure, of course."

They walked over toward the basketball court and Seamus leaned against the chain-link fence surrounding the playground.

"You've obviously heard about Ms. McAllister's murder."

He nodded, staring down at the ground.

"How did you know Shannon?" Seamus asked.

A lie followed Megan's slight hesitation. "Distant friends."

"I watch the news, *Detective*, I'm not stupid." Seamus McCann looked over at his students, checking on them. "I knew who you were right away."

"Let's just say I'm on a brief vacation but am still very interested in finding who did this."

Seamus nodded. "Okay."

"How many dates did you go on with Ms. McAllister?"

He didn't look surprised, but asked anyway, "You mean from Single Irish New Yorkers, right?"

"Yes."

"We had three dates. The first was at a coffee shop. I guess it went well because she said yes to a second one." His smile turned more serious as he continued. "We sat drinking coffee, and *more* coffee, for almost four hours. It was great, we really clicked."

"What did the two of you talk about?"

261

"Our work, our families, where we went to school. The usual first-date conversations."

"I don't know many first dates that last four hours. That's a marathon conversation."

"Tell me about it. Shannon was the first woman I met on the site that I found truly interesting. She had a lot of depth, and she was really…" Seamus started to get choked up recalling his first encounter with Shannon. "She was special."

"Why were you so surprised she said yes to a second date?"

Seamus looked at Megan and then back at himself, motioning up and down with his hands. "Detective, how many women enjoy dating a man thirty pounds overweight with bitch tits?"

Megan smiled.

"Yeah, well, anyway, our second date was dinner. We went for Chinese food."

"Another four-hour date?"

"No. Unfortunately. She said she'd had a long, stressful group session with her clients and was exhausted. She seemed distracted, like something else was bothering her, but we had a good time. She relaxed as the night went on."

"You didn't ask her what was bothering her?"

"No. I could tell she wanted to just switch gears and let it go."

"And the third date?"

Seamus stalled by yelling over to the kids playing soccer as if it were the World Cup, "Guys! Guys! Bring it down a few notches."

Seamus McCann was no killer, but there was something he wasn't quite sure how to share.

"Detective, may I ask you a question?"

She nodded.

"Have you ever met someone—" He placed a closed fist over his heart. "Met someone and in an instant there's a switch that just gets turned on? You just *know*. Conversations aren't worked for. You don't try to be someone you're not. All those stupid dating games go out the window."

Megan didn't have a convincing enough poker face to answer his question, and he knew it, too.

"I hope someday you feel that. I hope someday you know what I'm talking about, because that's how it was with Shannon. Immediate."

Megan hoped for that connection with someone, someday, but she wasn't ready to go all-in on a bet that it would happen any time soon.

"The third date?" she asked.

"I had a day off. I called her in the morning. I told her I'd bring lunch over. We could spend some time in between her classes that day. I picked up a few sandwiches and met her during one of her breaks."

"When?" she asked.

He looked Megan directly in the eye when he answered, "The day before she was murdered."

"You saw her the day before she was murdered," she repeated.

"Yeah."

"Where were you during this lunch?"

"We sat outside at the campus. We only had forty-five minutes, until her professor came by and asked to see her in his office about a project she was working on."

The word *professor* made Megan's stomach turn. "Do you remember his name?"

"No, he was a young guy, for a professor. At least it seemed that way to me."

"How did Shannon react when he approached the two of you?"

"She was completely annoyed. As soon as he walked away, she told me what a jackass he was. She was irritated he'd interrupted our lunch, let alone wanted her to stop by his office given how tight her schedule was."

"I see. I don't mean to be insensitive, but I have to ask, when I've spoken to some of Shannon's friends, and to her family, they didn't know about you. They didn't know she had started dating someone. Do you know why that was?"

"She said she'd just gotten out of a relationship and wanted to take things slow. It's funny, usually men say that, and women jump in. This time it was opposite—I fell hard, and she was being the rational one."

The soccer game across the schoolyard was getting out of hand at this point. The players seemed to be kicking the ball at one another rather than at either goal. "Guys! Guys!" Seamus yelled over again.

"Go ahead. Thanks for your time," she said.

As Seamus walked away, Megan couldn't help but add, "Hey, bitch tits or not, I think you're pretty cool. Teddy bear qualities, and all."

THIRTY-SIX

ICY RAIN SPAT DOWN on the skylight while Megan waited in the conversation room. *An odd name,* she thought, *"conversation room"*—it just seemed so peaceful for a place of such emotional and mental unrest. Her visitor's tag hung haphazardly on her leather jacket. She stood with folded arms listening to pages for so-and-so doctor, blue, yellow, red codes—extraneous considerations equaling that of elevator music.

Megan was cold. Chilled to the bone, actually, but she wouldn't display any vulnerability. With each breath she visualized a brick wall surrounding her, her personal castle without a moat. No one crossed, no one entered, not anymore. Not ever again.

A killer had entered her private world.

Only one person could give her answers, and it was the man who was being escorted by two orderlies and one fully armed guard. Her gut told her someone as sick, as heinous as he was, could give her a glimpse into the killer she now tracked.

The atmosphere of the room seemed to change as the man entered, as if the universe could accommodate only so much evil, leaving Megan to defend and honor the remaining miniscule space for justice.

Fintan D. Worth—his hair slicked back, his demeanor annoyingly confident—spoke with genuine appreciation, as much as a killer can. "Detective," he nodded, "as usual, a pleasure to see you. I gather you received my note."

Megan didn't contribute to his pleasantries. She sensed that a monologue was on its way. *Always place high bets on narcissists to enjoy the sound of their own voice*, she thought. He didn't disappoint.

Fintan fixed on her with a beady stare as he began his soliloquy. "Based on your body language and intentional silence, I'm to assume you've called on me for one of two reasons. Would you care to hear my hypotheses?"

Megan maintained her stance leaning against the wall.

"My first"—he pointed his index finger into the air—"and most hopeful hypothesis is that we're about to continue our conversation from the night you captured me. Now, I say hopeful because our discussion was surprisingly interesting, and great fun as well. *Fun* isn't the correct word, though, is it? *Fascinating* is more appropriate."

Fintan studied her reaction, or rather her lack thereof.

"Mmm. No takers on that topic. Color me disappointed. Now, that leaves me with my second possibility. I've been following the newspapers. The Tailor?" Fintan applied a thick French accent as he said, "Tacky *sobriquet*." He tapped his fingers on the table, humming a classical arrangement. His self-anointed grin was evidence that he took credit for her current professional achievements. "I have to assume you're not here to ask me about the recidivism rates in mental hospitals, and if I dare say, you are not here with anything to do with *my* world. You're here for much more personal reasons. Much, much more." He crossed his arms over his lap. "How did I do?"

He studied Megan before asking in a melodic tone, "Detective, you want *something* from me?"

"Are you done?" Megan's cool demeanor amused Fintan.

"Mmm."

Megan turned away from the wall, pulled out the chair, and sat opposite Fintan.

"What in the world happened to you, Detective?"

Her cut lip and blackened cheek were obvious, even in the poor lighting. She ignored his question. "I'm here to speak to you regarding the case I'm working."

"Is your handsome partner still by your side, Detective?"

"I'm asking the questions."

"Tsk, tsk." He waved his finger at Megan. "Now, you're here asking *me* questions, for all intents and purposes, asking for *my* help. Don't you think you could perhaps show a little gratitude? Or, at the very least, civility?"

"Civility?" Megan pushed back her chair hard enough for it to turn over. "After what you've done, you think you have the right to use a word like *civility*? Coming to see you was a mistake. Rot in here, Worth."

He turned his palm over. "Now, Detective, we're getting a little emotional, don't you think?"

"Go to hell." She pounded on the door. "Guard!"

"Megan." Fintan folded his arms. "You haven't figured out why he sutured poor Miss Shannon McAllister, have you?"

The fact Fintan had the audacity to use her name made her stomach turn, but what made her skin crawl was the fact he was right.

"He didn't just suture her, though, did he?" He traced the edge of the table with his feminine-like nails. "There's something else. Something only those working on the case know. Well, those working on the case as well as the girl's family, of course." He removed his glasses, polishing them with his shirt. "What was placed in the girl's body?" Fintan put his glasses back on. "Fine, don't tell me."

She acquiesced, knowing she had to give something in order to get something. "A wedding ring."

"Now, that's sick." His comment was barren of empathy or shock, not that Megan expected any different.

"What could be the reasoning behind it?" she asked.

"It's a religious symbol. Were there spiritual or theological overtones to the scene?"

Megan nodded. "Yes, but I'm not going into that detail with you just so you can get your rocks off."

"I'm not like that." Fintan shook his head. "A rude assumption on your part, Detective. I will say that ring belonged to whoever killed her, or someone related to whoever killed her. A personal memento. It sounds similar to Greek mythology. The dead had a coin placed over each eye to pay the boatman crossing the River Styx to ensure safe passage to the other side, their place in the afterworld."

Megan thought about what Fintan said. It did make sense, but she wasn't about to let him know that.

"Did he do that to you?" Fintan pointed to her face.

"No."

"How were you contacted?"

She couldn't hide her surprise regarding his question. "What?"

"Detective, I don't smell fear from you, but I do smell anger, like a wild animal whose private territory has been invaded. Marked by an enemy, so to speak."

They sat staring one another down until Fintan spoke once more. "You'll be contacted again."

"What makes you say that?"

"That's what I'd do. You're a part of the game now."

"This isn't a *game*."

"It's *all* a game, Detective."

Megan called for the guard again. He was opening the door when Fintan said, "I do look forward to our next conversation, Detective McGinn."

"*Don't*. There won't be another."

His tone flirtatious, he said, "Megan?"

It nauseated her to hear him use her given name.

"You *will* be back. I guarantee it."

Megan didn't look back at Fintan before leaving. What bothered her was the change in his demeanor at the end of their meeting. The only word resonating within her thoughts was *proud*.

And *proud* is an unnerving word when associated with a serial killer.

THIRTY-SEVEN

MEGAN INTENTIONALLY RAN INTO Nappa and Rasmussen at the corner of Matthew Garrison's address, and she rapped Nappa's shoulder. Hard. "Hello, Detectives. What a coincidence running into my coworkers here. Based on the address, I'd assume you're here to speak to the vic's friend from the summer camp program, the counselor?"

Neither men looked or were shocked.

Megan pointed to the Starbucks on the corner and in an ultra-sweet voice said, "I'll be right over there when you're done. I think we just have *loads* to catch up on."

"You're buying," Nappa answered.

Megan heard Rasmussen add, "She vacations at Starbucks?" followed by suppressed laughter from both.

Over one hour later, Megan saw Nappa and Rasmussen emerging from Matt Garrison's building enroute to the Starbucks she'd been seated at, now drinking her second cappuccino. "What the hell took so long?" Megan squinted up at Nappa's mouth. "And what is on the corner of your mouth?"

Nappa wiped both edges of his mouth with the back of his hand. "Curry."

Rasmussen shook his head. "I'll get us two coffees, be right back." He held out a palm, and Megan slapped a ten in it.

"Garrison's roommate was home, Garrison was on his way from the McAllister family gathering in Connecticut."

"I'm still at a loss for your curry mouth stains."

"The guy offered us finger sandwiches and Perrier while we waited."

Megan lowered her head and raised her eyebrows. "Oh-kaaay."

Rasmussen returned with the coffees—and no change.

"I'll start first," she said, as if there were any doubt Megan was to begin the conversation. "I heard from my friend regarding McAllister's laptop. I found out about the unknown guy Bauer spoke of. The vic met him on an online dating service: S-I-N, stands for Single Irish New Yorkers. Nice guy. Very upset about her murder. His name is Seamus McCann."

"Wait, you met with someone potentially involved in this case while you're on 'vacation'?" Nappa was visibly annoyed.

"Not as a detective, but as a 'friend'. And just so you know, he isn't a *part of the case*. A nice guy. So strike the SIN initials off the unknown list."

Nappa pulled out his notepad, flipping through pages.

"Tell me about Garrison," Megan requested in her usual tactful manner.

Rasmussen spoke up before sipping his black coffee. "I'll let Mr. 'I ate four finger sandwiches, and drank two Perriers' tell you."

"Nice," Nappa responded.

"Nappa, the 'roommate' offers finger sandwiches and Perrier, answers the door in spandex shorts and nothing else, and you still think they are only roommates. The floating candles, potpourri, and long hug with kiss when Garrison arrived home wasn't a bit of a clue?" Rasmussen wasn't homophobic, he was just amused at Nappa's naiveté.

Nappa ignored Rasmussen's goading. "Garrison and McAllister worked together at Sparta Camp during the summers for the last three years. That's how they met and became friends. Garrison's first thought was that Professor Bauer committed the murder, and we all know now that isn't the case."

Megan rubbed her back from Bauer's assault, but she didn't complain. "Did he have any idea about the unknown initials on the list from McAllister's datebook?"

"Nothing on BE or BD," Nappa answered.

"Well, we know BD is for blood drive, but the BE, that one I can't wrap my brain around."

"Nothing from the phone records, private or professional," Rasmussen added.

"There is one thing Garrison added. He mentioned McAllister became friends with some new staff counselors this past summer and he'd check with the office that runs the camp tomorrow morning, try to get a list for us."

"Good. Have you checked on the video from McAllister's building? Has the lab been able to identify what was on the unsub's wrist?" She could tell by his expression that Nappa felt it was a waste of time, but she pressed anyway. "Look, I know you didn't see anything, but I'm telling you, *I did*. I can't make the call, you have to, so just put pressure on the techs."

"I didn't see anything," Nappa answered.

Megan looked at Rasmussen for some form of support.

"I need to watch it a few more times," he responded. "Also, here's the copy of McAllister's last gynecologist appointment you wanted Palumbo to get."

While Megan read through the report, Nappa went on, "The sewing kit package was sent to you from the main post office on Eighth Avenue. Nothing more came up."

"Wait." Megan flipped through the file from Shannon's gynecologist. "What date is BE on?"

Nappa went through his notes. "The sixteenth."

Megan held up the folder. "We just figured out BE. She had a mammogram on the sixteenth. BE is for breast exam." Megan huffed, then handed Nappa an envelope. "Here, I printed out two sets."

"What's this?" Nappa handed Rasmussen a copy.

"From what Aunt Maureen told me about the crosses, being related to Saint Bridget? I did a search. There's a lot of information. Long story short, Saint Bridget is one of the three patron saints of Ireland, along with Saint Patrick and Saint Columba. She was known for her saintly stuff—feed the poor, help the sick, et cetera."

"Basically, all of *your* virtues," Rasmussen mocked.

"You should switch from detective to stand-up comic, Ras."

"So, what are you getting at with Saint Bridget?" Nappa asked.

"Okay, let's trace back a bit. McAllister was thoughtfully placed in that kneeling prayer position."

"Yeah, and I agree with what you said; it makes sense. She looked as though she were praying."

"Thanks, now there are a lot of different stories about Saint Bridget, but what kept coming up was that she refused many offers of marriage and decided to become a nun. She started the very first convent in Ireland and was the first female bishop. Her patronage covers, like, a million things: milkmaids, dairy workers, travelers, nurses, blacksmiths, children whose parents aren't married, poets. It goes on and on. Are you ready for this? Her feast day is February first."

Nappa looked confused, "What does that have to do with—"

"February first is Shannon McAllister's birthday."

"Son of a bitch." Nappa covered his mouth.

"Wait, there's more. The cross? The legend goes that Saint Bridget made the cross from rushes she found on the ground beside a dying man in order to convert him. The crosses are made to invoke protection in the home against fire, illness, and disease. They're made from rushes, sometimes straw. Each contains a woven square in the center and four radials, which are tied to the end. Every February first, the old cross is taken down and burned and the new one is put in its place, usually above a doorway or main entrance to the home. What I can't figure out is why not connect to Saint Teresa, or Saint Rose?" Megan felt a tinge of guilt when she heard herself say her mother's name, especially with the word *saint* before it. "The killer put time into making these. But why, and what is the significance to Saint Bridget? The cross is meant for protection, but he's already killed her, so what's left to protect?"

"Maybe in his mind it's not about protecting the home. Maybe he's protecting something else?" Nappa wondered.

Megan thought back to the memorial in *The Catholic Times,* "*Shannon M. You Have Been Returned.*" She slugged Nappa in the shoulder. "Motherfucker." The words flew out like darts thrown at a bull's-eye, making a direct hit, but she still whispered them: "Her soul. That's it, that's why he puts the cross up."

"Her soul? You mean he puts the cross up to protect her soul from the time he kills her—or, as that memorial says, 'returns her'—until she gets where? To heaven?"

"Possibly, or maybe he sends her to Saint Bridget." Megan held up the background on McAllister. "Look at Shannon's background, look at how much charity work she did. She volunteered at soup kitchens and a camp for sick kids. She was counseling drug-addicted, mentally fucked-up ex-cons, for Chrissake. How many people have we interviewed who have commented on how compassionate she was, how selfless? He could have some kind of fixation on benevolent women."

Nappa looked like he was starting to wrap his mind around Megan's theory. "Then this guy views women as saints."

"Not all women; only certain women. Women he feels possess attributes similar to Saint Bridget. I don't think it's a coincidence that Shannon has an Irish background or that particular birthday. Maybe that's the first thing that attracts him, and it develops from there. There's something else that's been bothering me."

"What's that?" he asked.

"When we spoke with the McAllisters, I asked Mrs. McAllister if Shannon was on birth control."

"When did you ask her that?" Nappa interrupted.

"When Mrs. McAllister went to get the contact sheet for the camp counselors. My gut told me it wasn't something to bring up in front of Mr. McAllister, so that's why I ducked out of the living room for a few minutes. I asked her if Shannon was on birth control. Mrs. McAllister said she was on the pill to clear up her skin and regulate her period." Megan tilted her head, mocking the reasons Mrs. McAllister had for Shannon's use of the pill.

Nappa winced at the *period* part of Megan's comment. The man could view mutilated bodies ten times a week, but when a woman mentioned menstruation, he got uncomfortable. "More like protect her when she was having sex with a married professor."

"Exactly, but here's the thing: Why didn't we find it in her apartment? Most women keep their birth control in a dresser or nightstand. Nothing was found. And on top of that, Mrs. McAllister said she would occasionally take a pain reliever for a back problem. So where are those bottles?" Megan asked.

"The Catholic Church is against birth control. If the killer found it in her apartment, maybe he got rid of it, so she didn't appear tainted in any way."

"Saint Bridget was a virgin. Maybe it's important that part of the illusion remains for him," Rasmussen added.

"If the birth control isn't found in the apartment or in her possession, then in his twisted perception, she remains pure, so to speak," Nappa said.

"The unsub isn't a stranger, because he's taken time to get to know her, or at least he thinks he has. I think it's someone who's been in her life a short time, maybe only a few months. And I'm willing to go out on a limb and say that the initials from her day planner, the ones we haven't been able to match up yet to any names or phone numbers, I bet he's one of those names." Then the irony of Shannon's murder hit her. "You know what's sad?"

"What?"

"If my theory about this guy is right, I think she'd still be alive. That is, if he'd known about the affair. It would have made Shannon impure, unwholesome in his eyes."

"Yeah, but she was still seeing the professor a few weeks before her murder, so there's a chance the killer knew about it and it didn't matter."

Megan rolled her eyes in amusement at Nappa's naiveté. "Nappa, a woman does not go shouting off the rooftops that she's sleeping with a married man. It's not exactly something you share with new acquaintances. If she met the killer a few months ago, Shannon was already weaning herself away from Professor Bauer during that time."

"Weaning herself away? What does that mean, exactly? You either dump someone or you don't."

"Hey, if the sex is good, it's hard to leave," Megan said, and then added, "Not that I would know, it's just the word on the street." She grinned.

"There's still one big question," Rasmussen said.

"What's that?" Megan asked.

"Why the rings, why the suturing?"

She shrugged. "I have no idea." She stared at him and repeated, "I have no idea." She checked her watch. "Okay, I have to go."

"Where are you going?" Nappa shook his head. "No, wait. I don't want to know. The less I know what you're up to, the better."

"Let me know when Garrison calls you in the morning regarding the info he's getting." He reluctantly agreed. "Thanks." Megan turned to walk toward the subway, adding, "Keep your personal cell on."

"Are you going to be okay?"

She didn't answer, just raised her hand as she distanced herself from his concern and formed an OK sign with her fingers.

"You better be," Nappa whispered.

THIRTY-EIGHT

THE STORE WAS EXACTLY in the vicinity where Megan had remembered. A green canopy with SHEEHAN'S IRISH GIFTS written in Celtic-style white lettering took up the corner of the Brooklyn street. Less than six months ago, she and Aunt Maureen visited Doreen Sheehan's store to pick out presents for the newborns of the Murphy clan.

The bell on the door chimed as Megan entered. Doreen Sheehan stood behind a glass jewelry cabinet restocking inventory. She was in her sixties, with a silver pixie cut. Her diminutive build could deceive one into thinking her personality was equal in size, but as Megan soon recalled, she was tough Irish stock.

"Hello, luv, what can I do you for today?"

Megan remembered Doreen was born and raised in Dublin, but she'd been living here for over forty years. She wondered if the woman put the Irish accent on a little thick to boost sales.

"Well, actually I'm here to …"

"Wait a second, I know you, darlin'." She shook her finger. "Yes, you're Pat and Rose's girl."

"Megan McGinn."

"Maureen Murphy's goddaughter, right?"

"You have a good memory," Megan said.

"God bless your father's soul. I didn't know him well, but from what I did, I knew he was good as gold, he was. How's your mum doin'? Maureen said she's in hospital. Holding up well, is she?"

Vacant of all rational thought. "Nursing home, actually. She's doing as good as can be expected, thank you for asking."

"Good to hear. Good to hear. I just saw Maureen two weeks ago at bingo." Doreen put one palm up to her cheek as if telling a secret. "Took home the pot, she did. But don't let it get around, especially to the mister."

"Cross my heart." Megan looked around the store and out of curiosity looked above the doorway. "I'm interested in that." Megan pointed up to the Saint Bridget's cross above the entrance.

"Ah, Saint Bridget, the Mary of the Gael. What exactly are you looking for, sweetheart? Jewelry? Maybe a necklace?"

Megan had temporarily forgotten the fact that her cross was missing, but the question was a hard reminder.

"Did you make that cross, Mrs. Sheehan?"

"Yes. Been making them since I was a wee girl in Ireland. My granny taught me how. It's a tradition, you know. Place the new cross above the door, take the old one down and burn it."

"Yes, I know. Where do you get the rushes from?" Megan asked.

"Darlin', that one isn't made out of rushes—yes, they're supposed to be, but I made that out of crepe paper from a craft store. Don't tell anyone, but it's been up there for eight years now."

"Your secret is safe with me. But if I wanted to get rushes, specifically from Ireland, how would I get them?"

"I have distributors in Ireland where I order my Saint Bridget's crosses from, but they come already made. I should think you could order the rushes from the same place and put them together yourself, if you wanted to go to all the trouble."

"Would you mind giving me a list of your distributors?" she asked.

Megan sensed Doreen Sheehan's hesitancy, not that psychic powers were needed. Doreen tapped the cash register with her pen a few times. "Oh sure, luv, that'll pay me rent."

"May I have a copy of the list while I browse around?"

"Of course, darlin', be right back with your information."

Knowing she'd be stopping off at the Murphys' before heading back to Manhattan, Megan was perusing the store for gifts when her phone vibrated.

Nappa's personal cell showed up on the screen.

"Hey," Megan answered.

"I checked with the tech guys on the video. It's going to take some time to get a clearer visual, but the tech guy agrees with you. He sees something on the tape, too."

She close fist punched the air. "I knew it!"

"Paige Gowan came into the precinct."

"The PG from McAllister's datebook. Anything?"

"Nada. She also assumed Bauer had something to do with it," Nappa answered. "One more thing, I just got off the phone with the lab. The second cross, the one from the sympathy card that had trace amounts of type AB blood, also had minute traces of paper towel."

"Paper towel? What for?"

"He said it was probably to keep the reeds moist. What little was found was near where the tips had been trimmed. The second cross also had traces of green sponge. But, again, very minute traces."

"Green sponge? Why would green sponge be on the reeds?"

"Foam brick, luv," Doreen interrupted.

"Hang on, Nappa." Megan turned to Doreen. "Pardon me?"

"Reeds are packed in saturated foam brick, like from floral shops."

"Who is that?" Nappa asked.

"I'm in Brooklyn, let me call you back." She flipped her cell closed.

"I received a shipment yesterday, let me show you." Doreen went into the back of the store and returned with an opened carton from Dublin. "See?" She showed Megan the moistened brick. "Same as a typical floral arrangement sent to ya."

Megan recalled all too well the number of recent sympathy arrangements sent to her and Brendan acknowledging their father's death. "Yes, I see."

She rang Nappa back. "Did the lab say if they came from the same bunch of reeds? The cross from the doorway and the cross from the card?"

"Couldn't tell, but they said if we want a more extensive workup, it could be sent to a university out of state. They could run more tests."

"What kind of tests?"

"Something about checking the pollen grains from the plant. It could identify the region they came from," Nappa said.

"At this point, go for it."

"It'll take some time, but it's worth a shot. Unless, like your computer friend, you have another friend, a botanist perhaps?"

"Any botanists I know deal with a certain other kind of plant."

"Information I don't need, McGinn," said the ex-Narcotics officer before ending the call.

"Here's the list, darlin'." Doreen handed Megan a paper of over twenty distributors based in Ireland.

"I didn't realize there were so many."

"And that's not even half of them—those are only the ones I order from. I go to trade shows in New York and New Jersey. They're always coming out with new things, so I like to use different distributors. It keeps the inventory fresh."

Megan looked at the names and phone numbers on the list. "What time is it in Ireland right now?"

"They're five hours ahead, so a bit after nine in the evening. You might better wait until tomorrow, if calling them is what you're needing. Can I wrap those for you?" she asked.

Megan had picked out a pair of silver earrings for Maureen and a Donegal tweed cap for Uncle Mike.

"Actually, yes. Gifts for Maureen and Mike."

"What, nothing for yourself, luv?"

Megan looked around the jewelry case. She already had a Claddagh ring, and still, in her mind, owned a cross necklace.

"Darlin', you asked so much about Saint Bridget, why don't you take that bracelet?"

A delicate silver bracelet had Saint Bridget's cross at the center of the clasp. Megan picked it up to check the price.

"I'll give it to you at cost, sweetheart."

"All right. Thank you."

Doreen removed the price tag from the bracelet before fastening it to Megan's wrist. She smiled. "Now you have Saint Bridget on your side, my dear."

———

As soon as Megan knocked on the Murphys' front door, she could hear the mayhem inside. Kids laughing, dogs barking, and at least two different people yelling, "Someone's at the door!"

Aunt Maureen greeted her with a grandchild on one hip and another tugging at her from behind. She had a warm, welcoming smile on her face until she took a look at Megan's. "Meggie, what happened?" She gently touched Megan's chin, turning her face side to side.

"I'm okay. Really."

"Come in here. We have a large group tonight: two out of the four boys and their entire crews—including the dogs."

A Jack Russell named Conan and a black Labrador named Daisy bombarded Megan with licks and tail wags as she entered. "Hey, guys." In a momentary lapse Megan bent over to pet the dogs, shooting currents of pain through her back muscles.

Aunt Maureen noticed her wince. "What else is wrong with you?"

"I'm fine, just pulled a muscle."

"The hell you did. Patrick, come take a look at Megan," Maureen yelled into the kitchen. Patrick was her second-eldest son, named after Megan's father, and he was also a doctor interning in orthopedics.

"Hey, Megs. Shit!" Patrick gave Megan a hug and a light peck on the cheek. He was the younger-looking version of Uncle Mike, only he now surpassed his father in height and not one gray strand could be found in the mop of black hair on his head. But the two men still shared the same warm smile.

"Patrick, the language," Aunt Maureen scolded. "Meggie's hurt her back, take a look."

By that time the rest of the Murphy clan in attendance had come into the living room to greet Megan: Patrick's wife, Moira; Kyle, the youngest Murphy brother; his wife, Veronica; and countless Murphy grandchildren.

Megan loved a full house, just not the medical attention. "Turn around, Meganator," Patrick demanded, "let me take a look."

"I'm fine, really."

"Patrick, take her in the kitchen. I'm going to put a video on for the kids until dinner is ready." Aunt Maureen received an enthusiastic response from the children, if not more so from the adults. The dogs, however, followed the scent of the roast cooking and joined the gathering in the kitchen.

Uncle Mike was checking on the roast when everyone crowded into the chef's quarters. "Genius at work, people. I need my space."

"Dad, Megs is here."

He wiped his hands on the kitchen towel, staring at Professor Bauer's handiwork. "So she is."

Megan handed him the bag of gifts. "This is for you, and this is for Aunt Maureen. As for all of you other Murphys, you're going to have to wait until Christmas!"

"That'll wait. Patrick, look at Meggie's back," Aunt Maureen ordered.

"I'm fine. Really." Megan's pleas fell on deaf ears.

Moira passed Megan a glass of red wine. "Drink up. You'll need it with this group tonight."

"C'mon, strip for me," Patrick joked.

"Patrick!" Maureen swatted his shoulder.

"Okay, I give up." Megan took her jacket off. "Patrick, I'm telling you I'm fine, but take a gander anyway."

Patrick raised her shirt up.

When Maureen saw her son's concerned look, she moved closer to see for herself. "What in God's name happened to you?"

Of course, this led to every adult in the room inspecting Megan's posterior region.

"I had a rather impromptu altercation with a suspect." She skirted having to tell the whole story.

Patrick felt around the bruise. "Does this hurt?"

"Only when you touch it."

"What about here?" he asked. He pressed hard into the bottom of the bruised area.

"If you push any harder, I'm going to turn you from a Patrick into a Patricia."

"Please do, three kids are enough," Moira chimed in.

"You should really get some X-rays, and a few tests," Patrick said.

Uncle Mike was uncharacteristically quiet.

"Do you want me to set up an appointment?" Patrick asked.

"Let me give it a few days. I promise, if it doesn't feel better, I will call you for some tests. Fair enough?" she asked.

"Hey, you're the baby sister I never had. I'm just trying to watch your back." Patrick messed Megan's hair. "Get it? *Watch your back.*"

"Your bedside manner sucks, but thanks anyway."

Uncle Mike spoke up then. "Megan and I are going into my study. Help your mother with the rest of dinner." He moved to the doorway and motioned Megan to follow.

In the study, Uncle Mike took out a bottle of whiskey and poured them each a shot. "Did this happen before or after your apartment was broken into? Before or after you started your *vacation*?"

"How did you know about that?" She thought to herself how stupid a question it was as soon as it left her lips. Though not on the force anymore, Uncle Mike had eyes and ears everywhere in the department.

"Drink." He handed Megan the glass. "Are you sure you're okay?"

"Bruised but not broken. It looks worse than what it is. Promise."

"Sit. Talk." Winning friends and influencing people were clearly not high on Uncle Mike's list during this conversation.

Megan went into full disclosure of every aspect of the case, from the moment she first arrived on the crime scene to an hour ago at the Irish gift store. Uncle Mike listened intently, though she could tell he badly wanted to interrupt and give Megan the riot act for not immediately acting the first time the unsub reached to her out via cell.

"So, there you have it." She finished her drink.

"That's not all of it."

"What? Yes, it is. I've told you everything."

"Everything but the fact that you're on leave and still working the case." He threw back the remaining whiskey in his glass.

"It's nothing you or dad wouldn't do, and you know it," Megan said with a level of certainty that could not be argued with, even by her father's best friend.

Mike sat forward. "I'm not going to waste my breath arguing the truth with you. You hear me, and you hear me good. You keep eyes open, front, back, sideways. You stay armed every second until this is seen through. Got it?"

"Dad, Megan, dinner!" Patrick yelled from the dining room.

Megan nodded. "I promise." She squeezed his hand. "I love ya, Uncle Mike."

He welled up and pulled a handkerchief out from his back pocket. "Just stay alive. Get in there, I'll be in in a minute."

———

A few hours later, the dining room looked as though a holiday feast had been enjoyed instead of a casual family dinner. The adults sat around the table drinking coffee and finishing off dessert, while the kids were experiencing food comas watching the end of the movie in the living room.

"So, Megs." Kyle threw a dinner roll across the table. "Saw you on the news this week."

"Oh, yeah." She returned the sentiment by throwing the roll back.

"I have to say, that partner of yours, Nappa, is *so hot*," Veronica chimed in.

"Definite eye candy," Moira added. The Murphy husbands moaned at their wives' observations of Megan's partner.

"I'll let him know you feel that way," she joked.

"We all think you should date him," Maureen said.

"Here we go!" Megan laughed.

"Okay, if that doesn't work for you, I tell you what," Moira suggested. "My girlfriend joined this Internet dating service. It's really been a great experience, and it's geared toward Irish New Yorkers."

"That's it, I'm outta here!" Megan started to get up from the table. "It's been lovely, just great seeing everyone, but unfortunately Manhattan calls."

The goodbyes took longer than the meal. Uncle Mike walked Megan out to the porch and gave her a gentler hug than normal. "Watch your back, kiddo. No pun intended."

"I will. Hey, you've been awfully quiet this evening. Are you okay?"

"I'm good."

"Are you sure?"

"Yep, and call me if you need anything. I mean it."

"You're on my speed dial." Megan gave him a kiss on the cheek. "Enjoy the cap. It looks good on you."

Uncle Mike smiled. "I know."

THIRTY-NINE

INSOMNIA HAD BECOME MEGAN's only bedtime partner since the McAllister case entered her life. She lay in bed hours after leaving the Murphys' house watching television, flicking from one channel to the next. Programming at that hour consisted of one infomercial after another. Megan watched as space-age technology shrank clothes down into zippered plastic bags. Then came the must-have, a set of kitchen knives that could slice anything in half, from a tomato to a Chevrolet. Of course, there had to be one self-help guru pushing his "Think positive thoughts, heal your inner child, eat a lot of salmon, and oh, by the way, none of this can be accomplished without buying my Guide To A Better Life Kit for three easy installments of $29.95 as long as you order right now" pitch.

She checked the clock next to her bed. Forty-five minutes until the gym opened. Working out was the last thing on her mind, but she thought a light swim followed by a sauna might loosen the muscles in her back. Megan sat cross-legged and placed her laptop on a pillow in front of her. It had been a few days since the last time she checked her personal email. She logged in and was bombarded with countless spam mail that she quickly deleted: offers for Viagra, personalized astrological charts, low mortgage loans, to name a few. Her personal inbox had far less mail. There were two emails from her brother. One had an attachment and she clicked on that first, assuming there would be pictures of her niece and nephew. The email said, "Megs, is this a carbon copy of your Kiddie Kampus photo, or what?" Kiddie Kampus was the preschool Megan and Brendan had attended. She got up to find the photo to compare the two. The 5x7 picture was near the front of one of the many photo albums she'd yet to complete. In the photo, Megan wore a black and red-checkered wool dress with a white, puffy-sleeve shirt underneath. She leaned on her elbows with one pudgy hand cupped under her equally plump chin, while the other rested in front of her. She held her picture up next to the one of her niece on the screen and smiled at the remarkable similarities. Both had long eyelashes and shared the same dimpled smile.

Megan tapped the photo as her memory returned to the day it was taken. She doubted her brother had as difficult of a time getting his daughter to wear a dress as Rose had with Megan that chaotic morning.

Megan was never a girlie-girl. Her wardrobe consisted of jeans, sneakers, and a baseball glove—a tomboy through and through. She had a doll she'd never played with, never played dress-up, and especially never wore dresses…until photo day for her preschool class.

At first, Rose chased her daughter around the dining room table, waving the dress and pleading for her cooperation. Like a gladiator stomping out the threat of an approaching opponent, Megan was quick, but when Rose was able to grab hold of her ponytail, it became a different match. Megan pulled the drop-to-the-ground move and lay on her back, using her feet to kick her mother away.

"Megan, you *are* wearing this dress. Your father and I picked this out especially for you. It's an important picture!" Rose pleaded.

"No! I don't wanna wear that stupid dress!" Megan flailed a last kick up at her mother when she was given the ultimate threat.

"You put your foot in my face one more time, young lady, and I'm calling your father."

Gladiators were never threatened with something like that.

Rose's exacting tone didn't leave any room for debate. "He'll be very upset with you if I call him with something like this. And I *will* call him."

Megan may have been young, but she wasn't stupid. Her father didn't put up with any bullshit from her at five, fifteen, or twenty-five. The threat of him being called at work was enough for her to concede but not, however, without a little bargaining on her behalf. Megan stayed on the floor staring up at her mother as she released a huff and said, "I'll wear the dumb dress but no shoes, no tights."

Rose glared down at her daughter mumbling to herself. She knew that was the best she was going to get out of Megan that morning. She got up from the floor, pulling Megan up with her.

One hour later they were at the preschool, standing in line with Megan's other classmates. Megan kept her promise and wore the dress and the white puffy shirt. She even let Rose brush the knots and tangles out of her hair. Rose stayed true to her end of the bargain as well. In place of tights and black shoes, she allowed Megan to wear a pair of jeans and purple sneakers under the checkered dress.

"People are going to think I'm color blind, letting you out of the house like this," was Rose's only comment.

Megan smiled proudly in the photo, more because of her partial victory than anything else.

"McGinn, you can really be a pain in the ass sometimes," she said to herself. She smiled, but it was more of a reprimand than witticism.

Megan started to pack her gym bag, wanting a cigarette now more than a workout, but she stayed the course. The lighting in the women's locker room, however, was less than kind. Alone, she turned toward the mirror to see the bruising on her back before donning her suit. She examined the marks on her face, momentarily relieved that her father wasn't alive to have seen her like this.

Megan patiently sat poolside, waiting for a lane to open. She wasn't concerned with how long of a wait it would be; she was just relieved not to be the lone swimmer this time. The Blue Hairs, a group of women Megan nicknamed a long time ago, were in the open section enjoying their morning senior water-aerobics class. Megan didn't give them the nickname because of their age; they wore water caps that had blue, feathery rubber hairs sticking out of them. The women talked more than they moved, but they always seemed to enjoy themselves. The lifeguard noticed Megan right away.

"Any word on your necklace?" he asked.

"Nope," Megan responded. Lengthy conversation was not part of her agenda.

"Well, with any luck it'll show up," he offered.

"Yep," she said.

The swimmer in the end lane finished. There was one woman in queue ahead of Megan, who turned around. "You can take that lane if you want. I'm waiting for the middle one."

Megan wasn't particular on which lane she swam in, so she took the woman up on her offer. Having other gym members around made her ease into her workout more comfortably than the last time she had swam.

She was so relaxed having other swimmers in the pool that she totally lost track of the number of laps she'd swum. Her shortness of breath indicated she'd accomplished more laps than her previous visit, but it wasn't until she flipped over and pushed off the wall that it came to a screeching halt. For the first time in her swim, she glanced to her side and was shocked to see no other swimmers beside her in the water. She stopped at the pool's edge and grabbed the side. She whipped off her goggles and cap, looking around the room anxiously. All the members of the seniors' water-aerobics class stared over at her.

"You all right, honey?" one of the Blue Hairs hollered over to her.

Trying to catch her breath, she answered in between huffs, "Yeah." Other than the women gossiping in the corner, there were a man and a woman standing at the water fountain.

"I'm fine," Megan answered.

"Enjoy, you have the pool all to yourself," the lady said.

"Great." Megan was less than thrilled with the notion.

"C'mon, girls, let's go take a steam. To hell with heart medication and doctor's orders."

When you're in your seventies and eighties, rebelling against doctor's orders must be as close to an uprising as you can get. It did put an idea in Megan's head, though. "Ladies, would one of you mind turning the sauna on for me?"

"Sure thing, honey."

In the locker room, Megan stripped out of her bathing suit, hanging it on one of the shower hooks. She wrapped a towel around her naked body. As soon as she opened the door to the sauna, she knew the ladies had done right by her. It was hot and relaxing. She could hear faint conversation next door from the steam. She was embarrassed to admit to herself that their presence was appreciated; though she was alone in the sauna, there were people nearby, and that fact comforted her. She discarded the towel, placing it on the top tier of the wooden bench. She moved gingerly onto her back, hoisting her feet up to the wall. Her creamy legs were sprinkled with pale freckles from her ankles to her inner thighs. Her body began to glisten with sweat as the jets sprayed down from above. She closed her eyes, breathing deep into her lungs. She pushed her hair back, but a few strands couldn't help but cling to her shoulders. The water hitting the rocks made a sizzling sound. She was on the verge of relaxing when the sound of Uncle Mike's demand leapt to the front of her mind.

Do not go anywhere unarmed.

It was enough to catapult her out of the sauna, forgetting her towel.

FORTY

MEGAN WAS HALFWAY UP 93rd Street to her apartment when her cell vibrated. *1 text message* was indicated. She pressed the *view message* button.

SWEET CAROLINE appeared. Megan stared down at the text. Her face, reflected off the phone's glass screen, made her look nauseated and faint. She knew her eyes were open, but her surroundings were out of focus; everything seemed to be spinning around her like an amusement park ride out of control.

"Please, God…no…" She took a deep breath and dialed the phone number the text originated from. Megan knew a woman named Caroline should answer the phone, but wouldn't. It was too late for Caroline, whoever she was.

"*Hi, this is Caroline. Sorry I missed your call. Leave your name and number and I'll get back to you.*" The sweet voice echoed through Megan's head. She hung up before the signal sounded to leave a message. She leaned against the railing of a brownstone to steady herself.

Her phone vibrated again. Her cell phone might as well have weighed three hundred pounds with how much energy it took to raise it into view.

"McGinn."

"I know."

He remained silent.

"Her name is Caroline," Megan said it as if she'd asked someone to pass the salt. "I *just* got a text."

"There's something else."

"What?"

"I need you to come over, *quietly*, and I mean *quietly*. Palumbo and Rasmussen know you're on your way. No bravado, otherwise it's all our asses."

"Nappa, what is it?" she demanded.

"We're at Two-Thirty East Eighty-Seventh Street. Caroline Dacey."

"Okay."

FORTY-ONE

PALUMBO LET MEGAN INTO the building. "Nappa and Rasmussen are up there. Third floor."

Megan nodded.

"You don't have long; I'm surprised the press isn't here yet."

"Thanks," Megan answered.

She was on the third step when Palumbo added, "Heads-up: this one is bad, if that's possible."

Megan looked back at Palumbo's pained expression, something she'd rarely encountered while working with him. There was nothing comforting she could say to ease a look she knew all too well.

The apartment smelled like a diner: anything and everything fried. Nappa and Rasmussen were at the end of the hall in the living room. She glanced into the kitchen. No in-depth search needed there, it was the size of most people's closets. Two dishes, silverware, and napkins topped a small butcher block in the corner, never to be plated. Never meant to be, for that matter.

"McGinn, I put a call out to CSU, but I wanted you to see the scene, short on time," Nappa urged.

Megan nodded. She stood over Caroline Dacey's dead body. "Oh my God."

She immediately understood why Palumbo had worn such a distressed expression. In the middle of the room Caroline lay on the floor in the position of Christ hanging from the cross. Her arms were spread out, bloodied hands nailed into the floor. Her legs were slightly bent, with two more nails lodged into her feet. The side of her head had been cratered by the bloody baseball bat positioned upright in the corner. Her hair was combed as if to hide the damage from the blunt force she'd sustained. One of Caroline's eyes stared up toward the ceiling; the other was swollen shut. Blood, not yet dried, exited her ear, nose, and mouth.

"The unsub used a bat to finish her off. Strangling wasn't enough?" Megan shook her head. "Who called this in?"

"Downstairs neighbor," Rasmussen answered.

"She fought like hell," Nappa said.

"And all it got her was a trip to Dr. Max Sutherland's slab for autopsy. She would have had a better chance at getting blood from a stone or having a month full of Sundays," Megan responded.

She looked around the apartment. Angelic was the theme for the living room (now, not so much living). There were pictures of angels and candleholders in the shape of cherubs, and angels' wings carved into two sconces hung in the hallway. Then, death reigned over the celestial setting. Two teacups were smashed to the floor, a wet mark on the wall, a crack in a wall mirror, the coffee table turned on its side.

"You need to see the kitchen," Nappa said.

Megan walked back to the small room and opened the oven. A traditional Irish breakfast consisting of bacon, fried eggs, fried mushrooms, and tomatoes filled a large cast-iron skillet.

"McGinn, turn around." She did.

A pen-and-ink drawing of Archangel Michael hung on the wall, signed by Caroline Dacey. Archangel Michael was depicted flying down from heaven in battle against Satan and his followers. *Who is like God?* was written in small letters at the bottom in Caroline's handwriting.

A handwoven Saint Bridget's cross was fastened to the corner.

"Her cell isn't here," Nappa said.

"Well, I can tell you the last number dialed on it," Megan bit her lip. "Mine."

Palumbo entered the room. "McGinn, time for you to go. CSU, press . . . it's getting busy out there."

"Okay."

Then Megan did a first at a crime scene: she made the sign of the cross before leaving the room.

FORTY-TWO

I THREW CAROLINE'S CELL into the middle of Third Avenue, just in time for a bus to crush it. I didn't get the euphoria I'd experienced in the past. What a shame. When the cashier asked if that was all, in truth it was, until I noticed the single wrapped roses in the bucket beside her. It was the last remaining pink rose among the red and white flowers. In that moment, I knew my destiny.

———

Megan went to the only bar she knew would be open at this early hour: Kinsale's. The same establishment where she'd hooked up with the stockbroker. She was hard-pressed to tell which patrons had been there all night and which had arrived for their morning "coffee." She didn't care either way. She plunked herself down at the bar and asked for a shot and a beer. She kicked back both and ordered another round while listening to the sound of police sirens coast by. It made her regret not fighting harder to stay on the case officially. The bartender turned the up the volume on the television—breaking news on the Upper East Side. No shock to Megan.

No matter what the idiot reporter conveyed, though, it could never match the scene Megan had just walked through.

"Ken—another, and please turn that off," Megan barked.

It wasn't just another. By noon, she was crocked.

Megan hailed a cab outside Kinsale's. She didn't have the energy to take the subway, and it was midday, so she knew the morning rush-hour traffic would have filtered out by now. She was grateful that the driver wasn't the chatty type. She wasn't in the mood for forced conversation. She leaned her head back on the seat and stared out along the East River as they drove south on the FDR. The water was calm, but the gray overcast day made the river appear dark and swampy. The screen in the cab played a similar breaking news report regarding the Upper East Side murder from a competing news channel. She muted the screen, wrapping herself up in her jacket and waiting for the last two shots of whiskey to send warmth through her system. Unfortunately, it was her bladder receiving the more significant effects. When they reached their destination, it would have shouted a "Praise God" louder than a Southern Baptist during service on a scorching Sunday morning if it had a voice.

Megan paid the cabbie and entered the front door to the hospital, but then had to be buzzed through the second door. The nurse at the front desk smiled the same fake smile she'd offered when Rose was admitted. Megan was in no mood to return it.

"Hi, I'm Megan McGinn, Rose McGinn's daughter. I just wanted to see my mother for a few minutes."

"I'm sorry, ma'am, it's lunch time. The patients are—"

Megan saw a ladies' room down the hall in the opposite direction of her mother's room. "I'm just going to use the facilities and I'll be right back."

"Ma'am, I need to see identifi—"

"McGinn! Megan McGinn!"

She left the ladies' room several minutes later feeling very relieved and ready to charge the nurse with verbal abuse for calling her *ma'am*. She walked up to the desk while the nurse was on an obvious personal call.

"Ma'am, I'm sorry, but during lunch the patients—" the nurse spoke while covering the phone with her palm.

Megan pulled out her badge, slapping it down on the desk. She didn't say a word. She stared the nurse down like a Rottweiler contemplating a Bichon Frisé as a snack. She put her badge back into her pocket and marched down the hall. But her slight buzz wasn't what prompted her to turn around to add, "And don't call me ma'am!" Megan would have said that stone-cold sober.

She slowly opened the door to her mother's room. She peeked in, not because she expected her mother to be awake, jump up, and yell *surprise!*, but out of courtesy. Rose was asleep. Megan smiled over her, then leaned in and kissed Rose on the forehead and whispered, "Hi, Momma. It's me, Meggie. You're all tucked in, I see." She walked around to the other side of the bed and sat on the edge. She pushed Rose's hair away from her eyes. "I had dinner with the Murphys, they all send their love."

She cringed at her own lie.

Okay, not really. But they would have if they'd known I was seeing you again so soon. I'll be forgiven, I hope.

303

There were so many lies being told lately, Megan hoped God was running a two-for-one special on absolution. She watched her mother sleep for a few minutes. She was happy to see Rose was wearing the new nightgown she'd bought for her. "The nightgown I bought looks nice on you, Momma."

Confession was a foreign concept to Megan, and one she had never taken seriously. When she was young and in Catholic school, she'd sit in the confessional, pop her gum, and tap the door with the tips of her shoes while formulating the most outrageous confessions for the priest to hear.

"Forgive me, Father, for I have sinned. It's been eight hours since my last confession. I'm really sorry I tried to suffocate my best friend's hamster with a pillow. I was just curious about how long it would take—but thanks for bringing him back to life. I'm sorry for the mean thoughts I had when I caught Sister Augustine drinking from the flask she keeps under her robe. And I'm sorry for the thoughts I had when Bonnie Jean elbowed me in the ribs during gym class today. I couldn't help that one—I'm better at dodgeball than her."

Megan would end each confession with that line of truth that made the priests disregard her skewed sense of humor. "And I'm sorry ... really sorry ... for being mad at my mom this week. I'll try to be a better daughter. Okay, that's it, I'm done."

Megan was sure she'd heard a few poorly suppressed laughs coming from the other side of the confessional, but that was when she was a kid. Now as a grown woman, she needed to get things off her chest that were a lot harder to admit. And she knew that if she lied this time around, she'd only be lying to herself.

"Oh, Momma, where do I begin?" Her heart felt heavier with every word she spoke. "See, there's this case I'm working on." She held her hand in the stop position. "I know, I know, you hated it when Dad would talk about a case, especially with me, but Momma…" Megan wiped the end of her nose with her coat sleeve. "Two young women were murdered, and it's gotten complicated on so many levels, and I'm not sure how I'm going to get through this one. Dad was always in my corner when it came to work. I could go to him with anything, and now he's not here." She leaned over and grabbed a few tissues from Rose's side table. "I'm not sure if you remember that part, but he died. Sorry if that's a shock." She blew her nose. "Brendan has his own life out in Ohio for Chrissake, so that leaves me and you." Megan's tears raced down her face. "The only problem I have with that is…" She pushed her hair back, giving herself a moment to catch her breath. "We never really got along. I'm sure it was more me not getting along with you. I was such a brat to you growing up." Megan felt a twinge of guilt telling her mother her problems, but the weight of them was taking its toll and she needed to do something to lighten the load.

"Anyway, like I said, I'm working these cases and one of the women who was murdered, well, I've been dealing with her mother quite a bit. I know it's wrong to feel this way, and I know how awful this is going to sound, but I'm jealous of them, Momma. I'm jealous of how close they were. It's a terrible thing to say, but it's true." Megan blew her nose for the third time and pulled out another tissue from the box. "I look at you and me—we were never close, not like that, anyway, especially after what you tried to do to yourself. Now you're here and… it's hard, Momma. It's hard for me to see you this way, and I can't do anything to help you. I feel so guilty. I know I wasn't the kind of daughter you would have preferred. You wanted a 'girlie-girl,' someone who played with dolls. Someone you could have had pretend afternoon tea parties with. Someone you could take shopping to Lord and Taylor. Instead, you got a tree-climbing, sneaker-wearing tomboy. I was so hard on you for that. I went out of my way to not be the daughter you wanted me to be. And whenever I screwed up, you'd let it go. You always forgave me." Megan looked up at the ceiling and thought, *Well, not always.*

"Okay, the thing with making me wear dresses once in a while, and grounding me for throwing eggs at cars on Halloween, and that time I was caught smashing the neighbor's outdoor Christmas tree lights, and when I put the candy bar in your purse and the grocer thought you'd stolen it. I admit it, that was wrong of me, and I deserved to be punished for that." She grinned at the notorious pilfering of the Snickers bar; couldn't help from laughing. "The candy bar incident was really wrong of me." Megan looked down at Rose, unsure if she should continue, but her words flowed as quickly as her tears, and she was unable to control either one. The odd thing was she was starting to feel comfortable talking to her mother.

"There's so much going on that it's starting to overwhelm me a little, maybe a lot. There's something I haven't told you, Momma. This case has gotten personal, and it's starting to worry me. Really worry me. And on top of that, Dad kicking when he did, and all the pressure of trying to do what's best for you, there's only so much a girl can take, ya know?" Megan leaned over, resting her head on Rose's chest. She gripped her shoulders, wanting the hug to be returned. "I miss Dad so much. I miss him so much."

306

Megan wasn't sure how long she been crying into her mother's arms when she felt a hand caress the back of her head, followed by a whisper in her ear.

"Baby girl."

Megan knew the voice, but it had been so long since it'd sounded this lucid. She lifted up her head and found herself staring into her mother's eyes.

Rose wiped one of the many tears from Megan's cheek. Her blue eyes met Megan's. "Time to buck up, baby girl. Be strong. Have faith. I love you." Rose held up a strand of Megan's hair, adding, as only a mother could, "You need a haircut."

Megan half laughed. She then cried on her mother's chest as Rose returned to sleep and Megan followed suit, though not without a moment of gratitude that her mother had recognized her.

FORTY-THREE

MEGAN FELT THE BUZZ from her cell phone. She lifted herself from Rose's embrace. Nappa was calling from his personal cell.

"Hello?" Megan was groggy, rubbing the crust out from her eyes.

"It's me. I'm with Dr. Max. How soon can you get here?"

"Um." She checked her watch, "Twenty, maybe twenty-five minutes? Why?"

"See you then." A dead line was his gentlemanly farewell.

Your phone skills are depreciating, Nappa.

Megan gazed down at her mother, appreciative for the lucid moment they shared. She got off the bed, making use of her mother's toiletries to freshen up, ignoring the truth facing her: this was probably the last time she'd ever have such a conversation with her mother. The sadness was too much on her sobering system. She needed to leave as soon as possible.

Buck up, baby girl.

"I will, Momma." She ran her fingers over Rose's hair.

Megan knocked before entering Dr. Max Sutherland's office, but her arrival was obviously expected based on their lackluster response.

"Shut the door." Dr. Max sat down behind his desk and pulled no punches. "It's your killer."

The term "your killer" sent a chill through Megan.

"Very little in terms of stomach contents: orange juice, a small amount of oatmeal. Her eye socket was fractured. She was struck on the side of the trachea, skull beaten in on the right side. No signs of sexual abuse."

Megan glanced over to Nappa. "Why do you think he was so rough with this victim?"

Sutherland interrupted, "This victim was a good twenty pounds heavier than the last. That may account for something."

"She put up more of a fight," Nappa concluded.

"I can say the killer is definitely right-handed based on the bruising around the neck. Time of death I estimate to be—"

Megan, reminded of the text, said, "I know when she was killed. Why am I here?" Megan knew there was something both men were hesitant to disclose. Formalities went out the window in moments such as these.

Sutherland handed her the small plastic Ziploc. "You need to see this."

Megan displayed an expression neither man had ever seen on her before. Her hands began to tremble.

"McGinn?" Nappa pulled a chair closer to her.

"This … is my necklace." Megan sat down, staring at her jewelry. "He put this in…" The thought of it turned her stomach. Sutherland finished the sentence for her.

"Yes. The piece was sutured inside her vaginal canal."

"Oh my God," she muttered.

"Are you sure it's yours? How would he get your necklace?" Nappa squeezed Megan's shoulder.

"I went to the gym to swim laps. I took it off. When I was done, I went back to get my towel, and it was gone. I thought it fell through a heating vent."

Nappa inspected the piece.

"Look at the back," Megan said. Inscribed in the back of the cross in tiny letters were Megan's initials.

"Jesus Christ." Nappa handed it back to Sutherland.

Megan walked out of the office shell-shocked, her stomach feeling as if a battering ram had plunged at her gut. "Wait a sec." She ran into the ladies' room and vomited out what little was in her stomach. "Oh my God!" She sat on the floor rubbing her temples. "You motherfucker. You motherfucker."

Nappa knocked on the door. "McGinn, you okay?"

She got up to splash water on her face. "Yeah, yeah, I'll be out in a minute," she called.

Megan sat a few minutes remembering what Fintan said to her, *It's all a game. It's all a game.*

Megan pulled out the business card from her back pocket for Detective Gold, the upstate New York detective who came to the precinct with a connection to what was possibly the first kill.

FORTY-FOUR

The buzzer sounded and Megan spoke into the intercom, "Yeah."

"Detective Nappa here for you, Miss McGinn." The doorman sounded more official than usual, perhaps because her apartment had been broken into and he needed to, at the very least, appear more professional.

"Send him up." She unlatched the door, though not without first checking her weapon, a precaution that was a part of her life more than ever now. She continued to fold clothes, stuffing them into a small suitcase.

Nappa's voice was scratchy and raw, emphasizing his exhaustion. "Going away?"

"I thought you didn't want to know my plans."

He sat down on the couch determined not to be defeated. "You're my partner."

She shook her head. "I'm not even doing a good job at being *that* at the moment."

"Here." Nappa threw her a cell phone. "It's private, paid for, charged, and I've logged the number into my phone as 'Pain in the ass,'" he said with a smile.

"You are such a douche bag."

He laughed. "Only you would use such vulgarity, McGinn. I'm meeting with Matthew Garrison's contacts tomorrow; it's a visiting nurse service. They hired people to work at the camp McAllister volunteered at. On your way to Elmira?" He'd noticed Detective Gold's card on her coffee table.

"Yeah, I need to see where this all started. I think it started there, don't you?"

"I should be going with you." Nappa stood up and stretched, back cracking. Less than a week on this case had taken a toll on all involved trying to find the perp. "Here." He threw her a box. "I'm heading back to the precinct; we're expecting more news regarding the security video. Some tech wizard is playing around with it, trying to impress the powers that be. Some college kid on his semester internship." Nappa laughed. "Whatever it takes, right?"

Megan caught the box. "I'll call tomorrow."

Nappa stopped at the door after half opening it and then turned back. "Get home safe, McGinn."

"You bet." When Nappa shut the door, Megan locked it and checked it twice. She sat and stared at the poorly wrapped box before opening it. A delicate silver cross lay on a miniature burgundy pillow. Megan's August birthstone, a peridot, was mounted in the center. Attached was a note in Nappa's handwriting: *Now is not the time to lose faith.*

Megan fastened it around her neck and decided she would never, ever, be the one responsible for removing it.

FORTY-FIVE

MEGAN HAD BEEN ON the road for nearly three hours. It had started raining two hours into the drive. The windshield wipers smacked back and forth, making a rubbing noise against the windshield. She had less than an hour to go until she reached exit 56, Elmira, College Avenue. Her racing thoughts took up all the space the mindless car radio music attempted to distract her from. There were brief moments when she felt she was fleeing, but she convinced herself otherwise. Because it was otherwise. She needed to go back to the beginning, what she thought was the first kill: Erin Quinlan. She'd phoned Detective Gold earlier and he was very accommodating, even borderline excited that this case may be put to rest.

This wasn't the first trip Megan had made to the Finger Lakes region; the fact that she'd be only thirty miles away from her own long-ago attacker weighed heavily on her mind, as her nightmare always reminded her. Like the one that recently woke her on her bathroom floor when she'd entertained the stockbroker, the nightmare never went away. Even though it was daytime, with every mile she drove closer to her friend's college town, the memory of that night edged its way to the front of her thoughts.

Megan was just a kid, a teenager thinking she was an adult, as they all do. Being grabbed had never entered her mind before it happened. She remembered the taste of sweat on his hand covering her mouth so she couldn't yell. His strength. Her fear.

How could I have been so stupid? she'd catch herself thinking. A cop's daughter, a New York City resident.

Dumb as a box of rocks.

When he dragged her into the vacant house, she was sure she'd be killed. What happened next was always foggy in her mind's eye. Maybe adrenaline kicked in and she freed herself, or the feeling of the blade invading her skin brought out her fight-or-flight response. Whatever the cause, it didn't matter. Somehow that night she'd gotten out. She'd have the scar above her breast for life, but Megan managed to do what Erin Quinlan, Shannon McAllister, and Caroline Dacey were unable to do: live.

She passed a car with the bumper sticker *Let Go, Let God.* When the most unspeakable thing has happened to you, it's time to help God out, because he was obviously busy when it happened. No blame, no shame, it was just a reminder that prayer is for the person you're aiming the barrel of a gun at. And Megan was registered and carrying two.

Godspeed, motherfucker.

Minutes later she got off at the downtown Elmira exit. The billboard had some familiar faces and some not so familiar: Mark Twain, Ernie Davis, Brian Williams, astronaut Eileen Collins,

Tommy Hilfiger. There were a few others that didn't register but who were apparently important enough to be on the town's billboard.

Megan pulled into the Holiday Inn on Water Street, registered, and went to her room to throw her things on the bed. The manager gave her a message. It was from Detective Gold wanting her to call when she was settled in.

Megan checked the cell Nappa gave her and wondered how he was making out with the nursing service.

———

Nappa arrived at the address for the Visiting Nurses' Society in midtown. He'd anticipated the location would be a hospital, but the building was a generic corporate high-rise. The company occupied half of the thirtieth floor. The other half was a law firm. He got off the elevator and greeted the young receptionist. "I'm Detective Nappa. I'd like to speak with a supervisor."

The young woman became flustered, not due to Nappa's request but his looks. Even with sleep circles under his eyes and a five o'clock shadow, Nappa still resembled a scruffy Prince Charming.

"I'm sorry, Mr. Warren is in a meeting right now."

"I'm afraid you'll need to pull him out of that meeting." He added a grin that could have had her on her back with heels pointed to Jesus in record time.

The receptionist picked up the phone and whispered something to the person on the other end. Her hand was shaking as she put the phone receiver back on its cradle. "He'll be right out," she said, trying not to make eye contact.

Mr. Warren soon came barreling into the lobby. He looked relieved to be pulled out of whatever meeting he'd been in. He was a big man, in his late forties. Looked like the type who enjoyed his beer and eighteen holes of golf every weekend—probably both at the same time, given the size of his gut.

"Detective?" He smiled, shaking Nappa's hand.

"Mr. Warren, thank you for taking time away from your meeting. I'm Detective Nappa."

"What can I do for you?" he asked.

"I just have questions for a few of your nurses."

He motioned Nappa to follow him, and they walked down the hall and into a conference room.

"Is someone in trouble?"

"Oh, no sir. Just routine questions, for the nurses who volunteered at a Camp Sparta over the summer."

He nodded. "Oh, sure. I know the camp you're talking about. I assigned the nurses myself."

"Great. I'll need their names and contact information."

"Not a problem," he said matter-of-factly. "Let's see, if memory serves there were three." He used his fat fingers to count. "Gary, Linda, and ... " He scratched his forehead. "There might have been a fourth. I'll go get the file." Before he exited the conference room, he swung back in, "Breton, that's the third, but there's one more I'm not thinking of. I'll be right back."

The smitten receptionist popped her head into the conference room. "Can I get you anything, Detective? Coffee? Tea?"

"No, thank you," Nappa smiled and then checked his watch, wondering if Megan had arrived in upstate New York.

FORTY-SIX

I thoroughly disapprove of duels … If a man should
challenge me now, I would take him kindly
and forgivingly by the hand and lead him to a
quiet retired spot, and kill him.

—MARK TWAIN

―――――

*I REMEMBER AS A teenager sitting at Samuel Clemens's grave, a stone's
throw away from my house on Davis Street, thinking of this quote,
never knowing anyone to challenge me, but always remembering I'd
be nothing but kind and forgiving leading up to the moment of their
surrender.*

―――――

Megan sat on the edge of the bed in the hotel room fidgeting with
her new bracelet, turning the Saint Bridget's cross to the front of
her wrist while re-reading the copy of the file on Erin Quinlan.

The final report listed where she was buried, eerily the same name of the place where Megan had just buried her father: Woodlawn Cemetery. There were brochures next to the mini coffeemaker mentioning Woodlawn Cemetery in Elmira. She skimmed through the information. Mark Twain was buried there. Megan read that Twain's wife, Olivia Langdon, was born and raised in Elmira.

Megan had certainly had her share of cemeteries of late, but she felt the need to pay her respects to Erin Quinlan's final resting place.

Driving up Davis Street, she passed Elmira College. The purple and gold college colors dominated the students' attire as they walked between classes. While waiting for a car to turn ahead of her, Megan couldn't help but notice a burned-out house among the middle-American porch-styled homes. The charred structure was intact, but all the windows and doors were protected with plywood.

She drove into Woodlawn Cemetery and pulled alongside two workers making space for a new "resident." She asked if they knew where Erin Quinlan's plot was and the one worker directed Megan. He told her she couldn't miss it. It was always covered in flowers, notes, the occasional candle. A few minutes later, she saw that they were right: Megan wouldn't have missed it. She parked to one side and walked around to the front of the headstone. She added a single white rose to the countless arrangements surrounding it. Megan noted sadly that she and Erin shared the same birthday. August 30th.

Megan didn't know Erin from Adam, but she whispered a promise to the dead stranger, "I'll get him. I'll get him."

A black lab ran up behind Megan just then, jumping and barking. "Hey, sweetie. Where did you come from?"

A woman in a red parka followed yards away. "Abigail!" for some odd reason, the lady was carrying a piece of cheese in a wrapper. "Abby! Get back here!"

Megan rubbed the dog's ears, but Abby turned over on her back; apparently she preferred a belly massage. "You're a sweetheart. Aren't ya girl?"

The woman approached, laughing at her dog's antics. "She acts as though she's not the spoiled rescue that she is."

The way Megan was crouched down displayed her gun, and she could tell the woman was a little uneasy. "I'm a detective," she explained, "from Manhattan."

"I noticed you were over at the Quinlans'." She tilted her head in the direction of Erin's headstone. "She was a nice girl."

"You knew her?"

"One of my classmates from Saint Jo's, she was her granddaughter."

"Saint Joseph's nursing school?"

The woman took off one of her gloves to give her dog a piece of the wrapped cheese, and Megan noticed her hand. She wore a ring identical to the one found sutured in Erin Quinlan.

"That's right." She patted the dog's head. "Come on, Abigail, it's time to get back to Davis Street."

"I just drove up that street, and I noticed a house not too far away. Was there a bad fire there?"

The woman nodded. "Very bad, in fact I live next door. A sweet, sweet woman lived there, a real rock for our neighborhood."

"She died in the fire?"

"No." The woman gave her dog the remaining cheese. "Bridget died later that night from complications. I'm sure it was due to the fire. She wasn't in the best of health to begin with." The woman continued talking about the fire that engulfed the house that night, but there was only one word that stopped Megan's heart: *Bridget*.

Motherfucker.

Megan thought, *You were right again, Dad. Angels come in many forms.*

FORTY-SEVEN

"Detective Nappa?" Mr. Warren walked into the conference room with paperwork. "I have the information on the nurses who worked at the camp this past summer."

"Thank you. Also, I have a few questions for you before I go."

"Whatever I can do to help."

"I'm investigating the McAllister murder and I'm sure you know she was a volunteer at the camp. Have any of your staff commented on her death?"

"We all were stunned when we found out." He put his hand to chest. "I don't want to seem indelicate, Detective, but we in the medical field deal with death, sometimes on a day-to-day basis. One of our nurses specializes in oncology services, so it's a part of the job, so to speak." He shrugged. "I will say this, Shannon was a sweet person. What an awful, awful thing to happen."

Nappa raised a suspicious eyebrow. "You knew her?"

Mr. Warren nervously laughed, "Well, no, not really. I went to the camp over a holiday weekend to help out. I didn't *know* her, so to speak."

"When was the last time you saw her?"

"At a blood drive we held. She was handing out juice and cookies to the donors. I think two of the nurses on that list were there as well."

Nappa took a page from Megan's Make-Friends-and-Influence-People booklet and left in a hurry. "I'll be in touch."

FORTY-EIGHT

MEGAN MET DETECTIVE GOLD at Light's Bakery. Permed hair and blue mascara dominated the waitresses' fashion, but for less than five dollars you received a sandwich with a side of coleslaw, a pickle, and coffee—with refills.

She went into detail with Detective Gold about meeting the woman in the cemetery and the Saint Joseph's ring, and requested more information on the house that went up in flames, especially the woman named Bridget who'd lived there. He knew what she was looking for and was all too eager to help.

"I also want to see where Quinlan was murdered," Megan said.

He nodded. "It's up on Seneca Lake. About a thirty-minute drive." He pulled out his wallet. "This is on me. Lori, sweetie, can we get the check, please?"

"You're a regular." Megan smiled.

"That's my daughter. That's the only reason I can get away with calling her sweetie," he said, smiling.

"I love small towns."

323

They drove through Watkins Glen at the base of Seneca Lake, home to NASCAR events and Seneca Lake wine country. Megan would have preferred a few wine tastings as opposed to a walk through a decades-old crime scene, but she was there for only one purpose: get into the mind of the killer. And she was certain Elmira had spawned this killer.

The driveway was steep down into the Quinlans' summer retreat.

"The family haven't been in the house since the murder. They tried to sell it for years, but it's hard to get rid of a place when the town knows of its history. I think they're planning on tearing it down and selling the lot this year."

Megan nodded, took out the Quinlan crime scene photos, and followed Detective Gold through the house. There was little to add to what was in the photographs. Megan didn't need a point A to point B tutorial. This murder mimicked the McAllister scene completely. After half an hour, she went outside on the deck to get a breath of fresh air. Detective Gold was returning a call on his cell.

Seneca Lake was choppy, white caps topping the water as the wind forced itself over the lake. A chill swept through the air, as if meant to warn her. In her gut she was nearing the end; she just wasn't sure how it was going to play itself out. And she was afraid to even guess at the outcome.

Detective Gold suggested stopping in Watkins Glen for a topper, his version of saying a drink. Megan rarely negated such an offer. They sat at the bar at the Harbor Hotel looking out on the basin of Seneca Lake sharing war stories of being on the job. Megan spoke of her father's tales more than her own. It was easier, and probably more interesting to Gold. After a few cocktails Megan excused herself to the ladies room. As she washed her hands, she looked into the wall mirror. A decoration made to look like a fisherman's net hung behind her. It held faux seashells, starfishes, and thick rope tied into knots. She whipped around, forgetting to turn the sink off.

"Bastard!"

She returned to the bar and opened the copy of the McAllister file. "Look." She handed the photos to Detective Gold.

"What?"

"What does this knot look like to you? Our ME hasn't been able to detect what it is, but it's different. Look at the suturing." Megan turned the photo on its side. "Look at it from this angle." She waited. "Did Quinlan have this done to her?"

"This is neat, hers was haphazard, but I see what you mean."

"Is it what I think it is?"

"Yeah." He shook his head. "I can't believe I missed that. I've been sailing for years."

"I have to call my partner."

"Bad reception here, better off waiting to get back to the hotel," Detective Gold suggested.

"Let's go through this again." Megan needed to be right before giving Nappa information that could be off the mark.

———

Megan woke the next morning on the tip of a dream. She was walking down a path through a park. The trees were green, the sky clear. There was a large picnic table in the grassy field at the end of the path. The table was filled with people eating, laughing, and toasting one another. They welcomed Megan with smiles, motioning for her to sit at the head of the table. The faces she recognized were familiar, but some of them seemed different: younger, happier than the last time she'd seen them. A woman put a hand on her shoulder. When Megan turned, it was a face she'd recognized immediately: her grandmother, her dad's mother. Megan looked up curiously at her, wondering what the purpose was for all of this. She pointed for Megan to turn around. Pat McGinn stood a few feet behind Megan, doing what he always did at family picnics, manning the grill. He looked peaceful and younger than the man she'd buried so recently. He smiled.

Megan walked over, wrapping her arms around him, holding him so very tight. She heard his voice as clear as if he were standing right in the room: *Go to her*. He turned Megan around, and the only person now seated at the picnic table was Rose. Not a youthful version of her mother, but the woman she was today: sick and confused.

The cell phone Nappa gave her rang like an old-fashioned telephone, but really loud. Megan tunneled her way out of the mound of pillows she'd covered herself with and answered, "What."

"Nice. You were supposed to call me when you arrived in Elmira."

She rolled over on her back, rubbing her eyes. "What time is it?"

"Six thirty."

"Christ." Megan climbed out of bed and started the mini coffeemaker while she relayed the last twenty-four hours to Nappa. "We're close, Nappa, really fucking close."

"The Bridget connection is no coincidence."

"No shit." Megan poured four Splenda packets into her coffee, along with the creamer packet. "What about the nurses?"

"I've been able to meet with two out of the three: Gary Palmer and Macey Spevack. Both met McAllister, both worked at a blood drive with her. I double-checked all donors on the day McAllister volunteered, no AB–blood type matches. I've left two messages for the third nurse. Rasmussen is heading over to meet with her this morning. I also got word from the computer whiz kid. He said the best he could come up with is it looks like a bracelet of some kind. The quality is terrible."

"Great fucking education Cornell is giving him." She ran her fingers through her hair. "I'm hitting the road as soon as I'm more awake." Megan started the shower for the water to warm. "Can you do me a favor? Reception is shit here, and I got a text from Uncle Mike, will you call—"

"He called me as soon as he was unable to reach you. I covered for you."

"Thanks. Meet me at my apartment later, I'll text you when I'm close."

FORTY-NINE

Megan dumped her overnight bag on the couch. She poured a glass of red wine and threw herself in front of the television waiting for Nappa to arrive. NY1 had the city's latest news, and it centered on the McAllister case, highlighted by the recent Caroline Dacey murder. A public relations nightmare that Walker had clearly thrown Nappa into the middle of.

Nappa arrived and, much to her surprise, didn't flash a judgmental eye when he saw the glass of wine at noon. In fact, he joined her.

"Love the latest interview, Nappa." Megan motioned to the muted screen. She clanked his glass. "You're a natural."

"Thanks. Here." He handed her a copy of the latest file on the case. "This is some background on the nurses who worked at the camp with McAllister."

She scanned through the papers. "You could have gotten in a lot of trouble for doing this, Nappa."

"I left Rasmussen and Palumbo out of it. They don't know."

"I'm sure they assumed," Megan said.

"They didn't ask, I didn't tell."

"None of these nurses' backgrounds are from upstate."

"I noticed that, too," Nappa answered.

"Rasmussen is meeting with them?"

"Yeah, Walker had me doing damage control with the press. I gave it to him. I think the first on the list is Buddington, then Daly."

Megan brought the wine bottle out from the kitchen, filling their glasses. "Nappa, why does Walker have you on television? You're so damn ugly."

He laughed. "Fuck off, McGinn."

They sat at opposite ends of the couch, but each had the same idea in mind. Their hands found their way to the middle, the neutral zone. They intertwined fingers. "Glad you're back safe," he whispered before her phone rang.

"Me, too." She didn't want to let go, but she had to—and not just to answer the phone.

"McGinn."

"Detective McGinn, it's Detective Gold. Something has been bothering me ever since you left. That sailor's knot."

"Don't beat yourself up over it, we all miss things."

"I know, I know. It's not so much that. I went back to the Quinlan site. There were a few photos on the wall of she and some friends boating on Lake Seneca. If you don't mind, I'm going to scan them and email them to you."

"I'm not sure why, but that's fine. Do you have anything more on the house fire on Davis Street?"

"There was a break-in the night of the fire, that I know."

329

Megan's cell clicked in her ear. "Can you hold on, I have another call."

"Take it. I'll send you the scans soon. Thanks for your time."

Megan switched over to the other line. "McGinn."

"Is this Megan McGinn?"

"Who wants to know?" she asked curtly, assuming it was the press.

"My name is Ani, I'm a nurse at the Olsen Facility."

She cringed. If her mother had heard how rude she'd just been, she surely would have earned a smack on the hand. If Rose had a few Manhattans in her, Megan would've gotten smacked in a few other places. "I'm sorry, I thought you were someone else. Yes, I'm Megan McGinn, Rose McGinn is my mother."

"Miss McGinn, I'm sorry to call, but the next of kin appears to be Brendan McGinn, in Ohio."

"What's wrong? Is my mother okay?" Her unnerved tone startled herself more than Nappa.

"I'm sorry, I should have said from the start, you're mother is fine. She did, however, have an allergic reaction to a medication."

Megan's hands began to shake. "Where is she?!"

"She's in her room. We administered Benadryl to stop the allergic reaction. However, she's still very agitated. I think it's best you come." Nurse Ani had a calming voice, more importantly the sound of reason. "She's so new here, I think a familiar face might help. She's calling out for her baby girl. I assume that's you."

"I'm on my way." Megan hung up, grabbed her jacket, and grabbed Nappa's arm without hesitating. "Come on, Mom's in a state." *Of course she probably thinks it's fucking Nebraska, but what the hell.*

FIFTY

MEGAN OPENED THE DOOR to the Olsen Facility. The nurse at the front desk greeted her. "Hi, Megan."

"How's my mom doing? Better?"

"She's calmed down a bit. Do you and your husband mind signing the visitor sheet?"

Megan laughed. "*Hon*, do you want me to sign your name?"

"I can handle it, *sweetheart*." Nappa rolled his eyes. "I'm going to use the facilities, then I'll catch up with you."

"Don't be long, *honey-poo*." Megan's cackle followed Nappa down the hall to the men's room just as her cell phone vibrated, signaling an incoming photo message. Detective Gold's picture. She started the download, and the first words on the note were: *Quinlan and both Dalys.*

"Daly?" Megan said aloud. The picture was of Erin Quinlan, another girl, and Fintan D. Worth.

Both Dalys?

"Just so you know, Miss McGinn, your mother has a visitor."

Megan stopped in her tracks. "Who?

"Breton Daly. The day nurse who admitted her."

Megan stared down the hall, feeling as if the length had just expanded into a mile between her and her mother's room.

BD. BD. BD. Not blood drive. Breton Daly.

And Fintan Daly Worth.

She ran toward her mother's room just as an orderly entered the hall with a stack of trays. She knocked him over like a linebacker. She flung open her mother's door to see a nurse pressing a pillow down over her mother's face. "*Noooooooo!!!*"

The nurse's possessed glare intensified as she tightened her hold.

"Stop! Police!" Megan flew around the bed, shoving the nurse into the wall. She moved to pull her gun as the nurse pushed off the wall and knocked Megan down. Megan's gun flew out of her hand, landing with a clatter only a few feet away from her. The nurse then threw a roundhouse punch that connected with Megan's already bruised jaw. Megan fell to the side, clawing for her gun, but the nurse hung on to her leg, dragging Megan back to her. Megan turned, kicking at the woman's face, then grabbing at her shoulder, but the motion only served to rip the nurse's uniform shirt.

Breton Daly's scars were now in full view, something that startled as much as disgusted Megan. The nurse was momentarily stunned as her entire secret life became exposed.

"What in God's name …?" They stared at each other a moment as if a referee had blown a whistle for them to stop. Megan kicked the nurse in the chest and pulled her backup pistol from her ankle holster. Their struggle forced Breton's fresh scabs to open and blood began to seep out of the wounds on her shoulders, her chest, and her arms. Her body was virtually weeping blood.

Megan was completely shocked at what she was seeing. "What kind of monster are you?" She was so close to the nurse that she could smell the faint traces of antiseptic soap emanating from her.

With a last, desperate move, the nurse twisted her entire body in an attempt to use leverage to her advantage. Suddenly, a shot rang out. Then another. The nurse slowly let go of Megan and began a long, slow, bloody slide to the floor.

Megan kicked herself free and ran to her mother's bedside. "Momma! Momma!"

FIFTY-ONE

MEGAN SAT BY HERSELF in a small waiting room down the hall, staring at the blank green wall. Nappa was outside in the hallway speaking to Lieutenant Walker. Uncle Mike and Aunt Maureen rushed down the hall; Nappa had notified them.

"Where is she?" she heard Maureen ask.

"In there." Nappa pointed to the door. "She's hasn't said anything, not to us."

"Where's the perp?" Uncle Mike demanded.

"She's still in surgery," Nappa answered.

A doctor approached Nappa. "Excuse me. We have Mrs. McGinn intubated. She's on the eighth floor. I've checked her chart. It seems that her son, Brendan, has the power of attorney. We'll need his signature to proceed."

Uncle Mike interrupted, "I've spoken with him. He's getting on the next flight possible. He should be here, if not late tonight, first thing in the morning."

"When will Ms. Daly be out of surgery?" Walker asked the doctor.

"They've closed her up and are moving her to recovery now," he answered.

"I want men posted up and down this entire hospital and on whatever floor she gets moved to. Nappa, I want you there when she wakes up," Walker said.

"No." Megan's voice was loud and clear when she approached the group. "I'm going to be there when she wakes up. Me, not Nappa. *Me.*" Megan walked down the hall, then turned. "Nothing happens until I get back. Do you hear me?! *No one* speaks to her until I get back!"

"McGinn! Where are you going?" Walker demanded.

Megan didn't answer. She slammed her middle finger on the elevator button to go down to the lobby.

———

Fintan entered the conversation room with a glint in his eye. "I told you, you'd be back. Oh, by the way, shame about that Dacey girl." He rested his chin on his clasped hands. "Your luck just isn't changing, is it?"

Megan stood against the wall, arms folded. She stared at him, a nice long, silent, cold gaze waiting for the appropriate moment. Like when a lion pounces on a gazelle. "I killed your sister today."

It was the first time Fintan didn't have a witty remark. His eyes filled with rage, then he quickly pulled back. "I don't have a sister."

"Joan Breton Daly. Shot her twice in the heart. Slow death. Very painful."

"I don't have a sister!"

"When I caught you, the only file we could find on you said your father died in Vietnam and your mother of a drug overdose, and then you were placed in foster care. The family that adopted you, their last name was Worth, but not yours." Megan walked around to the table so she could look down at him, eye to evil eye. "Now, what didn't come up in the file was who put you in foster care: Bridget Daly, your grandmother."

"Fintan *D*. Worth." She leaned one hip on the formica table, "Let me see if I can surmise as to why. You had a younger sister and you started to *do* things to her. Very *bad* things. Your grandmother caught on and got rid of you."

Fintan's face reddened.

"She had you removed because you were a threat." Megan squinted. "How am I doing so far?"

"I *don't* have a sister," he repeated.

"So, what? You consider her your wife? Lover? *Southern* cousin," she said, using a sarcastic drawl. "You both have the AB blood type."

He clenched his teeth.

"Here, look at this picture." She held her phone out for Fintan to see the photo of he, Breton, and Erin Quinlan. "Take a good, hard look; it's the last time you'll ever see her." Megan raised two fingers. "Two shots. Right through the heart." Megan knocked for the guard. "Oh, Fintan." She turned. "Such a shame about Breton, your luck just hasn't changed, has it?"

Before Megan left the Hudson Psychiatric Center, she bribed a few of the orderlies for Fintan not to be allowed television privileges for a few days. She wanted him to get a taste of what he'd put the victim's families through, thinking Breton was dead. Not surprisingly, the orderlies were all accommodating; some didn't even take the cash.

FIFTY-TWO

"I WANT TO BE alone," Megan said before opening the door to her mother's room.

Rose had been hooked up to life support. Megan sat down in a chair and stared out the window. She needed to be near her mother, but she couldn't bear to look at her connected to the medical apparatus. The sound of her forced breath was nearly too much to handle.

A light knock was followed by, "Can I come in?" It was Nappa.

"I said I want to be alone."

He politely ignored her before shutting the door behind him. "Brendan will be here in a few hours. He caught the last flight. You need to know a few things we've uncovered."

Megan met his suggestion with silence, then handed her cell over to him with the photo of Quinlan, Fintan, and Breton filling the screen.

"I know everything I need to."

Nappa looked away from the photo and handed Megan back her phone. "No. You don't. There's more. I'll leave it with you and when Daly wakes up we'll both go in, together. *Together*," he emphasized.

"I'll give you the broad strokes of it. So far we've found out that Daly was Caroline Dacey's mentor. Palumbo and Rasmussen went through Daly's apartment. Lots on her computer, pictures of her and Shannon at the kids' camp. She paid a search site and got all of her information on you from there. Palumbo went to *The Catholic Times* with Daly's photo ID. They identified her as the person who placed the ad. The blood on the cross matches hers."

"And Fintan's."

"No one could have seen this coming." He was out of words. Nothing could ever fill the void deepening in Megan with every moment that passed.

"All the pieces coming together, huh, Sam? All but one." It was the first time Megan made eye contact with Nappa since he'd walked in. "Can you tell me why I'm sitting here next to my mother, who has a fucking machine breathing for her?" She turned back toward the window. "I didn't think so."

———

Four hours later the doctors moved Breton Daly to a private room with two policemen guarding the door. Megan stood staring at her through the glass. Breton was beginning to stir but was not yet fully awake.

"Ready?" Nappa asked Megan.

"Where's her lawyer?" she asked.

"She waived her rights to having a lawyer present. When she awoke in recovery, she asked only for one thing," Nappa said.

Megan knew intuitively what Breton Daly requested.

"She wants to see you," he said.

Megan stared through the glass at the woman who'd changed her life forever.

"I can't believe the killer was a woman. It never even crossed my mind. A fucking female serial killer. That would have been last on my list."

"Her full name is Joan Breton Daly. Born upstate, in Elmira, New York. Both parents deceased. She was raised by her grandmother, *Bridget* Daly." Nappa emphasized her first name when he spoke. "Attended nursing school at Saint Joseph's in Elmira. There was a report on her grandmother. You may want to take a look at—"

"She's up," Megan interrupted. "Let's give the woman what she wants."

A nurse was in with Breton. Her wrists were strapped to the bed, handcuffed. The nurse was giving her water through a straw.

Nappa put a hand on Megan's shoulder, preventing her from entering. "Give me your gun," Nappa said.

Megan stared Nappa down, then took her gun out, opened the chamber, emptied the bullets onto the floor, and closed it, placing it back in her holster. She took the file from Nappa and they both walked in.

Breton was groggy, but she knew who was standing across from her.

"Hello, Megan," she said.

"You will refer to me as Detective McGinn."

Breton glanced over at Nappa. "Does *he* have to be here?"

"Yeah, I do," Nappa said.

"Be grateful for his presence," Megan added. "He's keeping me from killing you."

Breton sighed, "Meg—I'm sorry, Detective McGinn. How's Rose?"

"Do not speak her name again while I'm in this room," she demanded.

"The nurse said she's on life support. Is that true?"

Megan ignored her. She opened the file, pretending to re-read it so she didn't have to maintain long eye contact with the woman. "It says here both of your parents are deceased. Did you kill them, too?" she asked.

Breton smiled at her sarcasm. "Come on. Don't be silly. You're reading my life story—you know my father was killed in Vietnam, and you know my mother is dead, too."

"She was a hooker. Died of a drug overdose. You were raised by your grandmother, Bridget Daly," Megan stated.

"I've looked forward to this moment. I never really knew how it was going to come about, but on some level, I was positive we would meet. My little mouse made it through the maze. Tell me. Was it luck or good old-fashioned detective work?"

"Witty. You know you're brother once said that exact same line to me."

Breton's smug demeanor transitioned to a careful mask. "I don't have a brother."

"Funny, when I spoke with him a few hours ago, he first said he didn't have a sister. But, then"—she waived her finger—"he told all. Boy, those family Thanksgivings must have been *eventful*."

With each step Megan took toward Breton's hospital bed, Nappa became more vigilant. He wasn't about to protect a murderer, but he'd protect Megan's career at all costs.

"After he was taken out of your grandmother's home, how long was it before the two of you reconnected?"

Breton stared up at the ceiling. "I don't have a brother."

"Fintan molested you, sodomized you, fucked you, and then groomed you for . . . for what? Exactly what was the purpose?" Megan walked to the corner of the bed. Strapped down, Breton had few vantage points to choose from. "Wait. Maybe it was your grandmother? Did *she* touch you, hurt you, make you do things?"

"Are you sick? Of course not!" Breton snapped. "She was a saint, my grandmother, an absolute saint. You have no idea how much she sacrificed for me, how much she loved me. She was the most giving, kind, selfless woman in this world."

"It's interesting you say that. Those were the exact words the family and friends of the women you murdered said about them."

"Why do you use that word, *murdered*?"

"That's what it's called when one human being unlawfully and with premeditation takes the life of another human being."

Megan stood over Breton, slowly folding her hospital gown up each arm, exposing the self-desecration. Breton could do nothing to stop her. "Nappa, look at this." Megan grinned, knowing she may not have her gun, but she was sure as hell not leaving without her own lasting mark on the monster lying in the hospital bed before her.

"Nappa, this sick shit is all over Ms. Daly's body. How fucked up is that?"

The self-inflicted scars made Nappa wince.

"What are you doing?!" Breton screamed.

"Did Fintan do this to you?"

She wouldn't answer.

"You did this to yourself, didn't you? Penance for your sins, perhaps?"

Breton looked away, replaying in her minds' eye how she relieved herself after each kill…

Blood-soaked fingerprints marred her reflection as she wiped steam from the mirror. Her naked body stood on the green bathroom mat. Her body was unspectacular. Thin, pale more than an anemic. A ten-year-old boy had more muscle tone, but nothing matched her force when she was on a mission. Her one attractive perk was her face, ironically angelic. Rarely noticed by either sex. Invisible to the world unless her abnormal strength was focused around one's neck: not someone who would make you go gaga, unless she was pinning you down, throttling you, laughing at the end, all over you. But that was merely her outside; her inside was a different story, hence the blood.

The nail clippers were new, as they always were on days such as these. She didn't really need them, as she always wore two sets of gloves. Ten clips, the pointed cuticle instrument underneath the nail bed, and she was nearly done.

She turned the shower on, tilting the knob over to hot. The bathroom mirror steaming over cued her entrance. The scalding jet streams smacked at her from all directions. The horse brush lay next to the bottles on the floor near the soap. She didn't like to use soap; not on these mornings, anyway. She held the brush as gingerly as a woman nestling her newborn in her arms. Slowly moving her fingers over the uneven acrylic bristles, staring down, she closed her eyes as she poured the rubbing alcohol over the bristles. She slashed herself with the vigor

*of a sushi chef against a piece of mahi-mahi. The brush crisscrossed
over old scabs while the tips of each bristle dug under the dried clots of
blood, excavating the fresh skin from underneath. She felt them rip
open, but it was always the fresh cuts where she felt a small level of ac-
quittal, if there were such a thing to find in her soul. The stream of
water hit her skin like pellets of acid spitting down on her. Dead skin
and dried crusted scabs mixed with fresh lacerations. Her grin
emerged with each swipe, right up until the last hurling stroke. She released a deep groan, something she assumed an orgasm would sound
like, if she'd ever experienced one.*

*She rested her head on the shower door, staring down at the
feather-like wisps of skin floating into the drain. Moments later she
stood in front of the full-length mirror watching the blood snake its
way over her nipples, stomach, then her bare vagina, trickling down
her legs. There were more of them on her left side, since she was right-
handed. It would be hours before she would get sleep. The endorphins
running through her system made her feel as though she'd just downed
a few uppers, followed by a black coffee chaser.*

"This was a good morning," she breathed.

———

Breton sighed while opening her eyes after recalling the ritual.
She was determined to change the course of conversation.

"You know, when I'd visit your mother—" Breton paused. "You
don't seem surprised. Well, she and I had some nice chats. She
wasn't in a fog through all of them. She told me some great stories
about you. Her memory was quite good when I was there, quite
good. Tell me more about the time she taught you how to drive, or

343

the time she dressed you up for that class photo. Now, *that* one I loved." Breton started laughing.

"That's enough," Nappa yelled. It caused one of the police out in the hall to open the door. That's when Nappa noticed Walker waiting nearby.

Breton ignored Nappa's outburst to focus purely on Megan. "You don't get it, do you? I was doing those women a *favor*. I helped them, just like Fintan helped the people he returned to God."

"You helped them?" Megan flipped through the papers in the file until she came to a police report from the Elmira Police Department. She read it while Breton spoke.

"What kind of life do you think those girls were going to have? Tell me! You didn't know Shannon. She was as green as grass. She had no clue. No clue about how disgusting people can be, and usually are. About how selfish this world is." Breton was getting more agitated the longer Megan refused to give her direct eye contact. "Shannon was…" Her anger was making her trip over her own words. "Shannon was so good. She didn't deserve to be treated the way she was by some people—like some of the men she'd meet. She was too sweet for this world. I sent her to a better place. I saved her from all the world's pain and disappointment."

"Uh-huh." Megan's nonchalant tone continued into her next question. "Tell me about November 16th, 1986." She had everything she needed to know about November 16th right in front of her.

Breton's cheek began to twitch. Her fingers tapped the bed under her bound wrists. She didn't answer.

"Young white male broke into your grandmother's home. She was beaten. Raped. Her home burglarized. A fire consumed the

344

house. It says in the police report she was rescued and taken to Saint Joseph's Hospital. She died early the next morning. The man who did it was never caught."

"I'm feeling very tired. I'd like for you to leave," she said.

"What else happened that night?" Megan's instincts told her to keep pressing. "What? You got a phone call. You rushed to her side. Then what?"

Breton shut her eyes, fighting off the memory of that night, but it wasn't enough. She heard Bridget Daly begging from her hospital bed.

Breton, please. Breton, please. I've never asked anything of you. Please help me. Take me out of my pain.

"What was she like when you saw her? When you finally got to her?"

"I want you both to leave now," Breton demanded.

"She was bruised. Bloodied. Soiled. A man had *raped* her. It says here the man had sodomized your grandmother, in her own home, her own bed. You're a nurse. You know what 'sodomized' means."

"Stop. Stop it!"

"The woman who gave her life to you. She was a saint, that's what you called her, right? Saint Bridget. What did you say to her that night? When you finally got there? That you were sorry you weren't there to protect her. That you *failed*," Megan goaded.

"I did the one thing that you weren't able to do for your own mother," Breton hissed. "She begged me. She begged me!" She fought against the straps and handcuffs. "She did everything for me; I couldn't say no. I couldn't let her stay that way. I was not going to let her down. It was terrible to see her, to see her lying there. She was in so much pain." She turned her head away from Megan.

Megan closed the file and threw it on the tray table in front of Breton. "You smothered her with a pillow, didn't you? Just like you attempted to do to *my* mother. You fucking psycho bitch!"

Breton kept looking away.

"You don't have the right to play God, Ms. Daly. You don't have the right to decide who is too good for this dirty world and who isn't. And you didn't have a right to kill your grandmother."

Breton's head snapped in Megan's direction. "Tell me, Detective McGinn, when that button's pressed, and the machine keeping your mother's pulse beating stops, what will you be then? Her savior...or her murderer?"

Megan walked closer to Breton's bed, spurring Nappa to go to her side.

"McGinn, no. No!" he said.

Megan bent over the guardrail of Breton's bed. She pressed her hand into the bandaged bullet wound to her shoulder until blood ran through the gauze. "Someday. Someday when a jury finds you guilty and you're issued the death penalty—and you'll get it, believe me—when that day comes, rest assured, Ms. Daly, you will not be reunited with Saint Bridget. Returning to God will be the last place you go."

Just before Megan was out the door, Breton asked, "Detective? When can I get my grandmother's ring back?"

FIFTY-THREE

THE DOOR TO ROSE's room was opened slightly. Megan could see her brother Brendan speaking with the doctors and then signing a clipboard. Nappa, Pearl Walker, Mike, and Maureen all stood nearby. Megan stared at her mother through the doorway. The life-support machine pushed fresh air in and suctioned old air out. It sounded like a clogged vacuum cleaner was doing the job for Rose's lungs. Her neck was heavily bruised, with pockets of broken blood vessels running up and down her skin.

"Momma, I'm so sorry. This is all my fault."

Brendan heard her comment as she came into the room. "No, it's not, kiddo. It's not." He walked over to his baby sister. They cried in each other's arms. "It's time, Megs. It's time," he said.

One of the doctors stood in the doorway. Brendan nodded for him to come in. When he turned off the machine, Megan got up and held her mother the way she had one night before. She remembered that nagging feeling she'd had when Rose came to and held her: that the moment was going to be the last they'd share.

Megan hated herself for being right. She let go of Rose, gently placing her head back on the pillow. She walked out of the room, heading toward the elevators. She glanced into other rooms—patients smiling at the receipt of flowers. One older woman was packing a bag, happy to be leaving the hospital. That would never be Rose McGinn, ever. Seeing the handful of smiling faces made Megan feel hollow, more than she ever could have imagined. Guilt capsized her very being.

"McGinn? McGinn?" Nappa called out after her. "Where are you going?"

The elevator doors began to close between Megan and the hallway.

"Where are you going?" Nappa asked again.

"Away."

ABOUT THE AUTHOR

C.J. Carpenter was born and raised in upstate New York. She has spent the majority of her life living in Manhattan and now divides her time between NYC and Philadelphia, where she is currently working on her third novel.